Portrait of Emlanjeni

A novel by

TSITSI NOMSA NGWENYA

First published in Great Britain in 2023 by:

Carnelian Heart Publishing Ltd
Suite A
82 James Carter Road
Mildenhall
Suffolk
IP28 7DE
UK
www.carnelianheartpublishing.co.uk

Copyright ©Tsitsi Nomsa Ngwenya 2023

Paperback ISBN 978-1-914287-34-3

eBook ISBN 978-1-914287-35-0

Proofread by Lazarus Panashe Nyagwambo

Cover design:
Artwork – OKing
Layout – DanTs Media

Typeset by Carnelian Heart Publishing Ltd
Layout and formatting by DanTs Media

To my children Shingai Vuyisile, Nqobile Anele and Zoleka.

Chapter One

To reach Emlanjeni, one has to plan a three-hour drive from Ematojeni, about twenty kilometres south of Bulawayo. Ematojeni Hills of the famous Njelele Shrine and Matopos National Park, a national heritage site, lies on the village's north. You drive on a strip road, curving, turning and meandering around huge rock boulders, past the balancing rocks on the left till you cross a narrow bridge on Hove River. That is the bridge that makes bus drivers forbid women and children from occupying the front seats. As the bus descends, fearful passengers on their maiden trips to Bulawayo, koNtuthuziyathunqa, let out shrieks which sometimes cause the driver to lose control of the steering wheel. On the eastern side of the road, on huge rock boulders, still lie the remains of Cecil John Rhodes, uMlalankunzi. After the park, the road narrows all the way to Khezi, a small business centre with a court and shops dotted on either side.

The place is dry. One can smell its dryness. Acacia bushes dot the flat landscape which is littered with little, whitish, dusty stones. The whole surrounding area, all the way to Mwewu River, is mostly gullied and dry, giving the impression of a place being frequently cleaned by nature's maids. The road widens past Maphisa Growth Point, past Bhalagwe Hill, beyond the mine dump at the bottom of the hill. Wary travellers look at the Bhalagwe Mine dump with sorrowful eyes. Silent drumbeats echo from the mine dump, evading through the leaves of the trees dotted around it, pervading the rocks, past the rivers and the vast sands and into the hearts of Emlanjeni inhabitants.

Sorrow. Fear. Anger.

These feelings are the people's well-kept secret. They do not show them to strangers. They say nothing to them about the men, women and children who were swallowed by a moment in the country's history, a moment that is spoken of in hushed tones. When they travel with strangers in buses or *malayitsha's* vans, they look at Bhalagwe Hill, shake their heads, mumble something, shedding a tear or two before they look at their hands or laps. The harrowing memories are always there even if most of the elders who witnessed the horrendous events are gone. Memory has legs. Even when the treacherous pens of dubious historians deceptively omit facts, memory creeps in the underbrush of people's minds, whispering, sighing, popping its head on the surfaces of their amnesia. The hill itself looks tormented. It seems to be yearning for forgiveness, for relief, for freedom. Its folds contain a dark history, a burden that a simple hill cannot carry alone. Yet sometimes it seems to be blaming the irresponsive, incurious, insensitive dump lying at its feet.

Emlanjeni itself is about forty kilometres south-west of the infamous Bhalagwe Hill. If one cared to imagine the aerial view of the two rivers bordering the village, Simphathe and Marabi, with the Kwanike hillocks on the south, the picture would be a breath-taking one, the kind you find framed as a monument in a museum. The sandy loam, some patches of black clay on some areas and red soils on the other, holds the ground together. Grass slowly dies of thirst after the February-March rains only to come to back to life during the October-November planting season.

Houses of all shapes and sizes sit on that flat plain, receiving every assault of the sun's rays during the hot season. Thatched round huts huddle silently through it, shoulders hunched, as if existing on this monotonous landscape has taught them the benefits of stoicism. But the same cannot be said about the zinc roofs. They glare back at the sun with a blinding shine, and when you sit under them during the day, the sound of this invisible combat comes in the form of irregular crackling as if a mischievous boy is throwing pebbles on them. The zinc roofs have increased in Emlanjeni because many enterprising young men and women have trekked down south. If they had not decided to go and work at eMakhitshini, eGoli, the village would have perished from incurable poverty.

Rain is sporadic here. Crops wilt and die of dehydration before ripening. Most people who worked in the industries in Bulawayo are back home after the factories either shut down or were run by people with no clue what they were doing. The farming they came back to hardly sustains them. The most common form of transport are *malayitshas'* vans, pulling trolleys loaded with groceries in *tshangana* bags, bicycles, empty twenty-litre buckets, fencing wires, zinc sheets – anything their customers give them to deliver to those taking care of their children and homesteads. Because of the rain-gnawed dongas chewing what is left of the road, *malayitshas* have improvised with their own dust roads which run parallel to the main untarred ones, branching to some villages far off.

Emlanjeni village can be accessed from whichever direction one chooses. From Maphisa-Mphoeings Road, one can turn left after approximately five kilometres from St Joseph's Mission into the old Tribal Line Road which separates two chiefdoms. Chief Mlotshwa's village takes the right side. Emlanjeni villagers live the way their ancestors have lived since the year dot. They welcome whichever new developments come with the modern times but never uproot what holds their community together. In happier times, their life partakes a flattering fancy like the heaven preached by Christians.

Most young boys in Emlanjeni do not take school seriously. The schools are far apart such that pupils walk long distances. Even if some, especially girls, want to pursue education, they fail to do so because idlers and school dropouts wait for them on their way from school. These girls are persuaded and forced into love affairs which lead to pregnancies and hastily planned marriages. The young fathers then disappear to eGoli with local *malayitshas*. Once there, some, after failing to get employment, turn to crime. From time to time, the people gather to bury these young men shot dead by South African police during cash-in-transit heists. In some instances, parents only know that their sons were criminals after their deaths. They die on top of bank notes, their blood staining the precious papers. Still, the young boys do not learn from these shameful deaths. They envy the stolen top-of-the-range cars and the cash which those criminals show off at the local township, especially during Christmas and other public holidays.

These men, with their characters miraculously revived the moment they come back to Emlanjeni, do not lose their sense of community. They talk to elders with respect. They attend community events and participate in whatever work that needs to be done. With other village men, they cut branches of trees to weave field walls. They carry stones and mud to rebuild roads, dams or a community pre-school. They plough the fields and mend kraals and goat pens. Some go on to become pastors and prophets in their churches. Congregants believe what they preach, judging by the material blessings they display. One such man, who went a step ahead to be the local philanthropist, shocked the village when he was shot dead by the South African police in a botched cash-in-transit heist. He sponsored football and other community-building activities such that those who believed anything had regarded him as a hard-working, humble servant of God. The ambitions of these men are to build beautiful homesteads, own livestock and drive flashy cars. Most Emlanjeni men never think of persuading their children to be educated no matter how much money they acquire.

Malayitshas bring groceries in big *tshangana* bags, blankets and any other items given to them to take home. Some mothers, upon receiving these parcels, forget their disappointment. Those whose daughters send a *malayitsha* frequently are seen wearing beautiful *izishweshwe* dresses, berets and sneakers to village parties and other communal meetings. A year or so later, *malayitshas* will bring babies, as young as six months, as part of the parcels. These babies are named Amara, Kagiso, Booysens – any name the mothers and fathers find interesting. From time to time, some Malayitshas arrive on Saturday mornings, pulling trolleys with dead bodies underneath groceries. Some of the bodies are buried as soon as they arrive after enduring over twenty four hours on the road.

Those are mostly bodies of people who die from "the disease." The villagers do not say its name. If one asks the cause of death, they are told the deceased had "*ubelomkhuhlane.*" Most die before forty because of recklessness. They ignore anti-viral drugs which, if taken regularly, would have preserved and prolonged life. Those who are lucky enough to be brought home breathing go to queue for the medicines at the local mission-run hospitals where doctors are paid salaries that are not even enough to enable them to live comfortably. Mothers of the sick become home-nurses, making sure their children eat healthy homegrown foods, not the metropolitan deep-fried meats and fat-dripping potato chips. They do not give them fizzy drinks but home-brewed *mahewu* made from the powder of rapoko and sorghum. Once the patients get better, *malayitshas* come for them. Off they disappear, only to forget to take their nutritional medicines. When they return, they too will be in trolleys underneath groceries. In some cases, senile grandparents are the only available guardians left to look after children of their grandchildren, thereby making it impossible to discipline them. Such children do as they like. They become *umhlambikazelusile.* Their mothers do not see this. Those who hear the messages from the children's guardians do not believe it.

From October to February, it sometimes rains so much that Simphathe, Marabi and Semukhwe overflow for days or even weeks. When the sun comes out, it burns all the grass and the July winds blow away all the finer particles of dust from the sand till the grains that remain are so clean that one could pick them one by one. The glare of the sun on the sands affects the girls and their mothers who fetch water from the wells they dig on the vast sands of the riverbeds. Scooping scooping and scooping sand with enamel plates till mounds of it appear dotted on the river beds, the women talk animatedly, laughing out loud. They share secrets. Some husbands report their wives to their in-laws because they shaved their pubic hair, a practice that is still taboo to them. Some younger women, ignorant of such matters, wonder at that. They stop scooping water into their twenty-litre plastic containers, hold their tummies or their heads, their mouths agape. They exclaim, "I can never allow him to do that to me, it's my body!" Older women justify the men, pointing out that they are right because that hidden precious part was what the husbands paid cattle for, including other marital benefits. Daughters-in-law also share the latest gossip; whose mother-in-law is always intruding, whose mother-in-law is a witch, laughing and exclaiming as they do so. Mothers-in-law indulge in their own gossip; whose daughter-in-law followed her husband to eGoli and left young children with a *geli*, whose wife fell pregnant when her husband had been away for four years and so on.

During the Emlanjeni spring, when rivers go dry, cattle, donkeys, sheep and goats drink water from ponds along the river. When these run out of water, villagers dig deeper wells on the riverbed and then collect water which they pour into huge basins for the livestock to drink.

The weather is a regime with its own caprices. Sometimes, the sun comes out with a rapture of joy. Cicadas sing when it is visible and Mopane leaves look freshly green. But when the sun withdraws into its shell, bullied by dark clouds, the cicadas stop singing and remain on the Mopane trees. Young children celebrate the disappearance of the sun. With empty packets of sugar in their hands, they shake the cicadas from the trees. After picking these insects which are a delicacy to them, they quickly rush home to roast them in frying pans before their mothers, grandmothers and guardians start preparing evening meals.

During the season of harvest, when the rains have been good, scotch carts bulge with mealies, finger millet and sorghum. After all the grains are garnered home, the scotch carts carry pumpkins, melons and watermelons to be kept nearer the homesteads. Donkeys pull these carts slowly when they are full and at astonishing speeds when empty. Sometimes young boys challenge each other to impromptu races while the elders watch with apprehension as the empty carts hurtle towards the fields at lightning speed. On their way to the homesteads, the carts sometimes drop tufts of sorghum, maize, finger millet, rapoko and millet. Birds line these paths to peck on what corn has fallen to the ground. After harvesting, field gates are left open for cattle to feed on the stalks of the harvested crops. This lasts only a few weeks.

* * *

In the afternoon, after the harvesting season, MaMoyo would sit in the shade talking to MaNcube, her mother-in-law, if she was not at one of her beer binges. She would darn, darn and darn, her hands moving softly, slowly and carefully. She was very experienced in handwork since she had studied Home Economics before getting married. She also led the women's club in

Emlanjeni. The members of the club did a lot of handcraft. They competed with other women's clubs even at district level. There, they also learnt cooking, sewing, baking and knitting while singing village ditties. During their meetings, men did not want to pass by their club house, built of home-made brick moulded by the women themselves. The house was near the pre-school. There was a huge *umwawa* tree in front of it. When it was too hot or raining, they sat in the tree's shade. MaSikhosana, despite her age, was also a club member. She and two other women often started singing obscene songs which described sexual performances. One afternoon, whilst on leave, Hloniphani Hadebe, MaMoyo's husband and a member of the Chief's Council, thought of paying the women a surprise visit but quickly changed his mind when he eavesdropped on them singing one of their favourite songs. He heard the song and saw two women kneel down to dance. He heard them say they were going to imitate a mating lion and lioness. MaSikhosana was the lead vocalist:

Uziphathe Ntombi, zibambe ntombendala
Bayekele babone ukuthi ulinina, ubunjiwe
Helele ma… helele ma
Ungayekeli bakubambe, bakuthinte

Be in control, girl, be in control of your life!
Let them see what you have
Helele ma… helele ma…
But do not let them touch.
Helele ma... helele ma...

Ntombazana nanzelela
Indoda kungayifikela
Ingalandela umfazi esambuzini sikazulu

Kumbe ngemva kwesiduli
Esibayeni sembuzi
Loba ngaphi otsho khona wena

Girl, beware,
Sexually aroused men
Can follow a woman
To the public toilet,
Behind a gigantic anthill,
Inside a goat pen,
Anywhere a woman suggests.
Helele ma... helele ma...

Uma befika okufikwa khona
Helele ma... helele ma...
Bakhohlwa konke, kanye lebizo lakho
Helele ma. Helele ma...

Once they ejaculate
Helele ma... helele ma
They forget the girl's name
Helele ma... helele ma

Other women responded to the song, sewing, crocheting, knitting, nodding their heads in rhythm. On hearing that, Hadebe did not dare proceed. He walked backwards, face looking ahead till he was safely hidden by some thick foliage. He never mentioned the attempted visit to his wife.

Everyone cycles in Emlanjeni village. Women as old as seventy cycle to church, miles away. They are serious about attending these church services where they give God the love they could have been giving to their absent children and spouses. At the local St Joseph's secondary school, bicycles can be seen balancing on each other, piled on trees within the school premises. Younger women cycle to clinics with babies strapped on their backs. Some experienced women even cycle balancing beer calabashes to village parties. At the Chief's court and anywhere where people gather, except of course at the dip tank where men drive their cattle on foot, there are hordes of bicycles.

Chapter Two

The old women worked with deft hands and mechanical minds, singing and mixing the fermented cornmeal powder with boiled water. The huge earthen pots, products of expert work from three decades ago, stood imposingly on the earthen stoop inside the hut that served as a kitchen. After pouring the paste into the pots, the women added more boiling water, stirring the contents with long wooden spoons. Their calloused hands told a story of years of toil, of their regular commerce and their friction with mortar and pestle. They bore rough traces of the hoes and sickles they worked with most of their lives. The night was ominous; heavy clouds, black with the promise of a downpour, gathered sullenly at the base of the sky. Occasionally, thunder shook the world like the roar of an angry god. But rain did not come. The people hoped and prayed that the ceremony for which this beer was being brewed would tip the elements in their favour. They hoped that the chiefdom would be rid of the menace of hunger. It could not be any other way with the rain god appeased.

All the four villages under Chief Mlotshwa gathered to brew the ceremonial beer at a homestead selected by the rain god herself through the rain messengers from her shrine at Njelele in the hills of Ematojeni. Emlanjeni's beer was to be brewed at Hadebe's homestead. Nobody questioned the voice of the Njelele god. It was said that those who did risked having their homesteads struck by lightning. Everything, including the cattle in their kraals, would be burnt. Those who asked a lot of questions too risked being mentally retarded for life. The god only received beer brewed by these old women as well as tobacco for her appeasement. According to custom, the ceremonial beer could only be brewed by old women who, at the time of the brewing, were supposed to be beyond child-bearing age. Long back, the messengers walked to her shrine. In modern times, they travelled by bus or any other available transport.

Among the laws passed from Njelele was that of respecting Wednesdays. People were not supposed to work their fields, plough or harvest on this day. Just like Saturday or Sunday for Christians, Wednesday was set apart for the Njelele god. Those who chose to work did lighter jobs around the home. Even after a heavy storm, people were supposed to down their tools and not enter their fields to plough.

Since the people of Emlanjeni knew that rain in their area was like an unreliable lover, they knew which type of sorghum, finger millet or cow beans to plant. They planted drought-resistant groundnuts and roundnuts and just a small section of maize on wet parts of the field. Once it had rained, women walked as if dawn lived in their arms. They entered their fenced fields at four in the morning and waited there for their men to come, the latter brandishing long whips to guide ox or donkey spans, ready to till the land before the sun rose. MaMoyo used to in-span with her father in-law when he was still alive. Back then, MaNcube snored away in her bedroom hut till the risen sun cast short shadows. That was way back before MaNkomo and Siphamandla came to live in the village. She also used to plough with her husband's younger brother before he left for eGoli. Sometimes she partnered with other villagers. Having been raised in a family which valued education, she was determined to have her children graduate with university degrees and earn a good life.

It was said that no one had ever seen the rain god. The few who could talk about her with some knowledge had only heard her voice echoing from the rock cave. Her voice boomed with authority as she spoke in the language of the particular messengers. She listened to each messenger from inside the rock cave. No messenger was supposed to behold her. The lives of the people rose and fell with the enchanting cadence of the rain god's voice. She was the deity from whose ancient depths the laws and taboos of the land were issued. She was, at once, the lawgiver and the spiritual fountain of her people. Chiefs and kings came from all corners of the country to seek counsel from the paramount lawmaker, the rain god at Njelele.

The cruel heat had cindered the veld. Not even dry corn leaves could be seen in the large open fields which made the beholder think they had never been green. Even the previous season's late harvest crops had languished in the unforgiving heat, wilted and dried just after their tender leaves had sprouted from the earth. The cattle and donkeys at the salt lick on the plains of Kwanike were skeletons in bags of hide. The remains of the animals that had already been claimed by the drought lay scattered across the land, their white bones picked clean by hungry vultures. Days on end, the thirsty lands of Matobo, also known as Ematojeni, lay under a thick cover of dark clouds that gave the peasants false hope about the season. The rain still did not come. Fearsome claps of thunder often rent the night sky's silence even as the dark clouds rolled by, only to roll back and beyond again, leaving the sky a clear diamond blue. There were no rain birds in the sky yet the villagers hoped against hope that the rain would fall. Like distracted automatons, they prepared their fields for the cropping season. But thunder, the mischievous sadist that it was, echoed stories of impending hunger.

The women worked in unison as dawn slowly approached, revealing the pale gold of the veld. A jennet that had birthed a foal during the night stood nuzzling it in the vast open field east of Hadebe's homestead where the special beer was being brewed. Cattle and other domestic animals had nibbled on the last blades of verdure, leaving only the desolate aridity of the disused fields. The countryside, blacked out by low-lying clouds, was soundless but for the cawing of crows and bleating of sheep. The sombre mass of the night engulfing the village was hushed and hot. The villagers' insistent prayer was for rain.

* * *

MaNdlovu, the most experienced of the six elderly women, prepared the last mixture in the thirty-year-old earthen pot seated at the end of the row. The earthenware belonged to MaNcube, mother to the Chief's senior advisor. MaMlotshwa who had arrived first was the closest neighbour of the Hadebes but still had to be escorted to her sacred duties by her grandson, Zamani. She arrived when it was still dark. As soon as the boy saw her in, he ran back to the lure of sleep and wet dreams. Two more women arrived at the same time after MaMlotshwa. The women's homes were abreast of each other but separated by a small stream which flowed away with the village chickens when flooded. MaNdlovu, sister to the Chief's policeman, had come on her own, her apron heavily infested with the thorny leaves of a certain shrub which prided itself for sticking onto the flared skirts of unsuspecting old women. Her homestead was to the south of Hadebe's, behind a hillock said to be home to huge snakes, crawling villains, hyenas and other animals. Some herd boys had even seen a leopard sitting on the wayward branch of a tree on the same Kwanike hillocks.

The last to come was the friendly MaSikhosana. Her delay in arriving was understood by the other golden girls because the little path from her home cut through the ruins of Sithwala's homestead. Sithwala and family had been sent away by Chief Mlotshwa for practising daylight witchcraft, an accusation they could not deny. At the headman's court, the family admitted to wrongdoing. Of all these women, only MaMlotshwa's husband, Hlabangana, was still alive. He was a member of Chief Mlotshwa's council, together with other men from surrounding villages.

* * *

Earlier that night, young Zanele, on holiday from boarding school, sat on the floor, leaning against her bed. She had been writhing, heaving, surging like that animal with no name that her grandfather had told them about long back when they sat by his fireplace to listen to his ancient stories. She was vacillating between sanity and insanity. The whistling of tree leaves in the wind, the incidents of the village life, the mooing of cows and bleating of sheep and goats could not jerk her out of her painful reverie. Her cousin, Nonceba, and her sister, Ntando, were asleep on the bed.

Zanele's predicament was a reversal of the bright future that had begun winking at her. She wobbled between fear and anxiety, pain and shame, and something that she could not explain, something that haunted her day and night. Her deep-seated fear was not because she could not pass her examinations. The problem was that she would be unable to write them. The incessant noise of the barking dogs outside also made sleep impossible. To make things worse, there was a discomfort that she felt inside her stomach. The discomfort had roused her tormenting thoughts. Her fear was that she was running towards what she was supposed to be running away from. Truly, Dube's son had come to be her ruin. She fidgeted in her uncomfortable sitting position as she decided she would not worry about it anymore. But her resolve only lasted a few minutes. She had been enthusiastic about writing her exams and had felt determined to take the plunge. All along, she had imagined herself graduating from university and sitting in a citadel of power and privilege. But now this! How would she cross this Red Sea? Who would be her Moses?

The pain on the sides of her stomach made her feel like she was going to burst. She wished she could vomit, had tried all tricks she knew about inducing vomit, but still could not. Under normal circumstances, she would have blamed what she had eaten: too many boiled groundnuts and beans for lunch and *isitshwala senyawuthi*, a type of thick porridge cooked with finger millet, served with *amasi* for supper.

Her mind flashed back to the days when she scored 12 As at Ordinary Level, becoming the best 'O' Level student in the whole of Zimbabwe's Matabeleland South Province. Her school headmaster had arranged a party for her and every teacher had given her a present. Her parents too had given her a laptop to celebrate her success. Zanele was not only prominent in academics but had the limbs for sport. Despite her chubby body, she was very light on her feet. Her peers shouted themselves hoarse when competing against other schools, encouraging her on. After news of her outstanding results, even the governor herself had called her and spoken to her concerning her future.

And now this!

Sipho, her boyfriend, had warned her that if he ever saw her at Sibanda's homestead, he would skin her alive, so there would be no abortion for her. Her mother did not suspect a thing – nobody did except her friend MaNkomo and Hanani back at school.

She tried to sleep on her back and almost choked. She woke up and sat on her left side, still leaning against the corner of the bed. Thoughts about university shot up and she saw herself studying Law the following year. In her reverie, she was in Swinton Hall with Nonceba who was already at the Medical School. Nonceba remained her inspiration. Nonceba's brother was also at the university in his final year, studying Mechanical Engineering. Her academic consciousness had been enlarged when she visited those two at university in the capital city the previous year.

Even though she told herself time and again that she would let nature take its course, her head spun from this poignant secret. In that same awkward position, she fell asleep for a while, only to be awakened again by the sound of something hitting the thatched roof of their bedroom hut. A donkey hee-hawed in the night, reminding her of her appointment. She sat up at once. After making sure Nonceba was asleep, she tiptoed to the door, opened it softly, and made her way outside, careful not to alert her mother who was sleeping in the next bedroom.

She found Sipho crouching behind the tree in front of their homestead. Judging from the position of the moon and the stars, it must have been around midnight. They whispered to each other and then walked further away from the homestead, in case someone woke up and saw them. She complained to Sipho about the pain she felt and warned him about the old women who were coming in the morning to brew beer for the rain-making ceremony which was to be held the coming weekend. She was aware that MaSikhosana's eyes would not miss a thing. That one had embers of curiosity dancing in her eyes, always searching and asking questions about whatever she was curious about.

Sipho seemed not to have heard her. Instead, without any warning, he quickly pulled up her nightie and placed his hands under her navel, tilting her backwards till she reached the hard ground. She angrily gasped for breath. Before she could push him away, he was already breathing heavily on top of her after tearing away her panties and throwing them into the dark. She felt so much pain when he forcibly entered her that the agony in her mind was numbed. He began to thrust on top of her, groaning with selfish pleasure. To assuage the pain of Sipho feasting on her, Zanele's mind wandered to picture a future with him. She did not feel anything then, and she knew there would be nothing to feel in the future, except this weight dragging her life away from her dreams. After putting on his clothes, Sipho surprised Zanele by instructing her to spend less time at home with the elderly people and keep herself busy gathering firewood or doing laundry at the well. Too upset to answer, she just walked back home. She would come back before sunrise to look for her missing underwear.

To her surprise, she experienced a feeling of freedom, the same feeling someone experiences after giving up on something beyond their control. Sipho promised her that as soon as he found some money or a *malayitsha* that would give him a lift to South Africa on a pay-forward scheme, he would go. Once there, and as soon as he found a job, he would send her money. Zanele scoffed at that arrangement but as matters stood, there was no other way. In the end, despite the lengthy deliberations, she resolved that she could not place her future in the hands of Sipho.

On sneaking back into their room, she found Ntando and Nonceba snoring the night away, quite oblivious of her temporary absence. She tried to sleep but could not. The oddity of her present situation struck her mind again and again. Thoughts, like stinging nettles, released their fiery tongues on her. Sipho could still deceive her. Try as she might, she could never escape her situation. She had burnt her own future and its ashes brought a bitterness she could not swallow. Her carelessness was tantamount to disrobing her parents in public. For a short moment, she felt a titillating sensation, a light euphoric mood brought by the memory of the honour she had once received. Zanele told herself she would not lose hold on her future, but then felt panic creeping in as she imagined the same newspapers which had published her success now publishing her shameful predicament. At the same time, she did not want to deflate her spirits as her future was not exactly yawning blank. If Empandeni expelled her, the whole world was still there as long as she was still determined to earn her golden fleece.

Before going to boarding school, Zanele had been a skinny girl who appeared like one of those people on diet or wasted by a medical condition. After the first term at school, she had come back looking round and plump, thanks to the staple diet of cabbage and beans. Her stomach looked like that of a woman who was starting to respond to the excesses of pregnancy such that MaNkomo teased her by asking when she was delivering her baby. She had full legs and a big bust which ballooned when she was in Form 3, only to get slightly deflated when she was writing her 'O' level examinations. Afterwards, she regained her usual weight and even looked like a mature lady. Presently, her body weight covered her secret well. With time, sleep crept in and as soon as Zanele was snoring, the elderly women started arriving for the beer brewing. She heard them making a fire but still managed to steal a bit of sleep before her mother woke them up to fetch water.

She felt better when she finally woke up. She greeted the beer-brewing party and quickly disappeared, first to look for her lost underwear, and then to fetch water with Nonceba. Her thoughts wandered towards Sipho who did not have much of a family. When they first dated, she thought she loved him. Now she knew that it was not love but pity. She thought of the unpolished desperation with which Sipho used to write her letters and wondered what had really attracted her to him. She remembered how one of such letters had brewed a scandal in her dorm and made her feel ashamed. This had happened when she was in form three. One of her dormmates had stolen her letter and read it to others who fell on each other in hysterias of laughter. Despite that, her world had revolved around Sipho. Life then was without riddles and knots. She had looked at everything in light of their innocence. Now she was suffocating alone in her ordeal. She had allowed the devil to wait in the shadowy corners of her life and suffocate her personal development. Maybe the devil was a mere saint this time. She could blame no one but herself.

She was startled to see Nonceba opening the gate of the well. Lost in memory lane, she had not seen how they had arrived there. Sometimes her thoughts, which alternated between hope and fear, carried her out of this world to another and made her do whatever she did mechanically.

Zanele was someone who rarely cried, and when she did, one would think the whole earth was falling apart. Even from a young age, she was comfortable on her own. Unfortunately for her, from primary school, she had nobody of her age to walk to school with. Young girls who were almost her age were in classes that started in the afternoon while hers started in the morning. This arrangement was called 'hot sitting'. So from grade three, she walked to and from school alone. Lower grades were given morning classes only and dismissed at twelve noon. Even though MaMoyo worried about her, Zanele found the arrangement perfect because she enjoyed her own company. She did not talk much either. She acted her thoughts. Sipho attended school with her. Despite being much older than her, they were in the same class, so sometimes they walked together. Sipho started school much later because he had no birth certificate. If it was not for Zanele's mother who had visited Sipho's father to talk to him into doing something about the matter, he might have survived "like a wild animal of no registered birth," as the nurses put it.

In solitude, Zanele's immediate friends were books. At one point when they were in grade four, Sipho went to live with his maternal grandmother and attended school from there. During those years, Zanele walked alone. Later, Sipho came back to live with his father who had returned from eGoli with a new wife. So Zanele and Sipho's friendship grew. Zanele gave him the books the teachers lent her. She wanted Sipho to read after noticing that he was lagging behind in class and did not even know much about current affairs. Given a chance and encouraging environment, Zanele felt that Sipho could perform just as good as her. In most cases, Zanele gave him her own exercise books and other forms of stationery that he needed to save him from being chased out of class by their teacher who was already becoming impatient with him. It was not easy for him to be raised by a father who was as cold-blooded as a fish and a selfish stepmother. Nevertheless, Sipho wrote his grade seven examinations, even if he did not do as well as her. When his father told him he would not be able to proceed to secondary school, he ran away to his maternal grandmother who too could not assist him. Whilst the old lady did not understand why people went to school, she also wanted someone to help with ploughing, looking after livestock and just being around to run her errands. His uncles and aunts too, being uneducated themselves and working as gardeners and maids in eGoli, were happy to have him stay with their aging mother.

Sipho's gigantic dreams in small surroundings almost blew up his mind. Whilst tending goats and cattle, he read what he could find and wrote poems. Sipho's failure to proceed with school broke Zanele's heart. She felt so sorry and sad that when she was in form one, she brought him books that she had bought in second-hand bookshops and gave them to him after service on Sundays or when they went to clean the church on Saturdays. In those early years, they were just friends. Sipho then disappeared altogether. When she enquired from her cousins, each told a different story. Some said he was in South Africa while others said he had gone to Botswana. Two years passed without any communication from him.

Meanwhile, Zanele was doing well at school and was liked by every teacher including the headmistress. Zanele led the school choir and sports team. She was surprised to be among those called to see the matron after the Saturday morning duties which were carried out by every student. They included general cleaning of the school, fowl runs, dormitories and the dining hall. When her name was called, her heart skipped a beat.

Who could have written to her? She knew it was not a registered parcel or letter. It could only be a boy, but who? She did not entertain any boys or mischievous cradle snatchers. She knew that few boys would dare approach her. Most boys did not fancy girls who were cleverer than them. One teacher from primary school had once written to her, asking to meet her in town on a date. She had written him back telling him to leave her alone because she had bigger plans in her life. The good thing was that the teacher had given the letter to Ntando instead of posting it to her school address. She also sent her response via the same route.

As her turn to enter the senior matron's office came, she noticed that instead of the latter expressing anger at her, she remained neutral and did not show any emotion.

Could it be a letter carrying tragic news, she wondered.

Zanele composed herself and waited. The letter was addressed to 'the Matron/School Head or whoever read the girls' letters.' The forwarding address was St Joseph's. Zanele was the only girl from there. The matron gave her the letter to read aloud.

Dear You
This is a warning letter.
Stop reading my wife's letters. Right now I am failing to write my wife a sweet loving letter because I know you are notorious at putting your nose at matters which do not concern you.
Uyiyekele into yakho, stop it!
If you chose not to have husband, do not think everyone is like you. Again, this is a warning. I am boarding a bus to Chipinge to find medicine I will put in the envelope of the next letter I will write my

smomondiya. *Open letters and see if you will ever see again. Stop reading my wife's letters! I loved her since she was a baby girl. Right now I am waiting for her to write her O Levels. After that, I will take her eGoli and spoil her with rands. We will have babies every year. You will be jealous, I tell you!*

Stop reading my wife's letters!

Bye

Sizakufa silahlane ubukele!

Zanele could not finish reading the letter before she burst into laughter. Even the matron, who had remained quiet all along, could not hold it any longer. She laughed too.

"Ma'am, this person is complaining about someone who reads his wife's letters," Zanele said. "Honestly speaking, you know I am nobody's wife. One cannot be blamed for the actions of a lunatic," she added. Then handing back the letter to her, she insisted, "Please ma'am, it is not my letter."

"I think I believe you," the matron replied, her eyes pouring into Zanele's. "It cannot be your letter!"

Zanele was dismissed and the letter shredded, its pieces thrown into the bin.

Zanele had hands for making beads, wristbands and necklaces. Her grandmother, even if she did not do much of that craft anymore, had taught the trade to all her granddaughters. When they were younger, they collected some kind of tough grass which had long stalks and could bend easily. They wound that strong, flexible grass into bangles, necklaces and headbands. Sometimes Zanele also made beautiful earrings which resembled pumpkins, animals or anything which came to her mind at the time. They would wind three or four stalks of grass slowly while singing. Plait, plait and plait slowly they did, a three-fold, then another three-fold as they waited for their laundry to dry after taking a bath behind the village well. Sometimes they sat with MaNkomo, pricking their ears to hear her gobbets of gossip. Zanele was very much a child of nature. Sometimes, before MaNkomo came, when they were still much younger, they danced under the gentle but watchful eye of the moon after supper as adults sat talking about adult stories.

* * *

The elderly women finished the first stage of beer-brewing just before the sun had risen above the ridge of the eastern horizon. As others sat down in the shade of the hut, only MaNdlovu remained blowing chaff with a winnowing basket in a circular motion outside the temporary brewery. All the earthen pots with the shimmering liquid were covered with reed baskets to simmer and aid the slow but sure brewing of the contents in the gigantic earthen pots.

"How is the beer brewing going, my old wives?" Sikhwehle asked with comical intonation while throwing his knobkerrie down as he sat on the mud bench built around MaNcube's kitchen hut. He rested his back on the mud wall and sneezed hard, clutching his fists in an angry and impatient gesture. He picked his knobkerrie and, with its handle, scratched at a cobweb on one of the wooden pillars supporting the roof of the hut.

"*Hawu*! Son of Jiyane, where are you coming from this early?" asked MaNcube. She was washing a beer calabash in a fired open claypot. The claypot had a tattered beer strainer.

"I have warned you several times that I don't like dirty and lazy old women like you!" teased Sikhwehle. "What kind of a beer strainer is this? Do you want someone to swallow a strand and die coughing so that you can spread gossip in the community that he is suffering from AIDS? Shameless woman! I swear by my king

29

Lobengula, I would rather be buried with a rat than marry your type!" he added, pointing his finger at MaNcube who had risen to face him.

"Do not worry about that. MaNdlovu is weaving a new one that we will use to strain this beer. We were only using this to scrub the calabash, ha ha ha!" MaNcube answered him, feigning the politeness of a wife who tries to ease her angry husband. Sikhwehle's nascent ego made him puff himself up like a tiger marking its territory in the presence of would-be competitors. In that curious posture, he stood up and began pacing about, all smiles from ear to ear.

"Talk of MaNdlovu, I rejected her a long time ago," resumed Sikhwehle. "I don't want a woman who cannot make simple marula-nut sauce."

"Hawu!" exclaimed MaNdlovu, "that explains why you no longer visit me in our bedroom. I did not know that I have been sent off too, daughter of Gatsheni!" Then adopting a pleading tone, she continued, "Please do not leave me yet. Surely, we can straighten the bends. For dinner today, I will slaughter the hen that is laying eggs and prepare your favourite chicken stew. You will lick your fingers clean, I promise you."

Sikhwehle did not say anything but let loose that hollow laugh of someone who is wary of promises and has seen too many going unfulfilled.

"Sikhwehle, where did you sleep last night? Your feet are so dirty and cracked that one might think you haven't seen water in months!" MaNcube asked after she and MaSikhosana had put down the huge reed basket full of moist germinated rapoko. This was either to be pounded with pestles in mortars or ground with stones after it had been left to dry in the sun. At that moment, they were going to spread the sprouted rapoko on ripped grain bags and leave it to dry in the scorching sun.

"Hello, Kalanga woman! Did you give me water for my morning bath, you lazy old woman?" Sikhwehle asked defensively while scanning his feet.

"Didn't I tell you that your water was waiting for you on that rock behind the kitchen hut last night? Maybe you did not hear me. Let me warm some water in a tin just now for your bath whilst I make ready your breakfast," MaNdlovu spoke in a pacifying tone, caressing Sikhwehle's ego.

"I am not going to bath now, it's still early and cold. Maybe after the air gets warm. Are you going to serve braised rabbit meat in marula-nut sauce?" he directed the question to MaNdlovu with whom he had assumed friendship.

"Where will that come from? She will prepare dried pumpkin leaves in the sauce instead," MaSikhosana interjected.

"I do not eat vegetables, woman!" Sikhwehle retorted.

"Then go hunting and bring her the meat you like, so that she will cook it for you," echoed all the women in a chorus as if they had rehearsed their response.

"My husband used to beat me for cooking vegetables for his dinner, yet he did not provide the meat. He would wake me up at odd hours of the night to prepare fresh food for him whilst he watched me cook it, afraid I would put a love potion in his meals," MaNdlovu commented mournfully.

Sikhwehle stood up and helped her scoop up the litter she had been sweeping with a stiff besom broom off a hardened clay and cow dung polished floor. He used a half cracked calabash which he had picked near the hearth. He walked lamely outside the yard to throw away the litter.

MaSikhosana responded to MaNdlovu, "That's nothing! My husband did worse things. He never allowed children to eat meat, never went hunting for the meat he loved so much and never assisted in manly duties around the home. I had to brew beer for neighbours to help with putting up the roof of a hut, building a kraal or fencing a field."

"You sharp tongued, good for nothing old woman!" snapped Sikhwehle humorously. "The man was right. That was the reason why he married you in the first place. A woman who cannot even make fermented cow milk!" he shouted from the small gate, clicking his tongue as a sign of disgust. The old women looked at him as he walked to take up his previous sitting position.

"If that is the way you think, I doubt any woman would agree to marry you!" MaMlotshwa replied, looking directly at him.

"Ha ha ha!" laughed Sikhwehle spitefully. "I have a beautiful young woman with a full set of breasts still standing!"

Sikhwehle Jiyane was a fully grown man. Had things been alright with his mind, he would have made a wonderful husband and father. A man of medium build, rotund and as strong as a stallion, he never had to be reminded of his duties at his brother's homestead where he lived, not even concerning the communal chores in his village. His brother had built him a bedroom hut in his own homestead and he took his meals with the family. His brother and sister-in-law treated him like one of their own children even though they let him enjoy some grownup luxuries such as drinking beer and attending village parties. He had the dual character of a grownup and child at the same time.

Sikhwehle was not particularly fond of bathing. He cleaned his teeth all the time and could be seen from afar because of his wide smile. He would often defend himself saying he only bathed when he felt dirty. On such rare occassions, he went to Mahlasela Dam at his favourite spot near the dam wall, and there, under the cover of the branches of *mphafa* trees, he would scrub himself until his cracked heels bled. What baffled a lot of people was that most of the time his faculties seemed quite alert. This made some people think that he was alright after all, while others were not too sure of that. He was one of those people the villagers called '*umuntu kaMlimu,*' meaning God's person.

Suddenly, Sikhwehle changed his mood and confided with the elderly women reflectively, "On my way here, I saw MaNtini in a very sombre mood singing a funeral song and wiping off tears. When I greeted her, she did not even notice or hear me. She was walking in the direction of Headman Nkiwane's kraal!"

"You mean this morning?" asked MaMlotshwa with concern on her face.

"Yes, this morning," he said hitting the earth with the head of his knobkerrie, startling MaNcube and MaSikhosana.

The old women put their traditional utensils down and rested their hands on their waists, mouths agape, to listen to their friend who had begun a mysterious story. He misjudged their attention and felt he should defend himself.

"I greeted MaNtini, but she did not see me. I had nothing to do with her mood, so I let her pass," Sikhwehle explained to them, his shoulders hunched because of the discomfort caused by the morning cold and the story he was narrating.

"It must have something to do with that husband of hers. Mischief is not a stranger to MaNtini's husband, Khulumani Sibanda." MaMlotswa emphasised the latter's name in anger, throwing her arms in the air and adjusting her apron, though it was as secure as it could be. MaMlotshwa was sister to Chief Mlotshwa. She poured clean water into a gourd and washed her hands, muttering to herself.

"If it is something serious, we will hear of it as time gets by from the tides of rumours that never rest on people's tongues," observed MaNcube, pulling a reed mat to sit on. She opened her small pouch of snuff, mixed the powder in her left palm, stuffed it into her nostrils and sneezed vigorously. Sikhwehle extended his hand for her to pour some tobacco. After receiving a perfectly measured portion, he did exactly what MaNcube had done with hers. His sneezing was worse than MaNcube's. The women laughed. He was known not to take tobacco, especially that type.

"That is what happens to people who want to have a go at everything like a *tshangani* bag," MaNdlovu commented to the uproarious laughter of the women.

"That's nothing," Sikhwehle defended himself while trying to recover his blurred vision. "A man must be ready for anything. If you bring an angry lion here right now, it will tell you why I am called Sikhwehle. Then you hear a spoiled woman saying snuff wants to kill Sikhwehle. He he he he!"

One of the old women collected the last mound of litter and disappeared outside the yard through the little gate. MaNcube rose from her mat. She and MaSikhosana helped each other spread the sprouting damp rapoko on the ripped grain bags in circular motions. Next, they picked stones which they placed on every corner of the spread bags. These were meant to hold the improvised mats down so that the wind would not scatter their fermenting agent across the yard. The fermenting agent was also to be guarded from fowls, goats and stray pigs. There would certainly be no beer without this process, no rainmaking ceremony and no intoxicated effervescence for Sikhwehle and his usually inebriated friends.

Chapter Three

MaMpunzi, Headman Nkiwane's wife, was the first to see MaNtini enter their main gate early that morning. MaMpunzi went to meet MaNtini after sensing her sombre, tearful mood and quietly led her to the kitchen. After giving her a sheepskin mat to sit on, MaMpunzi greeted her visitor with calm, but instead of returning the compliments, MaNtini's cheeks became twin streams of tears that flowed unabated. MaMpunzi decided to let MaNtini cry her pain away, although after a little while, she began to feel her own tears welling up too. MaMpunzi then built a fire, placed a tin of water on the grill balanced on the three-stone hearth and went out of the house to check on her husband. She did not immediately find him. Headman Nkiwane had just woken up and gone to the cattle kraal, his first stop after waking up every morning. She had poured water into a zinc basin for her husband to wash his face and put some into a cup for his mouthwash. She had already arranged his towels and soap for him in front of their bedroom hut. But with the sudden arrival of MaNtini, MaMpunzi had to bring him back to the homestead when she found him.

"What is troubling you, daughter of Ntini?" asked Headman Nkiwane when he had seated opposite the visitor.

Several moments passed before MaNtini could answer. The old man looked at MaNtini, concerned, but let her compose herself. Sobs and streams of tears continued to communicate her grief. Even though MaNtini had a permanent look of nervousness, that morning her grief was much more pronounced. Besides her numbing grief, she was beside herself with helpless anger. MaMpunzi passed her a handkerchief, puzzled. And then MaNtini adjusted her skirt and forced out the heavy and painful words from her soul and heart.

"It is Sibanda, the man I am cursed to live with, Baba!" she paused as the tears streamed down her cheeks, down her blouse, on to her calico skirt, dampening it as well.

"Sibanda… hi hi hi… raped Khethiwe in the… hi hi hi… early hours of the morning… hi hi hi… in full view of me and her little sister Zinzile. Help me Baba, please help… I locked him up in their bedroom hut. Help us, Baba. He has destroyed my children. He has threatened us all with death. Hi hi hi!"

"He raped his own child?" asked the headman, dumbfounded. "This son of Mahlathini is a good for nothing hog. Oh, I am sorry I did not mean to, eeh… But how and why would he do that?"

"Please get him, Baba. I left him snoring. Every time he does that to me, he snores the whole morning." MaNtini spoke the last sentence in a mumble.

While MaMpunzi was consoling MaNtini, the headman was shaking his head in disbelief. After a brief moment, he sent his emissaries to Ndlovu, the village policeman. Ndlovu was ordered to arrest Sibanda, tie him up with a rope and bring him to the headman's court. MaMpunzi did not know what to do, so she just sat watching the flames of fire dancing crazily about. MaNtini's sobs were like a painful dirge in the background.

MaNtini, wife of Sibanda and mother of two daughters, Khethiwe and Zinzile, had had her physical appearance wasted by hardship, not age. Her face had premature webs of wrinkles, and her skin was loose and baggy like that of the old women brewing beer at the Hadebes'. Her strength always seemed to be sapped by her fear of Sibanda. She was not allowed to associate with other village women, especially her neighbour, MaNkomo, who was always hanging onto her husband affectionately even in public. Sibanda feared that MaNkomo would give his wife the same love potion she was presumed to have used to tame her husband. That way, he would be reduced to a puppy on a leash. MaNtini was never a member of MaMoyo's women's empowerment clubs.

Khethiwe, the victim of her father's lust and savagery, arrived later in a wheelbarrow. The wheelbarrow was being pushed by her little sister Zinzile and their neighbour, MaNkomo. MaNtini had left the girls under the care of MaNkomo and her husband Siphamandla Dube who was a nephew to old MaDube, one of the old women brewing beer at the Hadebes. She had sent instructions for them to let the girls come to the safety of the headman's homestead. Khethiwe sat in the wheelbarrow with tears streaming down her chubby cheeks, her hair standing up in grisly strands like a wild bush from tearing and pulling to defend herself. She was wearing a navy blue sweater on top of a light green dress which her father had shredded in his incestuous savagery. She asked MaNkomo and Zinzile to let her alight from the wheelbarrow outside the gate and was held by MaNkomo who led her to the hut of the headman's old mother. MaMpunzi rushed over with a wrapper to cover her blood-stained and tattered dress. MaNkomo and Zinzile had been grieving so much that they did not notice that Khethiwe was almost naked. On the way, Khethiwe had cried a lot when Siphamandla offered to push the wheelbarrow until he reasoned that maybe she did not want men near her and followed them from a distance. The headman's mother, almost blind and deaf from old age, sat near the fire, oblivious of anything, her dewlaps moving in a perpetual chewing motion. The 'golden girl', as the younger generation called her, felt the sombre atmosphere around her and asked who the visitors were and what they wanted. MaMpunzi did not explain anything to her but shouted every word in broken syllables for her to hear, claiming that the people had come to help her with the beer brewing. The ancient woman would forget whatever she was told as soon as her informant stopped talking.

Siphamandla and his wife, Varaidzo Sachirombo, or MaNkomo as everyone affectionately called her, had met in Mutare where Siphamandla had worked for the Mutare Border Timbers Company. Varaidzo used to bring lunch for her uncle who worked with Siphamandla and whom she lived with. She was a Manyika and bred in the Zimunya Communal Lands near the border town. Later, she came to Matabeleland with her husband when she could only speak a few Ndebele words that she had learnt from the Ndebele people who lived in the Dangamvura community. Siphamandla and his wife were the nearest neighbours to Sibanda and MaNtini, with their homesteads separated by a small stream, the same stream which flowed southwards past Hadebe's homestead. The couple lived a humble life full of love, running their home with adroit economy. They had two children, a son who was a toddler and a daughter who was of crawling age. They shared their chores fairly, irrespective of whether such duties were considered masculine or feminine. Even though they were neighbours, MaNtini's association with MaNkomo was forbidden by her husband who often accused MaNkomo of using strong love potions to turn Siphamandla into a woman.

"Where has one seen a man carrying a baby on his back, and where has anyone seen a man cook, bath children and fetch water for a wife?" reasoned Sibanda. "Those are a woman's duties!"

Siphamandla and MaNkomo would hoe their field together since they had no oxen and donkeys to harness for the plough. They weeded and harvested together. Both husband and wife drank beer, and carried their smart children to beer parties, MaNkomo leading the way, carrying the girl on her back and Siphamandla carrying the boy on his shoulders. They sang together, laughed, ate from the same plate and sometimes took their baths together behind the granary as the little boy watched unconcernedly over his little sister who would be sleeping peacefully on a soft sheepskin mat. Sibanda despised his neighbours so much that he only spoke to them when he wanted their help. They gave their help grudgingly, fearing his suspected use of charms which he openly boasted about at beer parties. The couple's small homestead had a kitchen, a bedroom and a granary at the back. They only had three sheep and pigs that MaNkomo raised for sale like other women in their community.

The sun had risen triumphantly when Ndlovu, the Chief's policeman, and Nkiwane's emissaries brought Sibanda to the headman's court. A group of men, including Siphamandla, helped tie Sibanda to a tree outside the yard before Headman Nkiwane, MaNtini and two other men went to report the matter to the Chief. He remained closely guarded by the Headman's officers who had gathered around him, heaping insults on him. It was well after midday when the headman's party returned and ordered MaNtini and her daughters to return home to refresh as Ndlovu proceeded to call the government police according to the chief's instruction. Sibanda was only going to be tried by the traditional court after the modern triburnal had done its justice with him. Khethiwe and MaNtini were escorted home by MaMpunzi and MaNkomo where they found Zinzile making ready some lunch of boiled cow beans mixed with precooked maize. The cobs had been left to dry in the sun before the rains. Khethiwe was helped to bath in salted water first and then in water with crushed *umsuzwane* herbs as they waited for the police. MaNkomo helped Khethiwe wear some leaves to help succour the wound and made her eat some herbed porridge to calm her nerves and make her sleep. Her mother washed her dress and undergarments as soon as she had fallen asleep in the shade of an Amarula tree. The women sat for a while, chatting solemnly with MaNtini who was still weak with grief.

The police came for the culprit in a Defender pick-up truck which they parked at Headman Nkiwane's homestead. They ignored Sibanda who was still tied to a tree like the devil that he was, mumbling unprintable curses to the singing women. Much to their surprise, the policemen warned them to leave him alone until he had been proven guilty. Headman Nkiwane stayed at home whilst Ndlovu and the two policemen walked across the stream to Sibanda's home. On arrival, Ndlovu removed his hat and the two policemen followed suit.

"We meet again our mothers!" Ndlovu said, startling MaNtini who had not heard or seen them entering the main gate.

"Oh! Good afternoon Ndlovu!" MaNtini answered.

"What is good about this afternoon?" quizzed Ndlovu.

"I am sorry you braved this blistering sun to come here!" she stood up to meet them. Zinzile brought three stools for the visitors to sit on.

"Today the sun is taking fish out of water!" exclaimed Ndlovu.

Frightened by the new male voices, Khethiwe woke up from the sheepskin mat and sprinted out of the yard screaming, looking back in the manner of someone being pursued.

"Khethiwe, wait! They are not here to harm you!" MaNkomo called in a pacifying voice while running after her. Zinzile and Ndlovu followed behind, but the pain from Khethiwe's wounds restrained her speed. Ndlovu caught up with her which made her scream even more for dear life. She tried to wriggle herself out of Ndlovu's grip but he held her with all his strength. She was getting too hysterical. The two policemen caught up with them, but as soon as Khethiwe saw them coming, she bit Ndlovu hard on his hand. Ndlovu did not let go until her mother and MaNkomo had taken over. The policemen lifted their hands to show that they were not there to harm her. She then held on to her mother in surrender and the party walked back home slowly.

"Khethiwe, we are here to help you. Please do not be afraid," the young, well-fed constable who looked as if he was in his early twenties said with a lot of sympathy in his voice. It could have been his first month of field practice in the police force.

"Maybe it would be better if you let her rest in the hut," suggested the older officer as they returned through the gate.

"She hallucinates more when she is in there. That is why we made her sleep outside," explained MaNkomo in a troubled and concerned tone as MaNtini and MaMpunzi agreed with her.

"My mothers, could you please take her to a shade behind the hut and keep watch over her as we speak to her mother," the younger officer said. Turning to face Khethiwe, he continued, "Khethiwe my sister, please do not run away. You will be fine. We are here to make sure you are fine."

MaMpunzi and MaNkomo held her and walked her slowly to the shade. Zinzile followed them with a rolled reed mat and the sheepskin mat they had been sitting on. MaNtini stood up, went to the kitchen and brought a gourd full of cold water. He handed it to Constable Mkhize, the younger officer, who was nearer to her. He bowed his head in a respectful gesture but then motioned for her to give the gourd to Sergeant Phakathi who drank and passed it to Ndlovu. Ndlovu drank the remaining water and handed the container back to MaNtini. As she quickly disappeared back into her kitchen hut to fetch more water, Sergeant Phakathi's eyes wandered around the homestead. The yard was swept clean up to the cattle kraal. Outside, in a clear line, neatly arranged stones circled the homestead like Bulawayo's Masiyephambili Drive. It was the work of Khethiwe and Zinzile who swept the yard and re-arranged the stones after being kicked out of line by stubborn goats and other domestic animals. The stones had been whitewashed with the ashes of *mutswiri* trees. The family's three huts stood in a row, with the kitchen at the centre. They were all plastered the same way, pitch black mud at the bottom and red antheap soil at the top. All the huts had a stoop or a mud bench hugging the wall from outside. A huge portrait was drawn on either side of the doors of all the huts using white ash, the same one which had whitewashed the stones outside the yard. Each drawing was the shape of a flying butterfly, their widespread wings dotted with black on the outside. The butterflies' antennae protruded further away from their little heads downwards to join words written in white, "God bless our family." The front of the kitchen had a mud wall enclave which distinguished it from other huts. Its thatched roof was darkened by soot. The enclave was also plastered in the same way as the walls, though it was shorter. The hearth which was at the centre inside the hut was beaten stiff, hardened by the sun and later polished with cow dung. The granary which showed up a little behind the hut in whose shade Khethiwe was sitting was also plastered the same way, looking neat and clean.

The fencing around the homestead left a lot to be desired. Cattle and donkeys could easily walk through the gate and devour grass from the thatch. There were gaps and patches. The cattle and goat kraals had the same gaps. MaNtini and Khethiwe had used acacia branches to block the animals from getting out and straying. According to Sibanda, that was a woman's job. The pigs made noise in their seemingly strong pen.

Zinzile took some water to them as soon as Khethiwe, who was visibly in an abyss of fear, pain and the torture of doubt, had settled into MaNkomo's lap, drowsed by the herbs which she had taken in the porridge. Fowls which had been standing on mortars and pestles, wings lifted, squeaked and flew about behind Zinzile towards the pig's pen under the illusion that she had something for them to peck at. Some remained pecking at the soft soil loosened by constant pounding in the shade of the nearby *mbondo* tree.

MaNtini passed the water gourd to Constable Mkhize, who first cleaned its edges with the back of his hand before drinking. He then handed it to Ndlovu who just drank.

"We are very sorry MaNtini about what happened." It was Sergeant Phakathi who broke the silence.

"I am very sorry too, Mama, for what happened," Constable Mkhize joined the conversation. "You just have to be patient with her; she is still traumatised. Most rape victims get damaged emotionally and mentally if they fail to get proper counselling on time. Others will hate men and not want to see them near them for the rest of their lives. Some withdraw from people and prefer to be alone. The other thing is you must not let people question her about what happened. The incident humiliates, terrifies and hurts her beyond imagination. What makes it worse for her is she was raped by her own father, a person she loved and looked up to for protection. Please, observe that she does not harm herself," Constable Mkhize advised.

"I hear you, son, and thank you for coming," MaNtini replied and then began to sob until MaMpunzi came to sit near her. She put her arm around her. Using a wrapper, she tried hard to wipe off her tears which were streaming freely down her face. They waited silently and patiently until she had composed herself.

"First, we would like to commend you for reporting such a heavy matter to us. Thank you for that courage because not many women can do it and we all know it is a difficult decision to make," Constable Mkhize paused and looked at the clear blue sky before proceeding. "I am sorry, Mama MaNtini, could you give us a statement of what happened and the evidence to support it?"

"What kind of evidence shall I give you?" queried MaNtini.

"All the clothes Khethiwe was wearing during the time of the crime and possible weapons used to threaten you and her."

* * *

Towards sunset, Zanele and Nonceba were chatting incessantly as they made their way to the village well. Ntando and her cousin followed behind them grudgingly. They did not want to leave the *inkente* game they had been playing and, after all, it hurt to carry water barrels on their freshly plaited hair. Zanele was expecting to sit for her 'A' Level examinations the following term at the Catholic run Empandeni Mission in Plumtree. After her came Mpiyabo and lastly Ntando. Nonceba was Zanele's eldest cousin from her paternal aunt. She lived with her parents at their Matshaemhlophe home in Bulawayo. Her father was a practising private surgeon who also served in government hospitals, and her mother was a nurse at Mpilo General Hospital. Nonceba usually visited the Hadebes during the holidays when she had no impending exams.

"Surely this world is coming to an end!" MaNkomo exclaimed as she moved her hands away from the logs she was removing from the little gate to open the communal village well from where they fetched water.

"What happened and where, MaNkomo?" asked Nonceba, moving closer.

"Anyway, how did the beer brewing go? I saw MaSikhosana returning home on my way here," MaNkomo said, shrewdly evading the responsibility of continuing with the story that she had started.

"We suppose it went well. How else would we know since we are not allowed to peep into their brewery? You have not answered my question," Nonceba pressed MaNkomo to reveal what had happened.

"I swear by my mother who is buried in the cold earth on the banks of Zimunya River, that son of Mahlathini should be banished from this village!" MaNkomo swore.

"Sibanda stole someone's ewe again?" Nonceba enquired curiously.

"This time he did something worse than claiming Sabelo's ewe!" MaNkomo replied, entering through the gate. It was an open well dug by the villagers. There was some open space around the water hole for villagers to stand around.

"What did he do? I'm scared now!" Zanele asked.

"He *kulungile*, Ntando and Zothile, could you please get me some leaves from the *umsehla* tree over there?" It was a trick just to get the young ones to a distance where they would not hear what she was about to say.

MaNkomo then lowered her voice and narrated Khethiwe's ordeal to them, almost in point form. Nonceba listened without interrupting but Zanele kept on throwing questions which MaNkomo ignored. She wanted to make sure she would have finished telling them Khethiwe's painful story by the time Ntombi and Zothile returned. She then indicated by way of a mock sealing of her mouth with her fingers to show that they must not talk about the matter anywhere. As soon as the little girls returned, Zanele and MaNkomo helped place water barrels on their heads and let them go ahead of them.

"How old is Khethiwe?" Nonceba asked as soon as the two were out of earshot.

"She is fifteen and is in form three at St Joseph's Secondary school."

"That is so bad, poor girl! She needs counselling, but do people here understand any of it?" Nonceba asked, her arms holding her stomach like someone experiencing labour pains.

"True, but people would mistake her trauma for the effects of her father's evil charms. Everybody in this village thinks he has very potent herbs which make him get away with every crime he commits!" Zanele said sorrowfully.

"And you think he does not?" MaNkomo screamed mockingly at Zanele.

"*Umh, ja*! Everyone here is morbidly superstitious, I see," Nonceba expressed her dismay.

"That I do not know MaNkomo," said Zanele. "I cannot confirm if he has such things or not, but Nonceba is right. Khethiwe needs professional help, like counselling. Victims of rape are often destroyed for the rest of their lives if they do not get help early enough."

"Of course, they are destroyed by their victimisers; medicine men like Sibanda!" MaNkomo said with confidence.

"MaNkomo, MaNkomo, hear me," Nonceba implored calmly and waited for her to listen attentively. "Rape is rape and a violation of human rights in general. There is no magic attached to it. Rapists are serious criminals who force their savage sexual urges on unwilling women. Rape is cruelty at its worst; it damages every faculty of the victim's brain as well as her physical well-being and also eats into the victim's emotional stability. So rapists should be given the longest prison sentences, sentences that are longer than those given to cattle and car thieves!"

"*Umh*, I hear you MaGodonga," replied MaNkomo. "What I am saying is that Sibanda's issue has always been there as a family secret. His late father also slept with his daughters. Actually, he is the one who broke their virginity and would continue having sex with them before they got married!" she emphasised the last sentence in a whisper.

"What! MaNkomo, where have you heard of a father who sleeps with his own daughters? That is incest!" Nonceba exclaimed.

"There you are!" MaNkomo said.

"Their mother was supposed to report him to the police," Nonceba said angrily.

"Women of those days could not do things like that because they feared their husbands, and even their clan would not come to the defence of such outspoken women. Instead, they accused the women of all sorts of things. Women who reported their husbands to the police could even be sent back to their families where they were illtreated for failing in marriage. Do not forget it was also shameful for a woman to give up on her marriage no matter the circumstances she went through. What was even worse in some families is that a bride had to have sexual intercourse with her father-in-law!" Zanele said remorsefully.

"*Nholowemizana*!" shouted MaNkomo.

"Zanele, you also know these things?" asked Nonceba, surprised.

"Yes, I know even though I do not necessarily agree with the cave custom."

"Tough for women!" consoled Nonceba. "Hands up to MaNtini! She is the type of woman we want in our society. Women should protect their children by all means possible and at all costs," she added.

"Let me rush to my baby who is not feeling too well. She is cutting her first teeth and I left her with her father who does not know what to do if she cries," MaNkomo said as she branched off from the path they had been walking along together.

"See you tomorrow morning then, MaNkomo. I hope she gets better," Zanele said almost in a shout.

Save for the noise birds made courting, chirping and building their nests which hung facing the ground from huge *umkhaya* and acacia trees, no other sound disturbed the calm sunset air. They walked on quietly now and entered the homestead to find MaNdlovu weaving a beer strainer. MaMlotshwa made the strands on her leg with fresh sisal fibre which Zamani and Mpiyabo had brought from Mahlasela dam. The old ladies were also taking turns keeping away the fowls from pecking on the sprouted rapoko they had spread to dry. For supper, which MaMoyo served early, they ate *isitshwala* with impala biltong in marula-nut sauce. Nonceba enjoyed both the biltong in sauce and calabash-fermented cow milk brought by MaNleya.

But it was double trouble for Zanele that night as she thought of her own ordeal and Khethiwe's. For Khethiwe, it was not her fault. That thought pained her and tears trickled down her cheeks. Was she really feeling for Khethiwe or was it for herself that she was crying?

Chapter Four

As the east was beginning to glow with the distant rays of the approaching sun, the beer brewing party made a huge fire with *mopane* logs. By the time Zanele and Nonceba had risen and gone to fetch water, the brew was almost boiling. When the two girls came back, the brew was simmering in a drum and the supporting earthen pots, much to the joy of Sikhwehle who also had just arrived. Sikhwehle's affinity for beer was legendary. The girls greeted him as they hurried off to collect firewood before the sun had risen too high into the sky. The heat then could be debilitating. They met MaNkomo near Sithwala's disused field, a clearing where the village cattle, donkeys, sheep and goats grazed. The village women used the time before the rains to stock up on firewood for their cooking during the expected rainy season. The rainy season was inevitably for ploughing and planting.

Not too long after the cropping, all other things having been done, it would soon be harvest time. The Easter holidays always had so much that needed to be done. Following the harvests, the villagers would thrash the grain and store it in their granaries. Most of these duties were done by women who generally accepted it as their lot.

The firewood gathering party had to wander further away from the homesteads since dry logs were becoming scarcer and scarcer. Besides, not all of the logs one came across could be used for home fires and cooking. Strange as it might have seemed to others, the women were actually very keen to go looking for usable logs; to them it was a splendid social expedition. Ntando, Zanele's younger sister, cried if ordered to stay behind. In Chief Mlotshwa's area, cutting down trees for firewood attracted the penalty of a fine. The fine was imposed depending on how many trees one had cut down. Certain types of trees attracted harsher penalties than others.

"By the way, Nonceba, which school did you say you were learning at?" asked MaNkomo.

"University of Zimbabwe."

"What are you studying?" she asked, breaking a piece of dry wood from a *muwawa* tree they were passing.

"Medicine. I am studying to be a doctor," Nonceba said, waiting for her to remove the dangerous spikey tentacles from the piece of wood.

"Yoh! A woman?" exclaimed MaNkomo.

"*Ki ki ki, he he he!*" giggled Ntando and her cousin. MaNkomo gave them a wink and smiled.

"Yes, what is wrong with that?" asked Zanele.

"MaGodonga! A doctor? When do you finish? You will soon be an old maid and fail to attract a man for marriage!" exclaimed MaNkomo, clapping her hands and looking at her in disbelief.

"You have started with your waffling. You want her to leave school and get married to who? Who will give her what education can?"

"It is just a comment, Za. She will get old and fail to attract a man! Anyway, do you build a home with books and injections? Can you talk to them and can they keep you warm at night?" MaNkomo said directly to Zanele.

"MaNkomo!" Zanele threw her hands up in resignation.

"I was not talking to you in the first place. What is a woman's job if not to get married, bear children and look after her husband?" asked MaNkomo with a wink at Zanele.

"That is the typical thinking of an unlettered, backward old peasant woman! Our first husbands would be our papers and degrees, Mama! We want to live in beautiful apartments first, before we can even think of getting married. We will buy our own cars and travel all over the world, shopping with our own monies," Zanele said mockingly.

"I want to become a doctor like my father. I love people, especially babies. I want to specialise in babies' health," Nonceba said.

MaNkomo shook her head in disapproval. Nonceba looked at her with candid wonder and curiosity. She smiled softly with an almost condescending intellectual subtlety. She then made off to break some dry twigs from a dry branch she had brought down from a nearby *mbondo* tree. They were assured of clean logs for the fires back home. MaNkomo stared at her as Ntando and Zinzile giggled. Nonceba found herself thinking about Queen Nzinga of Angola and Mama Asante Waa of Ghana. She wondered what MaNkomo would think of such powerful women as these two had been. Both women were notable military strategists with wisdom and diplomatic acumen. She smiled as she thought about how they had succeeded in keeping would be occupiers off their territories.

Queen Nzinga refused to sign a treaty with the Portuguese Governor Joao Corria de Sousa in 1922 for he had declared that the Portuguese were superior to her people. It is said the Governor had arranged that she talk to him while sitting on a mat just like one of his subjects. Queen Nzinga looked at her aides and bodyguards with a familiar contemptuous smile. They arranged themselves like a royal throne and one of her aids crouched on all fours for her to sit on his back. She held the meeting sitting on that man's back for three hours! Nonceba smiled at the thought of that act which would probably be baffling for MaNkomo who did not believe women could be anything other than wives and mothers.

"I have never seen a black woman who is a doctor," MaNkomo said honestly.

"She will be the first one you will see," Ntando said, smiling.

"I saw a European doctor at Mtshelanyemba hospital and –" Zinzile said.

"I saw another at Brunapeg Mission Hospital," interjected Ntando.

"Now you have heard her; she does not want to go back to Stone Age days, tilling the land, brewing beer for survival and delivering babies in kitchen huts," mused Zanele.

"That is inevitable for an African woman. As for your jealous Sipho, is he going to let you run wild? Remember he is not educated like you and he spends most of the time behind the tails of cattle. Unless you are telling me you will soon be leaving him."

"Yes. I am leaving him, MaNkomo. Let him find his type. Very soon he will be gone to dig for gold and diamonds in the mines left behind by Cecil John Rhodes's men in Johannesburg! I do not want a man I will see once a year for two weeks," Zanele said without conviction.

MaNkomo looked at Zanele and gave a quizzical wink that seemed to ask her if she was sure about what she was saying, if she really meant it. Zanele avoided MaNkomo's eyes. The pounding in her rib cage told her that her heart was racing. Try as she might, sometimes Zanele was just not able to hide her emotions, especially where MaNkomo was concerned. Why, the woman knew her better than her own mother! If someone who did not know her present predicament looked her over closely, she would pick the air of regret which Zanele was desperately trying to hide in the tone of her words. Alone, she shed tears that could fill an ocean.

"Nonceba Mahlangu, tell your mother, Zanele, to leave this Sipho boy. He is not good for her because there is an avenging spirit tormenting his family. It cries for compensation and retribution!"

"An avenging spirit, MaNkomo? Did a member of his family kill someone?" Nonceba asked, taken aback.

"Her prospective father-in-law and not just a distant family member! Since then, the Dubes have been dying like poisoned rats," said MaNkomo, trying to reach out for a dry branch from a *guwe* tree.

"I think it is just a coincidence, MaNkomo. People die! The Dubes are dying of different causes," Zanele said defiantly.

"When did the murder happen?" persisted Nonceba.

"Two years ago, MaGodonga. Since then, they have buried five people and Sipho's aunt lost her senses after she was chased out of her home by her husband's family over a trivial issue. She is the one you saw talking, singing and dancing at the shops last Sunday," MaNkomo said. She liked addressing Nonceba using her totem name, MaGodonga.

"Ah! That lunatic! She was saying funny things to herself about a baby who will not see his father!" Nonceba said.

"NakaThathabonke. The people from the shops have given her that nickname because she talks about taking everyone with her. Mostly she says things associated with Mxotshwa Ncube's murder and everybody in this village has heard her with their own ears. Zanele, nobody can say I did not warn you."

"Umm, MaNkomo, I wonder what you are on about!" replied Zanele adamantly. "The High Court itself cleared Sipho's father because he acted in self-defence. There is nothing sinister about the deaths, and that aunt of his was chased away because of laziness, so she is stressed out."

"Umm, stress? Do we black people ever know about stress?" teased Nonceba.

"Ask her that!" echoed MaNkomo.

"Zanele my love, please don't act like your father-in-law," MaNkomo warned but with a cooing vibrancy in her voice. Zanele wondered how late they had been when things were already toppled down as they were. Deep down her heart, she wished MaNkomo would let the matter rest.

"An avenging spirit does not respect the judgements of modern courts," reflected Nonceba. "Even if you do not want to leave Sipho, the avenging spirit will put an end to it," she added solemnly.

"Say it again, MaGodonga. If she won't, I will never open my mouth on the matter again," MaNkomo threw her hands away in despair.

"What exactly happened, MaNkomo?" Nonceba asked, moving her heap of firewood next to Zanele's. She had also made ready the strips of bark they were going to tie their bundles with from stripping young *mopane* tree branches. She placed four strands across on the sand for MaNkomo, three for each of the girls and gave the rest to Zanele who had the honour of arranging a bundle for her.

"It is said it was a usual Wednesday morning in January last year when this Mxotshwa Ncube took an axe and cut down a barren *Marula* tree near Simphiwe Dube's homestead. He wanted to carve a trough from which he would feed his pigs or goats. There was nothing wrong with that, but the deceased acted without respect by not greeting the Dubes and asking for their permission to do what he had in mind," MaNkomo spoke with a calmness that had a tinge of irony in it. Everyone, including MaNkomo, busied themselves with arranging their bundles of wood. Only Nonceba listened attentively and said nothing. "Dube, on the other hand, was working at his blacksmith's vice inside his homestead, chiselling and sharpening an iron rod he used to make holes on carved hoe handles, wooden spoons and other implements. He stood up inside his shed, surprised by this daring tree cutter. He decided to confront him. Sipho and his uncles who were at the cattle kraal branding some calves saw what was happening. They stopped and started to walk towards the homestead. Dube greeted Ncube who did not answer but continued to cut the tree down. Dube stood there waiting for an answer. Ncube, annoyed and without answering the greeting, hurled insults at Dube who remained quiet. Zamani's father, Mpiyabo and Zamani, who happened to be passing by in their donkey-drawn scotch cart at the time, also stopped to intervene, but it was too late. In the twinkle of an eye, Ncube had moved with his axe held high and ready. It almost sliced Dube, only missing him by a whisker. Dube leapt quickly to try and hold Ncube's hands but was overpowered. He fell to the ground on his back while still holding the sharp rod from his forge. The rod accidentally pierced through the heart of the advancing Ncube, killing him instantly."

"What a shame! Poor man! It wasn't his fault," exclaimed Nonceba,

"The Chief called Dube to negotiate a payment to appease the avenging spirit, but Dube has been making excuses ever since. He was acquitted at the High Court based on the evidence before the court, evidence that came from the people who were also rounded as witnesses," MaNkomo explained further.

"Of course, Zanele, a modern court would not charge him. The late Mxotshwa was at fault. The distance he walked to cut down the tree is questionable too. Why that tree?" Nonceba asked curiously.

They carried their firewood on their heads and walked back home under the already scorching sun.

"Dube is now hiding behind a finger. This court thing deceived him, but his family is perishing."

"He should just go and pay compensation. In the Bible, Abel's blood cried to God against his brother Cain who had killed him.

Spiritually, killing cannot be excused. I sympathise with him, but even though he is a victim, he must still pay!"

"You can say that again! According to tradition, he is supposed to pay a beast at the Chief's court to cleanse himself and ask for forgiveness from the spirits of the land. That way he will be forgiven," MaNkomo said.

"When did the mysterious deaths in the family start?" Nonceba asked in a loud tone. She was second in front of a single file.

"It was Sipho's grandfather who died first, a month before Mxotshwa's memorial service. NakaThathabonke went mad just after her father's burial. Sipho's brother was shot in South Africa a week later. That was when everyone began to be alarmed and the chief called him again. Two months later, a recently married niece of his, daughter to his brother, died soon after giving birth. She left behind a sinless baby, orphaned before she had so much as begun to suckle from her mother's breast. Dube's daughter with Sipho's stepmother drowned in the shallow Marabi River early this year. Last month, we buried his younger brother who was hit by a car in Bulawayo," narrated MaNkomo.

Nonceba, with a worried tone, said to Zanele, "Za, my mother, leave this Sipho boy alone, whatever the circumstances, and concentrate on your education. What MaNkomo has said does not sound good. I love you so much, Mama. I do not want to see you hurt. Boys like Sipho only think of being intimate with you. They will make you a scandal by getting you pregnant and leaving you to mind it on your own. What exactly do you talk with him about? You know what we used to do at the boarding school? We used to tease each other by marking and reviewing letters written to us by boys from Embakwe, Cyrene and Mzingwane! We knew that the boys did the same with our letters to them. It was just a bit of innocent fun, we did not sleep with them. But we didn't entertain Sipho's kind!"

"Tell her MaGodonga!" MaNkomo insisted exuberantly, "I want Zanele to get a good education. For her, a good job would certainly be guaranteed. She will bring me perfume, lotion and new pairs of glittering earrings. She will buy me bottles of Fanta from the shops on Sundays and a good selection of assorted biscuits."

"MaNkomo! *Ekudleni*! You love munching!" Zanele remarked playfully, choosing to ignore the advice Nonceba had just been giving her. The younger girls giggled, moving this and that way.

"Of course! What's wrong with eating, especially when you have worked for your own food? I work with my own hands so I will cook whatever I want and indulge," MaNkomo said, taking the path which led to her homestead.

Zanele tried hard to contain her anger. She suddenly went quiet. She walked slowly, brooding behind the others. Her face had gone ashen and morose, a mixture of unpleasant emotions and unexpressed aspirations troubling her. Her cautioned and controlled agitations made her feel like someone sitting atop a wasp's nest. She felt like throwing her bundle of firewood away and running into the forest where she hoped to be swallowed by something and disappear from the world. Suddenly, she gained some kind of inspiration from within and then decided against running away. Her thoughts wandered backwards and she saw, in her mind, a procession of events in her life after the return of Sipho. Years ago, after vanishing like a kite, she was surprised to see him at her party.

It was Ntando who spotted him parking his bicycle outside the gate. Sipho had grown big. His shoulders were wide and his arms displayed the masculine sinews of a body builder. After everyone, including MaMoyo, had greeted him cheerfully, Sipho naturally joined the group composed of his age mates. That was the first time he had seen Zanele's cousin, Nonceba, who had come with

Mandla and two other friends he was not introduced to. At once, he had felt inferior to Nonceba who spoke in English with her friends. Mandla's accent and clothes were there for Sipho to see; the car he drove at his age, his friend and girlfriend were enough to annoy him. He was surprised that they left at five in the evening. Sipho did not know that the big car that Mandla drove had been lent to him just for the day. He was glad when they returned to Bulawayo. He would have some private time with Zanele the following day on Sunday.

That night became long for Sipho who already imagined Zanele sweeping their yard as his wife. He fancied himself owning stores in every growth point and later, restaurants, and even hotels. In Botswana he had worked as a cleaner, waiter and then last, on a grill. With his love for cooking, he had learnt so many recipes. How he would do this, he had no idea. Zanele would stop going to school and marry him after Ordinary Level. It was set in his mind and heart, and come what may, he vowed to himself that it would happen. As soon as the girls appeared from across Marabi River on their way to church, his heart started beating faster than usual. He started rehearsing the sentences and words he would say to her, words which would not frighten her stiff. He was happy to notice that they had no elder among them. Even if he was oblivious of it, Sipho approached the group of girls, looking at Zanele with the hungriest of looks. Zanele herself did not notice it, but Khethiwe did. She just wondered if he really thought Zanele was his type of girl and then dismissed the idea.

After church, before they rushed home, Sipho quickly gave Zanele some presents which he had brought her. There was no time to play then since Zanele wanted to prepare to leave for school the following morning. She was excited to be going for Advanced level. Her brother and uncle would help her carry her luggage to the bus stop. Ahead in the city of Bulawayo, Nonceba, who was also waiting to start university, would meet her at the bus terminus. Even though Sipho could not get the chance to walk with her, he managed to be at the bus stop at the shops by the time they got there. Filled with excitement to proceed to 'A' level, Zanele chatted incessantly with her brother and uncle who were brimming with happiness for her.

During the following holiday, she came home for only two weeks. Her schoolwork had become so demanding that she needed a lot of study and research time. For the rest of the holiday, she stayed with Nonceba's parents.

Sipho did not want the gap between him and Zanele to become too wide. It had been widening as their lives ran in opposite directions. Soon, Zanele would not be persuaded to want the same things he desired in life. During the December holiday, Sipho was happy to come close to telling Zanele what he felt about her. Zanele had gone out for a Christmas party with Khethiwe and her cousins at a homestead near that of Sipho's parents. Even though they had not stayed for long, he had taken the chance to escort her back. Sipho did not divulge to her that his return was not voluntary, but that he had been deported. Instead, he lied that he wanted to take care of his sister for whom he had found a good school in Botswana, and that he was waiting for her passport and papers. He claimed his maternal grandmother mistreated his sister and that it would be worse for her to live in the loveless home of their father and stepmother. Zanele felt pity but could not do much except wish him well. The following day, Ntando gave her a letter. She was so taken aback by what Sipho had written in the letter, especially the rhymes that she read to Khethiwe. Impressed as she was by the poems, she warned Zanele to tell him to go and choke on the dirt of his own choice. What did they have in common? Zanele did not answer but just laughed it off.

"Sipho behaves like a man who beats up his wife till she faints, pours water on her, and when she comes to her senses, beats her again," Khethiwe warned matter-of-factly as they washed blankets at the village well the following afternoon.

"You should sympathise with him. He lacked love all his life!" Zanele protested.

"I do sympathise with him. I am merely stating his character. He is not the boy for you."

"He deserves to be loved too," Zanele said defiantly but without showing conviction.

"Certainly, he does but beware of mixing issues and feelings, otherwise you will suffer a permanent contract for a temporary feeling," Khethiwe said to her while looking at her directly.

Zanele merely nodded while feigning thoughtfulness.

After the conversation, she ignored the letter. Sipho sent another one, which also went unanswered. That oiled him more. He waited for them when they went to fetch water or firewood, but words just dried up on his lips. To Sipho, life was a sickness unless Zanele became his wife. He was only sure to find love and a listening ear from her among all the girls he had seen. He had lived all his life in a world which did not want or regard him. Zanele regarded and treated him as a human being, a person who deserved to be respected and listened to. Khethiwe, always sincere in her comments to Zanele, knew the pair would not make a couple. Zanele could not bear hurting anything living, either plants or creatures, whilst Sipho always carried a jack-knife which was so wicked looking that it threatened to cut the throat of anyone who wronged him. Meanwhile, Zanele had responded to his letter, accepting him with an impulsive penance. She kept the letter and decided to post it to him when she got back to school. She would see him in April during the Easter Holiday. She knew that she had hurried to conclude her decision without due consideration. It was a bad idea she was somehow vulnerable to. But she had never dated anyone before. Her curiosity of what it felt like to have a boyfriend also made her accept Sipho's clumsy advances. She would keep the affair a secret.

Chapter Five

The aroma of the cooked mixture, *umhiqo*, greeted them from outside the gate when they arrived almost at the same time with MaMpunzi. The Chief's mother had just arrived too. No doubt, before the end of the day, those who would have gorged themselves on the *umhiqo* would be drinking water like camels. That was what *umhiqo* made people do. Through the corner of her eye, Zanele saw that the beer brewing party had just finished pouring the hot thick liquid into various wide mouthed earthenware containers from where it would cool by sunset. Some fermenting agent made from rapoko malt would be added too once the *umhiqo* was cool enough. The fermenting agent had not dried sufficiently the previous day, so they had spread it again in the sun. Sikhwehle had helped keep watch of the fowls that came pecking at the all-important agent. That done, the old women sat on the ground in front of MaMoyo's kitchen, waiting for their first meal of the day and chatting about rain, firewood and mischievous children and grandchildren.

The Chief's mother was visiting MaMlotshwa, her late husband's sister, at her home, but when MaNleya told her that she was at the Hadebes, she decided she would go there and see other women in addition to checking how the process was going on. MaMlotshwa and her friends had finished working in the brewery for the morning, pouring clean water into the calabashes they would use to carry the beer to the dance shrine the following Saturday.

"Oh MaMoyo, I did not know we had a visitor! Why did you not send for us?" MaMlotshwa smiled and put the huge gourd down. She had somehow forgotten to leave it in MaMoyo's reed basket in the hut. She wiped her hands on her voluminous apron as her face beamed in an infectious expression of joy. She pulled a sheepskin mat closer and sat beside MaSikhosana. MaNcube had quickly rushed to her bedroom when she saw the woman approaching the gate. On emerging from the hut, she had in her hands a neatly woven and beautifully decorated reed mat. MaSikhosana and MaSibanda received it in her honour and laid it down for her to sit on. She manoeuvred herself onto the mat on her knees to sit comfortably. The woman was quite old and could now not remember her exact date of birth since no one bothered to have births recorded during her time. The things that she knew and the experiences she talked about made it a foregone conclusion that she was probably more than a hundred years old. She supported herself with a walking stick and her back had since arched.

"Do not worry yourself. I am just arriving. I am really impressed. I can see that you are still strong, and I can also see that you have finished sorting the mixture. That is the most difficult and important stage of the brew, and is what we call brewing beer," said the Chief's mother.

"He he he! What shall we say of you then? What time did you wake up for you to be here at this time?" asked MaSikhosana admiringly.

"I bet the second cock crowed when you were already on your way here!" MaMlotshwa teased.

"Not really," replied the elderly woman, "I was still sleeping. I walked fast before the air got warm!"

Greetings were exchanged between the ladies in polite reverence.

Zanele worked apprehensively, serving breakfast and the previous day's leftovers of boiled round nuts and huskless maize mixed with peanut butter. This was served cold. There was also some homemade bread baked by Nonceba the previous night. The bread did not have too many takers and only Sikhwehle and Ntando seemed to prefer it to the traditional delicacy.

"I am sorry about the incident that befell you yesterday! That son of Mahlathini should be banished from this community before he causes more grief and strife!" the Queen Mother said with heavy emotion. Everyone put their enamel cups down in confusion, except for Zanele and Nonceba who winked at each other.

"Did you see the girl, MaMpunzi?" she asked.

"Yes I did, Mama. It was terrible. She was so traumatised, I spent the day with her. It was the reason I could not come and help MaMoyo yesterday. MaNtini could not have managed the girl alone!" said MaMpunzi sorrowfully.

"When he stole the ewe and got away with it, he thought his charms would protect him, but now he will die in jail. Think of it, for raping his own child!" said the chief's mother, MaNxumalo, with grief.

"What happened?" MaNdlovu enquired on behalf of all the women.

Everyone stopped eating as MaMpunzi went into detail about what she had heard and seen. Sikhwehle looked at her accusingly as if she had something to do with the crime. Vigorously, he tousled his kinky hair, half closing his heavy lidded eyes, making MaMpunzi uneasy. It was as if they shared an embarrassing secret.

"Sibanda raped his daughter?" exclaimed MaNdlovu in shock mingled with pain.

"That is not to be wondered about. He takes after his grandfather who also did not know where to use the shameful burden between his legs. He was a man of great recklessness, showing the same tendencies, including being a self-proclaimed herbalist just like Sibanda," shouted MaSikhosana.

"Is he a herbalist?" MaMpunzi asked. Sikhwehle looked at her with an insulting and degrading look. She felt an unbroken colt's apprehensiveness rise and unsettle within her. Nobody noticed the war between the two.

"You do not know that he operates an abortion clinic in his wife's kitchen at night? His patients are young married women with husbands across the Limpopo. After sleeping with some of these young married women and impregnating them, he helps them to abort their pregnancies with his herbs," MaSikhosana said with great vehemence, much to the surprise of Zanele and Nonceba. Nobody else appeared surprised. She went on.

"It is said his grandfather used the same herbs on his own daughters after he would have made them pregnant."

"Right now, Simphiwe Dube's family is perishing because of him. He is the one who is giving him fake herbs and lying to him that he can reverse the avenging spirit," MaNdlovu added with annoyance.

"Talk about that MaNcube, his kraal is now flourishing with Dube's cattle and goats. It would have been better if he had paid the Mxotshwas with those," said MaMoyo sitting down next to the Chief's mother.

"This is the problem with us people; we do not always want to be bold and face the truth. When at last he opens his eyes, he will have lost his family and the wealth," the Chief's mother commented.

MaNkomo was full of fresh information and her sources always told the truth, Nonceba thought. They had kept that secret locked in their hearts. It had been their wish to visit Khethiwe but they did not know how to ask MaMoyo. But now they felt this was their chance since the matter was now in the open. Ntando kept watch over the fowls while Sikhwehle was having his breakfast. Sometimes stray chicks fell into the earthen pots containing the hot liquid. Some were rescued on time while others were scalded to death. Ntando made sure she kept them off the open containers.

The old sisters cursed as they continued eating breakfast and drinking tea with goat milk which Nonceba had reheated for them. Sikhwehle could not get his eyes off MaMpunzi who sat on a sheepskin mat a little further away from the rest of the women. Nobody bothered him about his strange ogling, Sikhwehle being who he was.

Tholakele Mpunzi was an extremely beautiful woman in her late twenties. She was the second wife who came aboard as a replacement for her dead aunt who had been Headman Nkiwane's wife. The headman himself was in his late sixties while his new wife was the same age as his dearly departed wife's last daughter. MaMpunzi was light in complexion and had a curvaceous body accentuated by a wasp-like waist. She had a medium sized bust and always wore a brassiere which most village women had no use for, even while they were breastfeeding. She was a beauty goddess with closet devotees among the village men. Her round face was decorated with high cheekbones under big eyes. MaMpunzi's nose stood high and was slightly pointed. When her lips parted, they revealed a set of beautiful milk-white teeth.

Besides her physical beauty, MaMpunzi was always cheerful, making people laugh everywhere she was. One could say she had a naturally warm countenance. Those who did not know her probably thought she was always under the influence of something. She was easily noticed and felt at meetings. Even her step exuded some cajolery about her. Her mother was constantly worried about her behaviour since she had been shepherded off to marry the headman. The claim was that Tholakele had developed loose morals, and her "I don't care" attitude reinforced a nascent disrespect for her husband. These remarks and scruples never weighed her down. Those who paid close attention to her said she seemed to be saying through her attitude that the damage had been done already and that there was no reason to worry anymore. One could say that Tholakele was rebellious. Nevertheless, her rebellion somehow disagreed with her undemanding existence. She appeared like a woman who was constantly looking for ways of fulfilling her life without much luck.

As the women chatted incessantly about all village successes and trifles, three men entered the homestead unnoticed. Two of the men were in police uniform. They were in the company of Ndlovu, the Chief's policeman.

"*E Hadebe, baba, bomama, ekuhle!*" Ndlovu led the greetings after removing his straw hat. The other men removed their hats too in respect.

"You are welcome, Ndlovu, you are welcome," MaMoyo answered them, her arms on her lap. Her arms remained held together against her abdomen to conceal her fright. The chattering from the old women stopped, for it was unusual for the police to patrol the villages. In spite of not fearing them, the Chief's mother despised their system. She did not, even in the slightest, approve of the new ways through which the system dealt with lawbreakers. She argued that people had managed their affairs from time immemorial without having to lock a lawbreaker in a cell for life, leaving the family suffering. She also saw the system as one with a lot of loopholes.

Nonceba and Zanele rushed with wooden stools from *ekhutheni* and gave them to the visitors.

"*Eh Ndlovukazi! MaWandla!* I am sorry my mother, I had not recognised you among my mothers who are here. How are you?" Ndlovu bowed his head in a show of special respect as he greeted MaNxumalo.

"I am fine, *mzukulu*, how are your children doing this morning?"

Ndlovu responded with an air of reverence. He beheld the familiar scene with undisguised excitement. He even went on to ask about the progress of the brewing. Constable Mkhize was fascinated by this display of respect and honour for traditional values and by the fact that everyone seemed to know what was happening in the community. He looked at his feet, then noticed as he raised his eyes, Nonceba coming out of the kitchen to get some plates from the stand made of wooden poles. His heart missed a beat. He felt his stomach move uncomfortably. His eyes followed every step and savoured her appearance from top to bottom. To him, she appeared like Shiva, the Hindu goddess with many arms, wondrous as she carried many things at the same time in her multiple hands. Nonceba had not seen anything but when she came out with a tray, her heart leapt a bit when her gaze and that of the young officer locked. She told her heart to forget it. What business would a medical doctor have with a village police officer, a dodecahedron like herself? Forget it!

"Do not be afraid, we mean no harm," Ndlovu politely told the women before introducing his colleagues and stating the purpose of their visit.

"Sergeant Phakathi and Constable Mkhwa…"

"Mkhize," corrected Mnqobi Mkhize, looking at MaSikhosana who obviously had a question for him.

"Where do you come from?"

Mnqobi did not hear MaSikhosana's question as his eyes, mind and heart had followed Nonceba into MaMoyo's kitchen hut. Sergeant Phakathi noticed his friend's misdemeanour and answered on his behalf.

"He is from Mzansi, Gogo, but he grew up in Mzilikazi, *koBulawayo.*"

"Does he know *umhiqo*?" asked MaMlotshwa playfully.

"Ha ha ha! Yes. My grandmother used to brew beer for my grandfather in Mzilikazi," Mnqobi answered affirmatively as a way of hiding and recovering from the reverie of his misdemeanour.

The remark loosened the tension and Mnqobi tried hard not to gaze at Nonceba who, at that moment, came out of the hut carrying a clean yellow enamel basin. Her coffee-coloured arms and legs appeared as if they would drip water if they were greased. He wondered how he could get close to the girl whose body seemed to give orders to his heart.

"MaMpunzi, the gentlemen of the law are asking for a private moment with you. If you can please come with us to the shade of that *guwe* tree. Please relax and bring the mat you are sitting on," Ndlovu said to MaMpunzi.

MaMpunzi's heart leapt a bit but she did not know why they wanted to talk to her; she had not committed a crime. She wished she had a shell like a tortoise. If she had one, she would withdraw into it and stay out of this trouble. The police showed their agreement with Ndlovu by nodding their heads and making ready their notebooks. They stood up to go towards the tree, carrying their stools with their left hands while the right hands held the notebooks and the hats.

MaNxumalo followed them with her eyes and considered them with mingled curiosity and revulsion. She had discouraged her granddaughter who wanted to be a lawyer after she had explained to her the nature of the job. Rich people committed heinous crimes and then hired lawyers to defend them in court where one man stood to pass judgement over all matters. That disgusted the old woman. She thought about the Sibanda and Khethiwe case. Sibanda could surely afford a lawyer, but who would pay for a lawyer if his daughter chose to hire one to represent her? There was that other issue of holding people who were suspects in a jail called remand prison. Her granddaughter told her that if a suspected criminal was caught, they locked him up there as they awaited trial which could take up to two full years or more depending on various factors concerning the case. The crimes they would have committed also had a bearing on the verdict. Sometimes the system did not have enough vehicles or fuel to ferry suspects from remand prison to court. Her granddaughter told her too, that some people were acquitted after being remanded for so long. Nobody cared about what happened to their families during the time the suspects were held in there. Who would compensate the productive times they would have lost while locked in remand prison? The old woman found everything disgusting, but worse still, it was said that they starved in those jails, and that some fell sick and died because of lack of medical attention. Why not try cases the way her fathers did in the old days, the traditional way? She often told her granddaughter that if she had power like Queen Yaa Asentawa of Ghana, that one her granddaughter had once spoken about, the only people she would lock up in there were those found in possession of guns, armed robbers, those who killed for ritual purposes and rapists. MaNxumalo sometimes wished she had the courage of the Ashanti Queen, Yaa Asentawa, who her granddaughter said had led the Ashanti rebellion against imperialists. She would lead the rebellion against this new judicial system which she felt protected rapists and other real criminals.

The men from the arms of law declined the tea Nonceba and MaMoyo had made for them, thanked the old women, and left after the interview.

"MaMpunzi! Why do they need the clothes Khethiwe was wearing on the day she was raped? Didn't every woman see with their own eyes that the girl had been raped?" complained MaSikhosana.

"As evidence, proof that she was raped, they said. They wanted her underwear as well!"

"MaMpunzi!" exclaimed the old women in unison.

"Sibanda has used his charms to cause confusion! Who cannot see that these men are on his side already before they go to court?"

commented MaSikhosana again, before she heaped insults on the culprit.

"If that sick-with-greed Sibanda thinks he can get away with this one, surely he is making a pet of a leopard. I will march with my own feet to testify against him in court." MaMlotshwa supported her remarks by hitting the ground with her fist.

"I suggest you gather the women who saw the girl and those who want to go to the courts in Kezi on Wednesday. Even I will talk to my grandson who goes to Bulawayo every Wednesday morning to buy some commodities for his stores. He will give us a free lift and bring us back!" the militant MaNxumalo suggested to wild applause and ululation.

"We will crush him, that dog's droppings of a man!" insulted MaSikhosana.

"If he is not stopped by us women, you never know what else he will wake up to do!" exclaimed MaNdlovu.

"Every abuser will learn from what they will see us doing to him. So, let's teach them a lesson," threatened MaSikhosana.

Mpiyabo and Zamani arrived with the herd of cattle, sheep, donkeys and goats from Mahlasela Dam just before lunch. They were with Sikhwehle who had left as soon as the policemen entered the yard. Nobody had seen him go. He was now in clean clothes, his hair trimmed and neatly combed. Somebody had warned him that the police could take him to Engutsheni, a prison for the mentally challenged in Bulawayo, if they suspected that he was mad. Some said those who were taken there never had their health improve; they got worse and often died. Others said most of the people who were taken there were not sick but were possessed by some angry avenging spirits who were ignored by their families. Engutsheni nurses never agreed that mental illness had any connection with evil spirits. As far as they were concerned, they had to be locked and stuffed with pills till they had sobered up. This, again, MaNxumalo hated.

"What are we having for lunch, my old women?" Sikhwehle asked, happy after looking around to check if the policemen had truly left the homestead.

"Where is the impala meat that you promised us?" MaSikhosana enquired.

"MaHadebe, bring me *umhiqo* with a lot of sugar. I know these old women always make it tasteless!" he instructed Zanele as he received the stool from her and sat stolid and lofty on it without answering the old woman's question.

"You did not even greet me and now you want my sugar! Look at you! Well done! These policemen should come here every day. If you stop bathing again, I will call them!" MaMoyo said playfully.

"You will not. My old man, Hadebe, will give them this!" Sikhwehle lifted his fist.

Everybody was then sitting in the shade of the timeless *guwe* tree. Zanele brought the *umhiqo* and sugar in a disused peanut butter bottle. Sikhwehle poured three quarters of the sugar into his favourite hot drink and stirred the *umhiqo* until it had changed its colour.

"Jiyane, this sugar you like so much is dangerous for your health. If you are not careful it will give you diseases you have never heard of or seen before!" MaMlotshwa warned him.

"Let him alone! He uses all of it by walking up and down in the sun, boiling himself like a goat," MaMoyo defended.

"Do not forget that he will walk all the way to Ematojeni the day after tomorrow," remarked MaNdlovu.

"The spirit mediums chose Siphamandla and Dingizulu for this particular journey," said Sikhwehle with unfounded conviction.

"Sikhwehle, you are not the one to decide on these things, you are merely a messenger for the people," MaNcube said.

As he was still drinking his syrup, Nonceba and Zanele walked from the kitchen to the shade, bringing the finger millet *isitshwala* served with dried mushroom stew. Those who did not eat mushroom had impala biltong in marula nut sauce and fermented milk brought by MaNleya. Sikhwehle was supposed to share his food with Mpiyabo who refused the offer and claimed that he was not hungry, much to Sikhwehle's delight. Mpiyabo later joined Nonceba and Zanele.

"MaHadebe, you are the one I am going to marry. You certainly know how to look after a man," he spoke while munching the food in his mouth and licking his fingers one by one. He truly enjoyed the biltong in sauce. The women too indulged themselves in their lunch and drank the *amahewu* they had prepared the previous day.

Chapter Six

Just after lunch, Zanele and Nonceba braved the merciless sun as they made their way to the well along a path that snaked its way down to the stream. The girls had decided to pay Khethiwe a quick visit after MaMoyo had granted them permission. They left their water containers hanging on the poles that guarded the well. No one would think of stealing them. The villagers knew and respected everyone else's property. There was no way anyone could get away with theft, no matter how small or petty. Singing and laughing gaily, the two girls crossed the stream walking carefully to keep hot sand from slipping into their sandals and burning their feet. Looking very much like mice that had come out to play because the cat was away, each of the girls held leafy twigs above their heads to keep out the sun.

They found Khethiwe lying on a reed mat in the shade with her mother and MaNkomo. The girls exchanged a few pleasantries with MaNkomo. Khethiwe looked down in shame mingled with a kind of silent and embarrassed anger.

"*Sabona*, Khethi?" Zanele greeted Khethiwe.

"*Sabona*, Sisi Za, *unjani*? Khethiwe responded looking at her hands.

"I am fine. Thank you, how are you?" Zanele asked her with concern.

"I don't know how I am," Khethiwe said in a low voice, tears trickling down her cheeks.

"This is my cousin Nonceba," Zanele said after a brief moment. She tried hard to fight back her own tears.

For a moment Khethiwe said nothing, twin streams of tears flowing down her face. Her mother let her be. MaNkomo was quiet too. Nonceba fidgeted as she looked up the tree where a bird was singing what sounded like nature's dirge to a girl whose only crime was to be the daughter of a sadist. Khethiwe tried to compose herself but failed. Tears continued to well and drop down her cheeks. Hot tears. She let them flow down her chest to meet between her standing breasts and continue down to her underwear. In no time, her blouse was wet. Zanele let her tears be, too. In the distance, crows crowed and doves flew past in a pair, as if the universe knew nothing of Khethiwe's horrendous ordeal. Only the singing bird seemed to care. After a while, Khethiwe thawed and wiped her tears away. She did not say anything immediately.

"I did not know that you were on the road to see me. I am glad you came with a singing visitor. How nice of you! How are you Sisi Nonceba? I am pleased to meet you." Khethiwe's face brightened as she carefully tried to balance on the two big pillows against the small of her back. Zanele smiled at her. Khethiwe asked about Ntando in response to her smile.

"How is she? Why did you not bring her along?"

"I can see you are good friends. We left her snuffling and fidgeting, tired of keeping watch over the chickens to keep them from pecking at the sprouted rapoko spread to dry," Nonceba said.

"So they have not started grinding it yet? Isn't it supposed to be used tomorrow?" MaNkomo enquired, surprised.

"Yes, probably they will start grinding it later today. Just that it had not dried well enough. I am sure they probably have started on it by now," Zanele said.

"Sisi Nonceba, did you enjoy *umhiqo*?" Khethiwe asked.

"Yes, I did. I like it very much but not when it has too much sugar. I like the sour taste," Nonceba said, looking at Zanele.

"We do not like it with sugar either," MaNtini said coolly.

"Oh! But I saw Sikhwehle pouring three quarters of a tin! And it turned brown. I would not drink it like that!" Nonceba said laughing. Zinzile laughed with her and the rest of the women.

"Talking of Sikhwehle, he can pour ten teaspoons of sugar in a normal tea cup!" Zanele said.

"Yet they send him for important responsibilities like calling for the rain!" Khethiwe said.

"Him and Dingizulu!" said Zanele.

"I would not say they are mad or anything – they are simply misunderstood. I do not know about Dingizulu," Nonceba intervened.

"You do not know those men," Khethiwe warned.

"As long as I am here, I will," insisted Nonceba.

"Be careful when you say you will know those men; do you know what *knowing* a man in our culture means?" Khethiwe said. Her mother had escorted MaNkomo back to her homestead via the village well.

Nonceba was amazed at Khethiwe's sense of humour. Nobody answered but they all giggled.

"Are MaSikhosana and MaNdlovu there?" Khethiwe asked.

"Yes, why?" Zanele asked.

"They promised to make me a necklace and matching earrings with beads. I wanted to tell them to make them for Nonceba instead."

"What about you?" asked Nonceba.

"What do I need them for?" she asked, tears welling at her eyes again.

"You are a girl. Girls love looking and feeling beautiful!" Nonceba said. She felt happy that the opportunity she had been waiting for had come. She wanted to know what Khethiwe's feelings were after the accident.

Khethiwe fell silent and went into deep thought as tears scalded her eyelids. Nonceba indicated in sign language to Zanele to let her cry to release the stress. She handed her a pack of tissues to wipe away the tears. After Khethiwe had cried for minutes and wiped her face dry, Nonceba hugged her.

"Anyway, thank you for coming to see me. I feel hollow and blackened within myself. I do not see myself coming out of this home. There is no reason for me to live. How can a person live with this shame, this... What if I have contracted HIV from my own father, or worse, what if I am pregnant, or worse still, what if I am both pregnant and diseased?" she said as she let out a wail. Zinzile cried with her. Zanele fought back her own tears.

"You will be fine, you will heal. We know this might be difficult as it is still fresh and sore. You will be fine. We are with you, my sister. We are together in your pain," Zanele said calmly.

"Zanele is right," agreed Nonceba. "We are together in this, even the old women. I heard them saying they are coming with you to court to offer support."

"Including the Chief's mother, MaNxumalo herself. We will fight this together. Hold strong baby girl," Zanele emphasised.

"That would be good," she replied. "I really appreciate the gesture. But how does a young girl like me fight her own father in court? Life is really nobody's friend. Had the crime been committed by a stranger, my father would have defended and protected me."

The two girls did not know what to say. After a short awkward silence, Nonceba spoke with calm counsel.

"Khethiwe, you are such a strong girl, believe me. The worst is over. I am glad you are talking with us. Do not even think of taking your own life; it is a sin, an unforgivable sin. There is so much which lies ahead of you in life. God and so many of us love you. I know right now you think everybody will be pointing fingers at you. I want to tell you this: people are feeling for you. They are sympathising with you. Our Lord Jesus Christ is looking at you right now. He knows all the pain there is in this world." She stopped briefly while fumbling with a sisal handbag that she had brought along. "Here are the books that I have brought for you to read."

Khethiwe smiled as she received the books.

"Thank you, Sisi Nonceba. Finally, I am going to read *I Know Why the Caged Bird Sings*. I performed Maya Angelou's poem 'Still I Rise' at the last Prize Giving Day at school," Khethiwe said with brightening cheer as she browsed through the books. She had formed an immediate bond with Nonceba.

"You seem to me to be one of those people keen on questioning social norms. I can see you are an artist. You will end up a professor and an artist," Nonceba said.

"Prof Khethiwe Sibanda," Zanele said smiling, happy that Khethiwe had something to look forward to reading. She knew that her friend was a bookworm, only that their library at school was not well equipped.

"Ha ha ha!" Khethiwe laughed. "What qualifies a person to be a professor and what do they do?" she asked, opening the pages of the book slowly.

"You know what, Khethiwe, I meant to ask Nonceba the other day, but then MaNkomo went on with her tales and I forgot," Zanele said excitedly.

"What does MaNkomo know about being a professor, ha ha ha?" laughed Khethiwe.

"It varies from university to university. Depending on your university's academic policies, you may need to write and publish about twenty or more books and researched scholarly articles in internationally recognised journals. You must be a holder of a doctorate as well," Nonceba said.

"What are scholarly articles?" asked Khethiwe, showing much interest on the subject.

"Articles written based on a specific subject. They can be research papers, for example, say the call for papers is about a topic such as 'Child Abuse in Zimbabwe'. You then go ahead to write what you think about it, supporting your arguments with researched material that can be proven. The research material could be in the form of citations from books, newspapers, interviews with people in the field who have a proven record and interviews with participants like you and me. Your paper or article is usually also used by other scholars. Therefore, it should be well written so that it can be published. You will be usually attached to a university as a lecturer as you write your papers," explained Nonceba.

"That is hard work my dear, but I am sure it can be done," Zanele said.

"You can accomplish anything you want as long as you put your mind to it," Nonceba said.

"I would love to be a professor one day!" Khethiwe said, fidgeting in the manner of someone who wanted to be left alone.

"And you shall be one!" they said in unison and laughed in a girlish banter.

MaNtini was relieved and happy to find Khethiwe laughing with her friends. She wondered what kind of magic those two had performed to make her daughter change her mood so suddenly. Both of her girls were as vulnerable as unweaned infants and she felt that they needed to be guarded from their father who could get his violent claws on them. Since the ordeal Khethiwe had gone through, the girls had been crying all the time to the extent that the previous night, they had gone to bed without eating their supper. When she saw her peeling an orange that Zanele and Nonceba had brought her, savouring the juice, laughing and talking incessantly, MaNtini's heart was filled with joyful relief. She asked Zinzile to make some tea and felt assured when Khethiwe seemed to enjoy the bread baked by Nonceba. Nonceba was so impressed with Khethiwe's response that she thought of sending her books at every opportunity she would get. Nonceba gave Khethiwe a consoling hug before they left.

The girls took the narrow path from Sibanda's homestead towards the well where they had left their water containers. As they descended into the ravine with stony banks before the stream, they met Motini Nleya on his bicycle. He was a brother to MaNleya, their neighbour and Zamani's mother. He was coming from the direction of the headman's kraal but was so well dressed that one would be forgiven for thinking that he was coming from a wedding.

"Hello, MaHadebe? Where are you coming from in this scorching sun?" He smiled at Nonceba, almost teetering and wobbling as he tried to dismount from his bicycle.

"Mind your suit, *malum'Nleya*!" Zanele jumped to assist him with the bicycle. Nonceba did her polite best to conceal her amusement as she watched him come to a stop on the side of the road.

"I don't suppose you will believe where I am coming from in this scorching heat!" he said with a slightly hoarse chuckle, mopping sweat from his forehead with the back of his hand.

"Where are you coming from, *malume*?"

"Maphisa, yes, eh from the General Hospital," he said as he again wiped sweat from his brow.

"That is far! Cycling all the way from there on a bicycle! Who is sick?" Zanele asked.

Zanele was wondering why he had taken this route because Maphisa was to the north, but he had approached them from the south. Since it was impolite to ask and she could not quiz an adult further, she let the matter rest.

"Nobody is sick as such. It's your aunt who is expecting a baby. She had complications at St Joseph's clinic so they referred her to the General Hospital where she will be under the close care of a doctor," he explained.

They parted and walked on cheerfully in the sun, plodding the sands of the stream with their sandaled feet. After a distance, their feet could not stand the heat as they sank so deep in the blistering sand. They crossed the stream hopping, jumping and giggling away. They did not see that along the streambank stood several somnolent donkeys hiding from the scorching sun. One flicked its ear to chase away flies and startled the girls. They ran away giggling. Three more beasts of burden were resting in the shade of the *muphafa* trees lining the stream and forming a continuous canopy. They stood so still that you could only hear them breathing, their eyes closed. Sipho too was hiding in the eaves of the trees, observing each and every move they made. Since morning he had been secretly following them to the well or when they were fetching firewood, eavesdropping on their conversation with the talkative MaNkomo.

They found another water barrel balanced upside down on one of the logs which were used to close the entrance to the well. They had no clue whom it belonged to. A pack of goats waited outside the well, smelling the water. One pushed the logs closing the well furiously with its horns. Zanele drove the goats away as Nonceba opened the entrance to the well, still singing a village ditty which had become her favourite. MaNkomo appeared, and she too hummed the same old village ditty as she walked towards the well, her baby strapped to her back. She was walking from the direction of the headman's kraal where she had gone to ask for some finger millet chaff to feed her pigs.

"How was she when you left her?" She passed her bucket to Zanele for her to fill with water. Nonceba greeted her first before answering her question about Khethiwe.

"A little bit traumatised but I feel she will be able to cope after our visit," Nonceba said.

"Nonceba gave her some lectures on hope and left her some books to read too," Zanele added.

"That was nice of you MaGodonga, eMahlangu. Please visit her more often before you return," MaNkomo said seriously.

"She is not going back to Bulawayo. She is coming to get married to your husband!" Zanele said playfully.

"Oh, that is nice of her. Please do come and help me with work." MaNkomo said.

"You say that as if you mean it!" teased Zanele.

"Why would I not mean it? If it was you, I would say no, but Nonceba can. I would not want a lazy cowife."

Nonceba's delicate personality made her easy to get on with. She had radiant contentment and genial warmth that was not expected from a girl whose parents had given her a fur cushioned life. Most people admired her humility and studious mind. She fitted so easily in any environment she was in, understanding and talking to everyone she met without judging them. She ate their food with them, listened to and participated in their talk and their activities. She even played with children whose runny noses were not so endearing and quietened crying babies who were yet to be bathed by their mothers.

As they prepared to lift their water containers onto their heads, MaMpunzi appeared from behind the shrubs along the stream. She seemed quite happy like somebody who had just been in a world of milk and honey.

"MaMpunzi, did you fall? What happened to you?" Nonceba asked innocently.

"*Eh, ah*, no. Why?" MaMpunzi restlessly responded, turning her head to check herself.

"You have dust and some leaves at the back of your neck, and your blouse is torn," Nonceba answered, dusting her with a cloth she was going to use to pad her head before placing her water container on it.

MaMpunzi did not answer those questions but instead threw her arms up in the air in despair. She went to take her water container which was still balanced on the log.

"Oh! The water container is yours?"

"Yes, I left it to check for some wild herbs." She scratched the nape of her neck, her words not sounding convincing even to her.

MaNkomo had an idea of where she could have been but did not want to pursue the matter further. At her homestead, her children had told her she had gone to visit Khethiwe which was obviously not true. She had seen Motini earlier madly cycling from the same direction. She hid in the shrubs and let him go without noticing her.

Zanele and Nonceba carried their water containers home, singing and feeling happy to have spent some time with Khethiwe. Zanele thought about having to carry water on her head like that all her life if fate did not turn to her favour. She felt really sad even though she could not show it in her singing. Her heartbeat of fear and anxiety returned at the thought of her future. She felt the lip-licking dryness in the air tormenting her even from inside her soul. She thought that maybe she should have gone to train as a nun after her Form Four. When she was younger, Zanele had wanted to be a nun. She thought that the white-veiled women were angelic and holy. She believed that they spoke with God. She even believed that they saw God, what with their cleanliness and soft singing every morning and evening. The problem came when she was taught by one in grade one. After spending hours with the nun

83

teacher, she discovered that her heart was full of hate and anger. Zanele's teacher made them carry heavy metal buckets to the borehole situated a kilometre away from the school in order to fetch water and worse still, she would make them bath with cold water outside her class in the school yard. She claimed that they all smelt of urine, smoke and dirt. Although she was always top of her class, the sadistic nun hated her. She caned her, and humiliated her even for small mistakes that any pupil her age was prone to make. The nun favoured boys over girls. She lashed at the girls as if they were grownups.

Zanele was so engrossed in her thoughts that she only came out of her reverie when she realised that she and Nonceba had arrived back home.

Chapter Seven

There was much sunlight after an overcast and windy morning. The clouds had rolled back eastwards where they had come from in the early hours of the day, leaving the sky to the sun. Zanele and Nonceba cut across Sithwala's disused field to collect firewood as usual. It was their routine duty every summer. That day, they were not going to do much picking as they had left some stacked heaps the previous day. They met MaNkomo where the path they had been following branched into smaller ones leading nowhere. They walked in a line across the field, chattering before meeting with MaSikhosana near the place where Sithwala's abandoned homestead stood forlornly.

At once, Zanele moved away from the others, afraid of meeting MaSikhosana face to face. She pretended to have seen a dead log on the right side of the road. She folded her arms under the jersey she was fond of wearing those days.

"Did you wake up well, MaSikhosana?" called MaNkomo.

"I woke up well if you did too, my girls. I saw *itshowe lakho,* MaHadebe, it is almost reaching the skies in height," cheered the old woman, directing her response to all of them. She was cutting through the bush because she was late for the important rainmaking ceremony. The other women were already in the brewery when Zanele and Nonceba left home.

"There would be no *itshowe* if it wasn't for Nonceba's industriousness. Zanele alone could be snoozing and dreaming in bed at this hour," MaNkomo teased in mock drama with her Manyika-laced accent which amused many in their community.

"Ha ha ha!" laughed Ntando.

"*Shamwari yangu*, MaNkomo, you will never keep a daughter in law with your uncontrollable meanness and nagging!" Zanele too indulged in mock argument in response to her statement.

"MaNkomo, who destroyed the shells of huts which were there the last time I was here?" Nonceba asked, ignoring the pair's usual jokes.

MaNkomo hesitated to answer as the traditional laws of the land passed by the rain god prohibited telling or explaining to the underaged some sacred activities and certain songs. It was believed that if these secrets were told to the young, they would be drained of their meaning and spirit. Yet MaSikhosana, who had heard Nonceba ask the question from a distance, persuaded MaNkomo to tell the girl. The old woman then disappeared beyond the thick acacia shrubs which dominated the vegetation of the disused field, her indelibly stained apron flying about in the windy morning.

"It was the village men on the day of *ijumo*. This is a cleansing custom which is performed before the rain dance ritual they are brewing beer for. All village men, including boys, wake up early to clean the forests of dead animal carcasses and bones, bringing down disused birds' nests, removing debris thrown on the riverbanks and destroying abandoned homesteads like these," MaNkomo explained.

"You said it is a…" Nonceba asked again after stopping to look at MaNkomo.

"*Ijumo.* They comb the forests and burn all the stuff and hunt along the way. As the men go about their business, the women would be at the rain dance shrine, *edakeni*, singing *amayile*, and waiting for the men to come back. When they do return, they skin their catch, roast the meat and eat it there, and nobody is allowed to carry any leftover meat home. Nobody participating is allowed to eat anything before the exercise and ritual. It is only the mature women who attend the ceremony, not necessarily those beyond childbearing age, but older women," MaNkomo spoke with authority over the subject.

It was amazing how she had learnt the customs of the land, even better than some who were born and bred here. She paused as she broke a dead protruding branch of a tree before continuing. "The elders of the land – in this case spirit mediums – select the day of the rain dance and the people who will go to the rain god, eNjelele Shrine at Matojeni Hills, now called Matopos, to ask for the rains. Those are sometimes accompanied by spirit mediums if there are serious matters haunting the people apart from the delays of the rain. It must and has always rained before the rain messengers' return. Those first rains are supposed to wipe off their footprints," MaNkomo explained.

"That is interesting, MaNkomo, thank you. Who provided grain for the beer? Is it the Chief?" asked Nonceba.

"No, the villagers contribute. We each take the grain to the selected homestead and pour it in large reed baskets," MaNkomo answered her while picking up a dry mopane branch.

"Has this been the way of life always?" Nonceba asked, walking further away to pull the dry branch of a mopane tree.

"Yes, since time immemorial, and nothing is going to change that. That is one of our few rituals we still do!" Zanele said proudly.

"Who allowed Cecil John Rhodes's body to be buried at such an important place? The site is not very far from the Njelele Shrine. I read too that the colonisers did something at the Zambezi on top of some Tonga kings' graves," asked Nonceba genuinely.

"Nobody, I guess!" said Zanele.

"The rain messengers usually leave for the shrine on the second day of the beer brewing so that they come back on time for the rain dance!" MaNkomo continued, unperturbed.

"The whole process seems so organised. I wonder why some people think we do not have order as a people. The other thing

MaNkomo, the people who go there, how and why do they select such characters?" asked Nonceba.

"Even in the Bible, God's messengers were the poor and those whom people despised!" Zanele said.

"Zanele! That is so true hey! I had never taken notice of it! Elijah, John the Baptist, Moses, even the son of God himself, were not born from rich families!" Nonceba said.

"It is still the same God. It rains when they go there to humble themselves, confess the people's sins, and offer sacrifices!" MaNkomo said.

"Umh... I will neither agree nor disagree with you on that one," Zanele said.

"It seems like God is closer to people like Sikhwehle and Dingizulu! I wish I could go and watch the rain dancers," Nonceba said.

"Never! No child is allowed there, even to take a glimpse," Zanele warned.

"Does Dingizulu and Sikhwehle dance with *iwosan*–"

Before Nonceba could finish her question, Sikhwehle had appeared from behind the bushes. He knelt beside Nonceba who moved in reverse towards Zanele. He then rose and started dancing the ancient dance of a suitor asking for a maiden's hand in marriage.

"Zalabantu ziyebantwini...
Ayikho eyagana inyamazana!"

He performed his dance act still holding a plastic bag full of *umqokolo*. He threw three round purple fruits into his mouth very fast and started sucking harshly from the sour and juicy fruit.

"I heard my name, what about Sikhwehle...*hi*?" he asked after spitting the seeds of *umqokolo* which had already coloured his teeth brown.

"From today onwards, I shall make you a skirt. Why is it that you are found where there are women, young and old?" teased MaNkomo.

"I have noticed that too. He surely is the ladies' man! *Emthonjeni, enkunini okuphekwa khona utshwala!*" Zanele echoed.

"Yet, strangely enough, he has no lady of his own!" MaNkomo laughed.

"Who said I have no wife?" Sikhwehle asked looking at Nonceba.

"If you have a wife, do you keep her in a granary, because nobody has ever seen her?" teased Zanele.

"I have a wife. She is as beautiful as the rising African sun. She is not even your type!" Sikhwehle laughed at MaNkomo and Zanele.

Sikhwehle then handed some *umqokolo* to Nonceba who looked at Zanele as if to seek some sort of approval for her to receive some. Zanele observed and leapt across to Sikhwehle, dipping her hands in the packet. She took out some which she cleaned with sand and ate one. She then gave a handful to her cousin who was watching everything in awe. Nonceba ate and then tried to imitate MaNkomo and Zanele in cleaning her fruits with sand. She loaded some sand grains in the mouth of the fruit and gave up. Sikhwehle watched her without blinking his eyes before handing her the whole packet of fruit.

"Eat alone my wife. Do not share with these two," he said.

Nonceba flashed her fabulous lashes and politely received the fruits, but her body shrunk as Sikhwehle moved closer and even tried to embrace her.

"Leave my child alone, she is not Tshedu!" MaNkomo said calmly but forcefully.

"Get away, old meddler! She loves me and I will marry her. I have cattle, goats and money! I can give her a good life while you two continue to fetch water and firewood! Look at your feet, cracked heels which leave marks on the road like the wheels of a tractor. You are tractors!" he paused and laughed from his heart, looking at MaNkomo and Zanele who continued with what they were doing, ignoring him.

Nonceba smiled and shook her head.

"Listen to yourself, indeed they should…" Zanele could not finish what she wanted to say. Sikhwehle kept moving towards Nonceba who was busy trying to clean and eat her share of *umqokolo*.

"Who should do what to me? I am marrying her; she is mine," Sikhwehle said seriously.

Sikhwehle moved closer to Nonceba who was still trying to remove bits of sand from the mouth of the fruit. She felt him breathing close to her and when she turned to look, he was an arm's length away from her. From his tone and look, it was clear that Sikhwehle meant his words. He seemed to indeed adore and idolise her. In his mind and blind passion, he did not even think he could never reach her heart. Blood rushed to his head as he came closer to this girl who could quite easily have stepped out of every man's dreams. He imagined being alone with her in his bedroom hut. Nonceba looked at his furrowed forehead and stepped back till she bumped into MaNkomo who received her with an embrace before turning round to shield her.

"Tomorrow, my darling, my men are driving a herd of cattle for the dowry to your father. Do not worry about these jealous two, women of suffering! I have been seeing you in my dreams and my ancestors agreed with God himself sitting on the clouds to bring you home to cook for me," he said.

"Sikhwehle, stop fantasising about my cousin! And by the way, who are women of suffering?" screamed Zanele trying to break a log with her foot.

"I am not going to elope with her at night. *Ngiyabhadala inkomo*! I am not the type who runs away with men's daughters at night," Sikhwehle laughed aloud.

He turned towards Nonceba and addressed her directly.

"My sweetheart, I am coming for you in daylight with a large herd of cattle for *lobola* walking ahead of me! I am g…"

"Police!" shouted Ntando.

Sikhwehle did not wait to check if it was true that the police were indeed there. He ran as fast as he could without even looking back as he disappeared into the thickness of the forest. MaNkomo clapped hands for Ntando's thoughtfulness. That was the only way which could have stopped him from doing what he was doing to Nonceba and delaying them.

Sikhwehle had quivered with excitement from the very first day he saw Nonceba, imagining her sweeping his bedroom hut as his beloved wife. He would get lost in thought for long moments, imagining a home with her.

"Here is a husband for you, my dear," MaNkomo teased.

"Yeyi, MaNkomo, leave my cousin alone! I have a pilot for a son in law. I will be flying like a bird in the sky very soon!" Zanele complained as she arranged her firewood.

Nonceba followed suit in arranging her own firewood. She had seen and learnt that they placed straight firewood at the bottom to make a flat base and that they left the sharp protruding tentacles for the top of the bundle. By so doing, one did not risk being pricked as the bundle sat on one's head. She then tied slippery knots with strips from the *mopane* tree bark that would be undone in a tug. In Filabusi, Nonceba did not have to worry about firewood. The man who looked after their home and cattle gathered enough for them to use during the holidays or weekends when they visited.

When the two girls arrived home, they put their bundles of firewood down and hurried to prepare breakfast. The beer brewing party had finished the task of mixing the fermenting powder with the *umhiqo* which had now cooled in large earthen pots fixed in the brewery. They were all sitting in the shade of the *uguwe* tree, helping each other to weave beer strainers. Nonceba and Zanele brought cow peas boiled together with precooked and salted maize cobs. These maize cobs were cooked whilst fresh and then left to dry in the kitchen smoke after the harvest. They served them with tea thickened with goat milk and then hurriedly prepared to go and clean the church. It was their turn to do so that week. MaNleya had since left ahead of them.

Chapter Eight

Zanele wore a blue and white summer dress. It had straps which hung from the top of the bodice which was huge enough to cover her growing bust and was flared from the waistline going down. She wore a white wide brimmed hat to shield herself from the sun and a pair of white canvas shoes that she used for sports at school. Nonceba put on a blue skirt which still exposed her curves in its flare and a white T-shirt with the words "University of Zimbabwe Christian Union" printed at the back. She had worn a hat on which the same words were printed but had decided to let her shiny shoulder length hair fall below her shoulders. Unlike Zanele, she wore stringed sandals which exposed her delicate feet. She balanced her sunglasses on the crown of her hat. MaNcube had given Zanele her wrapper and Nonceba was going to use MaMoyo's. They had them neatly folded in Nonceba's handbag. They rushed off quickly, afraid of being late, a crime which could invite scolding from both MaMoyo and MaNleya, their section leaders. They trotted till they entered the gate of the primary school before the Convent area and church, oblivious of two men ogling at them.

The two men sat at the veranda of one of the stores which lined the business area, facing the Mission side. They sat facing the east, the direction from which the girls were coming.

"Look who is coming, Sergeant!" Constable Mkhize said to his colleague.

"Who?" Sergent Phakati asked, though he had also lifted his eyes to look at the girls.

After a moment, he said, "Let them come close. I did not really pay much attention to them yesterday. I know Zanele, the Chief's advisor's daughter. It was my first time to see the one who left someone lovestruck yesterday. If I were not married, I would not waste my time too!" he said, emptying the contents of his bottle.

"Hey, you foolish men! Stop ogling at girls young enough to be your daughters! Silly men! That is all you know and what you always think of is the thing that lies between women's thighs! Nx... Rubbish! Who will you arrest here when you fail to arrest top thieves roaming the streets of Bulawayo and Harare? Hiii? What you know is stealing people's money from the banks and selling everything outside and under the earth. Shameless men! Shame on you! Go and arrest criminals and stop fantasising about young and innocent children!" the mad woman, NakaThathanonke, shouted at the two policemen before throwing stones at them. The two men did not answer her. Instead, they rose and walked towards the west, where a restauarant had been opened by one of the *malayitshas* the previous weeks. Everyone dispersed from where they were either sitting or standing.

The girls found MaMpunzi, MaNleya, and other women and girls from their section already sweeping. Without wasting time, they hurried on to do the mopping and were soon chatting, giggling and singing. In no time, the church was shining clean. The flowers were neatly arranged for mass. Once done, Zanele's friends stood in a group talking to Nonceba whom they had not seen for a while. They were happy to know that she had started her studies at the university. Some asked her many questions about campus life and her chosen career while those who did not understand the subject matter just looked on, admiring her natural beauty.

Khethiwe appeared from the corner of the old church, walking slowly behind her mother who was pushing a bicycle from the direction of the clinic. She wore a wide beamed sunhat and sunglasses. Nonceba left the other girls standing together and went to intercept Khethiwe.

"Hello, Khethiwe!" Nonceba opened her arms ready to embrace her. Khethiwe hesitated at first but soon came forward to embrace her with a beaming smile. Zanele joined them, leaving the other girls chatting among themselves.

"I am much better, Sisi Nonceba, thanks. I am actually coming from the clinic. I suffered hallucinations and fever. My temperature was so high that I could not sleep. I feel much better now."

"The pain will pass my dear sister. Time heals everything. You will be fine," Nonceba said soothingly.

MaNtini felt frightened at the thought of what could have happened had her daughter been impregnated by her own father. She sweated heavily and a drop of her sweat fell to the ground where it formed a small mud ball. It was a visceral feeling that made her stomach warm. Their religion was against abortion, and her conscience would have haunted her had the results of Khethiwe's tests come out positive. There would have been the usual stories spoken in hushed tones, stories about uncles who impregnated nieces left in their care. Nobody reported such cases because they believed they were shameful and would divide and destroy families. Babies who were born in such circumstances were deemed fatherless, *omazwihila* in Kalanga, a derogatory term which debased the babies for life. Some would deceive people and say that the boy who had made the underaged girl or niece pregnant refused responsibility or that the girl did not know him.

They all walked together before MaNtini cycled away ahead of them, carrying Khethiwe on the bicycle carrier.

* * *

The accursed Sibanda sat languishing in a Khezi police holding cell. He was to be tried at the court of law on the first working day of the following week. He was brought to the cells the very day he was arrested because the police had other business in Khezi where the district courts were found. His mind wandered back to his hut where he kept his strong medicine. However, he was relieved that he had his other herbal protection tightly sewn in a hidden pocket inside his trousers, near the fly opening. There was no way he would go to prison. He was certain. The first thing he would do was to chase away that wayward wife of his and remain with the children. It was good that they were both girls and his real children. He could do whatever he wanted with them. He smiled at that thought. After sealing his decision in his mind, he then thought about the concoction to fix for a ritual he needed to organise for Dube.

* * *

At the mini brewery, the old ladies sat to a lunch prepared by MaMoyo with the help of MaNkomo. They had boiled dried goat meat brought by MaNkomo and pounded in a mortar to make it good for soft stew. It had no nut sauce. After enjoying the meal, the old girls asked MaMoyo if there was anything she could let them do for her. She felt so relieved and appreciated their offer to help with the work. Hurrying off to her granary, MaMoyo brought a basketful of groundnuts for them to shell. She would need them as seed when it was time to plant. However, she would have to select the flaccid ones for the mortar and the earthen pot. As the other four continued with weaving the beer strainers, MaSikhosana and MaNdlovu shelled the groundnuts. MaMoyo sat with them too and darned on some material. MaNkomo kept herself busy, knitting her baby's jersey while the child slept on a sheepskin mat beside her. The women talked and sang old songs as their brew whispered in earthen pots, waiting to be strained.

"Hello, girls! We meet again!"

Zanele and Nonceba were startled as they had not seen the young man approaching.

"Hello!" they answered in unison.

"What an adorable dress you have on, Zanele!" the junior police officer smiled while speaking in an attempt to precipitate a romantic mood.

"Thank you. I am surprised, though, that you know my name!" Zanele protested.

"I am sorry. True, it is unfair; let me introduce myself," Constable Mkhize said lightly. He did not wait for their answer and fired on. "My name is Mnqobi Mkhize. I grew up in Mzilikazi Township, *koBulawayo*, with my grandmother. That is where I still live when I am off duty," he said.

For a moment he appeared not to know what to say next. The girls looked ahead and walked on quietly. He followed them but kept his gaze more on Nonceba even though he displayed an air of friendship with Zanele.

"I know your name, but it is your sister's name that I don't know yet," he said after some silence.

"She is not deaf and dumb," teased Zanele.

Mnqobi fixed his eyes on Nonceba and playfully said, "Oh, sorry madam, could you kindly remove your sunglasses? I might shiver and die if I don't get to see your eyes."

Nonceba replied after a long pause.

"My brother, are you an optician? If you are, I am sorry, but my eyes are perfect. They don't need an examination."

"I did not mean to offend you, but I would love to see your eyes. I feel better if I am able to see the eyes of the person I am talking to," Mnqobi insisted.

Zanele moved fast ahead and deliberately left a wide gap between her and the two. Nonceba called to her to wait for her, but Mnqobi cut her off.

"We will soon catch up with her," he said.

The silence was such that one could hear donkeys breathing on the banks of a nearby stream. They walked for a while without anyone saying anything. Sensing that the silence would make him lose ground and have the girls laughing at him, Mnqobi asked if he could speak with her.

"I thought we were talking already," Nonceba said calmly.

His knees felt weak at her response, but he gathered himself. The pair walked in silence. Hot and cold air wafted at him so that it felt as if someone playing a mischievous game had opened a refrigerator somewhere and let the cold air blow in their direction for a moment and then closed it again to fling open the gates of hell. The sky itself was diamond clear and only a few clouds hung still as if waiting for an instruction to move east or west. Everywhere, the cicadas were singing their loud, flat melodies as if to compete with the birds weaving their nests up high in the huge *umkhaya* tree which stood on the other side of the path. Nonceba applied some gloss to her lips and adjusted her sunglasses. The lemon scent from the lip gloss filled the air they were breathing for a moment. She accidentally stepped on a stick which was lying across on the ground, tripped and almost fell. Mnqobi rushed in to help her gain her balance.

"I am sorry!" he said after making sure she was fine.

"It's okay," Nonceba said, clutching her sunglasses with both her hands. She felt in control and then stepped forward, careful to jump over a rock protruding from the ground. Mnqobi's fear disappeared and he felt much at ease.

"Are you a Hadebe as well?" Mnqobi asked with confidence.

"No, my name is Nonceba Mahlangu. Zanele is my cousin."

"Oh, I see. Are your mothers sisters or…" Mnqobi asked sincerely.

"No, my mother is her father's sister."

"Do you also live here, or you are just visiting?"

"I live in Bulawayo, eMatshaemhlophe. I am visiting them this holiday," Nonceba said.

"*Yebo ke* MaGodonga, Nonceba, did I get your first name correct?"

"Yes, my name is Nonceba."

"You have a lovely name."

"I will take it as a compliment. I am tired of people who cannot pronounce my name correctly and sometimes want to call me with names they think suit me better!"

Mnqobi was taken aback when Nonceba told him she was at university and had done her secondary education at St James in Nyamayendlovu. He thought she might have been in Form 4 or even Form 3. She looked much younger until one spoke to her. He almost jumped out of his skin when she told him she was studying medicine. He was worried that Nonceba had treated him too casually, that asking her out might just as well be asking for the moon. The calmness in the girl's nature did nothing but bring him right under her skin. How he wished that she too could come under his skin! She was the sort of woman he could surrender everything for.

"So, when are you going back to Bulawayo?"

"On Monday," she replied with her lashes fluttering like the wings of a beautiful butterfly.

"So soon? Why don't you stay for a few more days and keep us village folk company?" Mnqobi asked desperately.

"I will give you my number and my email address so we may keep in touch," Nonceba volunteered.

"That would be great."

After a moment's silence, during which he was rummaging for what to say next, Mnqobi spoke.

"I have a cousin who was at St James some years back; her name is Sibusisiwe Tshabangu. She went to Hillside and trained as a teacher."

"I know Busi!" Nonceba responded with excitement. "She is teaching at Mtshelanyemba Secondary School now. I met her on the bus when I was coming here some time last year."

"You have an elephant's memory!" exclaimed Mnqobi, happy that they at least had something in common.

"How can anyone forget the beautiful and dimpled Sibusisiwe, the debate queen?" Nonceba said playfully.

"She is getting married this coming Christmas!" Mnqobi informed her.

"Oh wonderful! Who is she getting married to?" Nonceba asked with interest.

"A geologist from Kenya," said Mnqobi.

"That is lovely. I wish her all the best with the Kenyan!"

After another moment of silence, Nonceba looked at Mnqobi and asked him which school he had attended. He told her he went to Mzilikazi High School and that he wanted to study Banking and Finance at the National University of Science and Technology in Bulawayo. Having failed to get enough points to qualify, he was now thinking of applying to Rhodes University and the University of Cape Town, in South Africa.

"That is brilliant! Money, money, money!" said Nonceba in encouragement.

"I am glad you appreciate what I want to study," said Mnqobi smiling.

"Why should I not?" asked Nonceba.

"Well, you are studying medicine, which is a respectable profession."

"And so is Banking and Finance!"

"It is about money you know; it can sometimes mess up people's minds and make them forget life's essence," Mnqobi said.

"Well, it depends on an individual's values. If you worship and idolise money, it can play havoc with you, but if you keep true to *ubuntu* that cannot happen. Besides, we can't all be doctors," said Nonceba.

"I think being a doctor suits you well with your calm nature."

"I personally think that it is a heavenly calling for someone to become a true doctor. I do not know if I have been called to it," Nonceba said.

"I think you have been called to it."

"Are you a prophet or psychic?"

"I am neither of the two."

"Are you a philosopher then? Talk, Shakespeare."

"I would say Einstein."

Zanele called to Nonceba to walk faster. There were duties they needed to complete at home like fetching water and pounding finger millet for *isitshwala*. Hadebe, who was arriving that evening, did not eat any other type of *isitshwala* when he was at home. He was coming for the rain dance festival and to see the Chief about other matters affecting the people's peace in Emlanjeni, besides checking on his family.

Meanwhile, Sipho had followed Zanele and Nonceba from the hillocks near St Joseph's Mission, hiding behind the trees. He jealously imagined seeing that police officer with Zanele. His imagination grew and he saw them laughing together, holding hands, climbing hills, picking wild flowers, playing and even wrestling with each other to the ground in the corn fields, the crops caressing their bodies. He saw them playing with sand in the Simpathe and Marabi Rivers, rolling on it as they laughed the time away. With his wild imagination becoming almost real to him, his head warmed up and he felt the heat coming up to his brain, and his lips trembled with anger. He imagined that police officer, whose name he could not even mention, holding Zanele in his arms. The thought made him nearly break the branch of the *guwe* tree he was standing under. He walked faster ahead of them and hid under the eaves of the trees lining the Marabi Riverbank. He concluded that the young officer could only love Zanele, for what would a policeman do with a doctor?

Chapter Nine

On the third day, the day on which the old women added the fermenting agent to the brew, Siphamandla and Dingizulu, the rain messengers, left in the early hours of the morning, just as the stars were beginning to pale. The sacred offerings were ferried in a scotch cart by a pair of lethargic donkeys to a bus stop where the two men would catch the earliest bus and be at Ematojeni before sunrise. In the scotch cart were packets of anthill tobacco, squirrel hides and other offerings acceptable to the rain god. Mpiyabo and Zamani accompanied them to the bus in the scotch cart and made their way back after making sure that the messengers were safely aboard on time for the rain dance.

The old women anticipated that by midmorning, the beer would be ready for straining. MaNcube and MaSikhosana were not disappointed. On entering the brewery the following morning, they found the beer pots bubbling with much liveliness, ready for straining. They began to prepare as they waited for the final sign to show in the pots. The straining started around midmorning when they poured the frothy millet beer into the waiting calabashes. As soon as they had filled the pots with the fluffy froth that looked like a miniature pool at the base of a waterfall, the bubbles started flowing out of the small mouths of the calabashes, ready to be drunk by the village men and women. An old black goat that looked like a yak left the herd that was nibbling at the acacia pods and sneaked quietly to the solid residues of the traditional beer stored away on a large reed mat outside the brewery. The fermented smell of the traditional brew dominated the cool Saturday morning air, attracting the wayward goat and making the pigs cry with greed in their pen.

"Go away, you silly goat!" Ntando screamed, throwing stones at it.

"Leave him alone, Ntando. I mean the goat. Leave him alone," MaMlotshwa said.

"Gogo MaMlotshwa, the residues are going to be used to feed the pigs. If I leave the goat, it will finish them. Let him go and feed on acacia pods with the rest of his kind!" Ntando screamed while throwing stones at the animal.

"No, this is the Mpofus' special goat; just do not curse or beat it. We do not want to be called to answer questions tomorrow."

"This is just a goat, Gogo MaMlotshwa, an animal!" said Ntando, her chest thrust out, and her hands on her waist.

"Ntando, do not be stubborn! Now, leave *ubabamkhulu wakoMpofu* alone and go to your mother!" shouted, MaNcube her grandmother. In a righteous but sulking gesture, the girl sucked her small finger and went away, understanding nothing of what the old woman was saying.

According to the Mpofu clan, the goat was a spirit medium who conveyed messages to and from their ancestral spirits. They talked to it as if it was a human being. They brewed beer and made it drink from an open wooden or earthen pot, singing and telling it their problems in the dark night. Moyawezwe and his youngest uncle once beat it when they found it drinking water from their well and waited for a bad omen to befall them. They were still waiting; nothing had happened so far.

The goat nibbled at the residues of the rain dance brew. After chomping his fill, undisturbed, *Babamkhulu* then staggered to MaMoyo's kitchen to get water from the same water containers people drank from. He knew his way about very well. MaMoyo saw the goat coming and quietly hurled stones at its back, driving it even further to join the other goats.

After they were done with the process of straining, the old women washed their wrinkled arms and legs and changed into the cleaner clothes they had brought with them in wrappers fastened to their backs like babies. MaMoyo had made some breakfast ready for them. After the quick meal, they set off, Indian file, the beer calabashes balanced on their heads, to the rain dance shrine. The old women followed the road that meandered and turned, avoiding the homesteads and skirting around the fields. They walked along, chatting in subdued tones, but on approaching the shrine, they started singing the rain-calling song known only by them. MaSikhosana led the song:

"Ngitshiye abantwabami
Ngivalele endlini!
Ngitshaya amayile."

The rain dance shrine was situated on an open space to the west of Old Dube's homestead. This Dube was a senior member of the Chief's Council like Hadebe. The ceremonial beer brewed in four different homesteads was carried the same way to the shrine by old women coming from different directions. A number of drums lay on the ground, their hides facing the sun in order to make them taut. Nearby, a few older but strong men were collecting firewood in preparation for the ceremony. Small paths leading to the shrine from all directions were jammed with old women and men, all with one purpose: to sing and dance to the drumbeat of the rainmaker at Njelele.

Hadebe, who had arrived the previous night, would go to chat with the Chief that morning before the rain dance started. He would join the Chief's other advisors and they would set a date for the Dube and Mxotshwa case. The Dube family had reported the matter for trial at the Chief's court following the last death and after a daughter of the family had been sent away unceremoniously by her husband's family and mysteriously began to lose her senses a few days after arriving at the Dube homestead. Sibanda's case also upset Hadebe but, as things were, it could not be discussed at the Chief's court since it lay under the jurisdiction of the magistrate's court. There was also talk about water harvesting and repairing of the road. A new dam project was on schedule but would only begin when, once again, there was peace in the village. There was even talk about rebuilding the Marabi River Bridge. The old one had collapsed, making it difficult for people to cross to hospital and for children to go to school, especially during rainy days. And there were plans to build more roads to link the villages together.

* * *

That Friday night before Hadebe's arrival, Zanele barely slept. Her father would arrive in the last evening bus. After arriving, he would not come home straight away. There was a bottle store just near the bus stop which opened till the early hours of morning. There, he would talk to his friends whilst Mpiyabo and Zamani carried home his parcels after leaving a bicycle for him. Zanele heard Mpiyabo and Zamani arrive from the bus stop. Her heart started beating fast. *What if her father found out? What if her mother knew and pretended not to know anything? Was her mother afraid of her father also? What if they were waiting for their father to return before they asked her?* It would be a disaster if they did and if he refused to pay her school fees for the third term. Her body being tired, she fell asleep just before midnight and as soon as she did, she was awakened by her father's arrival. She waited to be called but after some silence, she fell asleep again, only to wake up after an hour. She never slept after that. *What if they knew but were just quiet? If her father was to chase her away, would her aunt take her in? Would she assist her with her examinations so that she would go on to become the lawyer she always wanted to be? Where else could she go?*

Her uncles and aunts in Masvingo would not understand. They would escort her straight to Sipho's people as their culture demanded.

Her father was a strict man who was so proud of her and did not, in the least, expect any nonsense like that from her. She finally fell asleep again around 03:45. She dreamt of being a destitute who was living with her baby on the streets. She was on her own, and even Nonceba did not want to be associated with her. She felt better when she was awakened by her father who was calling Mpiyabo to bring the donkey harness to him.

Nonceba and Ntando were out first to greet him.

"Oh MaGodonga, you are here!" he exclaimed, laughing aloud.

"*Yebo malume,*" Nonceba answered, smiling.

"*MaMoyo, yibukhwele!* Why did you not tell me the first wife was here?" He shook her hand while laughing from his heart.

Hearing that, Zanele quickly sorted herself and went to greet him whilst he was still happy.

"*Salibonani, Baba?*"

"*MaHadebe, yikuvuka lokhu. Ayi lapha uBaba waswela umfazi...* ha ha ha!"

Zanele was so relieved to hear him chat so jovially with them. Hadebe entered his room and brought them sweets. Usually, he gave all the sweets to Ntando. Despite being very strict, Hadebe was loving. He acted love; he did not preach it just as he never went to church, except for weddings, funerals and baby christening. He did not discourage those who chose Christianity. However, he disliked the sanctimonious.

"Hadebe, my chief!" Sikhwehle put down his knobkerrie as he proceeded to shake Hadebe's hand. Hadebe had just sat down for breakfast.

"*Awu awu* … big man!" Hadebe put down his cup to shake Sikhwehle's hand. Before Hadebe could ask about anything, Sikhwehle had proceeded to get a cup from the standing wooden table built for placing all kitchen utensils to dry.

"MaHadebe, pour some tea, with plenty of milk and sugar. My chief is here, so today I am not going to entertain any funny excuses!" he mirthfully commanded while sitting on a stool near Mpiyabo.

"How is it, my chief? You have lost so much weight. Were you sick, *mdala*?" he jocularly asked Hadebe who was at that time washing his hands again so that he could eat some pumpkins. MaMoyo had stowed away some under the cool shade of the granary. Some years they lasted till October. Other family members were eating bread with jam and margarine.

"I want bread!" shouted Sikhwehle before Hadebe could answer his question. It was true that Hadebe had lost weight. Nobody else had managed to ask him.

"*Mdala,* you can take me along. I will cook for you whilst you are at work. Maybe you are not eating well!" Sikhwehle said while impatiently looking at Zanele who was placing slices of bread in a plate for him.

Hadebe smiled, placed his cup on a saucer, before answering: "It is age, *nduna yami*. Age. You cannot come to cook for me; you know you are the policeman here. You leave this place, disaster will happen. People will do as they like."

Hearing those words, Sikhwehle smiled. His smile had the wideness of the mouth of a river pouring its contents into a dam. He munched on more bread before speaking. Sikhwehle loved his bread. He savoured its taste, chewing loudly, his cheeks inflating and deflating from the bread rolling in his mouth.

"There is a strange man clearing a field on the banks of Marabi River. I told him not to do that without being cleared and officially introduced to the community!"

Hadebe put down his cup to listen attentively to Sikhwehle. He waited for him to take a bite from the bread Nonceba had just given him in a plate. Seeing that he was not going to continue soon, Hadebe continued eating slowly, shaking his head.

"Where is this man from?" Hadebe asked impatiently.

"From across," Sikhwehle said before drinking all of the remaining contents in his cup and giving the cup to Zanele to pour more tea.

"Across where?" Hadebe was becoming more and more impatient. Communal disputes always made him restless.

Sikhwele loaded huge pieces of bread in his mouth and attempted to chew. His cheeks bulged. He closed his eyes and faced up, enjoying the bread and jam. Zanele, Nonceba and Ntando giggled, looking down. MaMoyo too looked at Sikhwehle and smiled.

Seeing that his impatience was not going to move Sikhwele, Hadebe waited for him to eat his fill.

"*Ezizweni, umkhwenyana wakoNdlovu,*" Sikhwehle said finally, still trying to chew.

"Jiyane, please speak clearly. *Umkhwenyana,* coming to build here?" Hadebe asked again, concerned.

"Yes, *Lihole.* He is building a homestead and clearing a field. He came with his wife, Nozimanga and several children who do not speak or understand isiNdebele," Sikhwehle said while dipping bread with margarine into the hot tea and munching it.

Hadebe shook his head.

"*Amahole sehluphile.* Their children have no manners. They answer back to their father and even challenge him, saying 'Daddy you are a liar!' The funny and sad part is that both the father and mother do not see anything wrong with it. One morning I saw the oldest boy threatening to beat up his mother for failing to give him some money for marijuana!" Sikhwehle said, looking at Hadebe.

"*Si si si… lafa ilizwe,*" MaNcube said, shaking her head.

"The other day as I was passing by, I saw the big boy threatening to cut his father's throat with an okapi knife because he was refusing him permission to use his bicycle for his leisure trips. I did not waste time. I hurried in and gave him this!" Sikhwehle said lifting his fist. The girls smiled and looked at each other.

"When he fell to the ground, I wrestled with him and took away that knife. I beat him unconscious. I warned him that we do not tolerate children who disrespect their parents. They should never ever talk back to them. And I promised that if I ever heard that they raised their voices to their mother or father or any adult, I would come there with my cattle whip! I took the knife, here it is!" He took the knife from his back pocket to show Hadebe. Ntando covered her mouth with her hand in fear.

Nobody spoke for some minutes. MaMoyo then applauded Sikwehle, calling him her true son in law.

Hadebe rose without commenting, still shaking his head and seething with anger. He had to prepare to go and visit the Chief before attending the rain dance.

Chapter Ten

As the elders were making their way to the rain dance around midmorning, Zanele and Nonceba were taking heaps of laundry to wash at the well. Ntando helped by carrying the lighter packs in plastic dishes. Zinzile, who was five years older than Ntando, brought hers along too. She told them that she had left Khethiwe with their mother and maternal aunt who had just arrived to check on her. Once at the well, they filled the zinc dishes with water before selecting and grading their laundry. Nonceba threw Ntando's stinking, ammonia gassed blankets into one of the dishes and proceeded to stamp on them with her bare feet. Instantly, the water turned brown, but she continued stamping on the blankets while singing a mbira-jazz song.

"MaGodonga, you should have put in the lighter ones first. We normally do your mother's stinking ones last. You do not want your nose to be blocked so early in the morning by the bad smell. After all, we wash her blankets with soapy water," Zanele said, priding herself in hanging out her clean bed sheets to dry. Yet she was trying very hard to conceal that she was having difficulties with performing any chores that required her to bend her back.

"Ntando is better than Mgcini. Even if you wake Mgcini up ten times, he will still wee in his blankets. Mother makes me sleep with him so that I wake him up, but I have since evicted him from my room!" Nonceba spoke and laughed loudly.

"How old is Mgcini now?"

"Twelve. And if he does not stop weeing in his blankets at this age, I wonder how he will manage at Mzingwane Boarding School where he is going for his secondary education next year."

"*Yeyi, yeyi*, leave those children alone. You were worse than them at their age!" MaNkomo's voice boomed from behind them.

They had not seen her coming. Nonceba smiled her ever near smile which Hadebe said reflected her heart.

"How did your baby sleep MaNkomo? We heard her crying yesterday as we were rushing home from cleaning the church," Nonceba asked.

"She is much better, she is asleep. I left Farai to keep watch over her."

"By the way, has your husband gone to the shrine at Njelele?" Nonceba asked.

"Yes. He is not back yet… and the old girls, what time did they leave for the dance shrine?" she asked after placing her water container down.

Zanele told her. "I saw Hlabangana and Headman Nkiwane on my way to see how Khethiwe had spent the night. Unfortunately, I found her sleeping and I did not want to wake her up. How did she sleep MaDawu?" she directed the question to Zinzile, calling her by her totem name.

"She was hallucinating and sweating, so we ended up making a fire in the kitchen and sleeping there with her the whole night," Zinzile said sorrowfully.

"You see now Sibanda's medicine is working on her. He wants to drive his daughter mad!" MaNkomo said while helping Nonceba rinse the blanket she was stamping on.

"Nonsense! There is no medicine, it is trauma," Nonceba challenged her.

"MaGodonga, we all think it is his magic. This is what everybody is saying," MaNkomo persisted adamantly.

"Everybody might be saying so, but does that make it true? Our neighbour's daughter who was raped by a herdboy in Lupane has never talked to this day. The worst thing is that the herdboy was a relative and the matter was never reported," Nonceba said.

"What, Nonceba!" Zanele exclaimed from behind the shrubs.

"That is what made her not talk. You know her Zanele, that beautiful girl. She withdrew herself from the world. She does not talk to anyone, yet we used to play together before the incident. She was a bubbling, intelligent girl but now you will think she was born dumb and angry!" Nonceba said angrily.

MaNkomo and Zanele shook their heads in a mixture of pity and disbelief.

"You are indeed in the right profession. Where do you know all these things from?" a voice suddenly broke from the nearby shrubs.

MaNkomo almost jumped with fright. Zanele, on recognising the speaker pushing a bicycle, winked at Nonceba and smiled. Ntando and Zinzile took advantage of the situation and disappeared to the well unnoticed. They were usually not allowed near the well which was deep and dangerous.

"Are you not supposed to be at work, Mnqobi?" Zanele asked, but Nonceba's mouth remained aghast, not understanding how he had known they were at the well.

"Yes and no. I am not feeling well." He turned and greeted MaNkomo after picking her accent.

"*Makadii zvenyu Maiguru?*"

"*Ndinofara kana muchifarawo,*" MaNkomo looked at him for a long time, surprised by this young man who had greeted her in her own language.

"You look familiar, have we met before?" MaNkomo asked Mnqobi. She did not know that Mnqobi had picked her language from her accent.

"Maybe. I live with you in the area. *Ndoshandira hurumende,*" he said seriously.

"Oh, I see. Maybe a teacher, a district officer or something of the sort?" enquired MaNkomo.

"MaNkomo, leave him alone, *usulijoni*? Are you a policeman now?" Zanele teased.

"*Sizayicela isivuthiwe*," she winked and disappeared to the well where she filled her water container and left.

"You did not answer me, Nonceba. I got here the time you were talking about ammonia!" Mnqobi said after greeting her in a cordial voice.

"What! Shameless eavesdropper!" she laughed gaily, trying to think about what they had been talking about earlier.

"You are studying sciences but you seem well versed in social issues too. Isn't that fascinating!" Mnqobi said.

"I cannot claim to know much as yet. I live in the world with people, but most information is written. It is in reading that you get to know things," Nonceba said casually.

"I can see that you have a passion for knowledge!" Mnqobi said, without taking his eyes off her.

"True. How are you doing?" Nonceba asked.

"I am fine but lonely when I am without you girls, which is why I asked for these three hours off, to see you."

"That is nice of you. We really appreciate your visit," Zanele said.

"You girls are very hardworking. Do you ever sit down and rest?" Mnqobi asked.

"Have you ever heard of village women resting? Their rest is nothing more than weaving, knitting, sewing and any job that they can do while sitting down!" said Zanele seriously.

"Ha ha ha! You know Za, I had not realised it but it is the truth! Yes, it is. Even the old women who were brewing the beer, when they sat down it was either to a meal or to weave or do this and that! Let's be serious with books my dear, otherwise we will be in trouble," Nonceba said.

"Zanele, what do you want to study?" Mnqobi asked.

"Law. Community Law," Zanele said, taking clothes from her dish to spread them on some shrubs nearby.

"Quite impressive! You girls inspire me a lot. I am tired of meeting girls who just want to meet rich men and get married. I am not saying getting married is bad!" Mnqobi said while breaking a twig from a *mopane* tree.

"Don't worry about that. We hear you. We have seen it too. It is not their fault, they are brought up in a society which teaches girls that they need a man to validate their existence on this earth!" Zanele said, bending with difficulty.

"I wonder if I will be able to raise the fees. I want to study too," Mnqobi said sadly.

"You are not satisfied with your job?" Nonceba asked.

"Hell no! I am not! I want to go to Rhodes University or UCT. Zanele, you want me to die kicking dust following those who steal cattle and rape their own daughters in the village! It was just a starting point in my life, you see," Mnqobi said carelessly because he did not know that Zinzile was in the vicinity. Zanele looked at him with eyes that seemed to say, "How could you?" as Nonceba looked around to see if Zinzile had heard the remark. Satisfied that she was out of earshot, she cautioned Mnqobi about his lack of sensitivity.

"That is good. Where is Rhodes by the way?" Zanele asked.

"It is in Grahamstown in the Eastern Cape Province of South Africa," Nonceba answered.

They talked about this and that until his time was up. He left them as they were beginning to pack to go back home. As he cycled back to work, Mnqobi was worried that Nonceba treated him with artificial cordiality, showing no affection for him at all. He had dreamt of her the previous night and could not think of anything else until his superior granted him the three hours leave. He cycled back half satisfied. Nevertheless, his feelings remained the same. No matter what, that girl was his for life. The cicadas were singing from the *mopane* trees as Mkhize's son cycled away, a love hunter in a pair of blue jeans that went just below the knee and white training shoes. He was in a striped, blue golf shirt on the back of which was woven a picture of a man ready to tee off a ball. His white cap had the same picture. Try as he did to save himself from it, the scorching sun still shone in his eyes, almost blinding him.

* * *

Simphiwe Dube's matter was introduced to the men by Siphamandla a week before the old women had started the process of beer brewing for the rain dance ceremony. It was a Wednesday morning. This was the day on which they went to clear the forests before the preparation of the rain dance. For this sacred expedition, the men from the villages met on the banks of the Simphathe River, a mile away from the rain dance shrine. They were grouped according to their villages and shown the area to clear. Siphamandla was busy clearing a heap of debris along the banks of the river. He stopped suddenly, as if he had seen something in the debris.

"You see, Dube, the day you open your eyes about this matter between you and the Ncubes, your whole family will have been wiped out by this avenging spirit."

"If the courts cleared me, then who are you to tell me about the Ncubes, unless you are now a judge? The courts ruled that the late Mxotshwa was wrong, so what are you now talking about?" Dube answered defiantly.

"We all agree it was not your fault, but in our culture, killing a person and not apologising is an abomination. You must apologise to the family for spilling their blood," Siphamandla said, proceeding to destroy an old nest with the handle of his knobkerrie.

"Siphamandla is right, you ought to pay," advised Old Sikhukhula, indicating with the handle of his knobkerrie that the younger men should destroy a crow's nest they had not seen up the nearby *umkhaya* tree.

"Why can't you people understand? Are you the law now? If he was locked up in jail today, will you go there and tell him to pay the late Mxotshwa's people? Anyway, who has proved that the avenging spirit is the one causing the deaths?" asked Sibanda with an air of superiority.

Everybody looked at him with anger. Sikhwehle struggled to remove a tough piece of cloth which had become wound around the roots of a *mphafa* tree. He carried it to a heap of burning debris and threw it on the fire before speaking.

"Son of Mthembo, what do you say then of people who are falling like over-ripe *amarula* fruits? Do you suspect some kind of foul play?" he directed the question to Dube, addressing him with his totem name, ignoring Sibanda completely.

"*Uthi baloyiwe?*" asked Dingizulu who was sceptical about all the talk of witchcraft.

"Foul play? Do people not die? His wife died before the Mxotshwa incident and his father died of old age. Egoli people always stab each other to death!" shouted Sibanda from the riverbank where he was relieving himself of urine behind a tree.

"Sibanda, stop being casual for once and show some seriousness and respect. You know what you are doing and you should stop it at once!" Hlabangana's caustic words prompted Dube's brother to speak.

"He says he does not have cattle to give to the Ncubes as an apology. That's incredible and incomprehensible! He would rather have cattle go to another man's kraal whilst our family is perishing!

Now even our dogs and cats have run away, fearing that they too will die. Who knows who is next?" the brother said, lifting his arms and letting them fall in resignation. He then looked at his toes, blinking away tears that were threatening to escape through his eyelids.

"To Sibanda's kraal. He is happy to drive his cattle there!" said Sikhwehle in a strange falsetto.

"*Wena* Sikhwehle, what can you tell me? Do you have a wife and children? You call yourself a man? You have no home to talk about. You have nothing of your own!" Dube barked at him.

"Leave him alone! What home do you still have without children and kinsmen? Are Sibanda's useless herbs more important to you than your family? He has your wealth and yet your people are still perishing," warned Hlabangana.

"Be man enough and accept correction! Your sister is suffering, sleeping in the open and eating dirt. You need help. This Sibanda, your friend, is only confusing you for his own gain," Siphamandla advised.

"I am better off without a wife and children. Go and apologise and pay quietly. That is the only thing that can make us and the world forgive you!" Sikhwehle shouted from up a *mbondo* tree which he had climbed to light the tobacco he had folded in a newspaper.

"Shut up you vagabond before I eh, eh…" Dube charged at Sikhwehle with his knobkerrie raised. Sikhwehle made good his escape by jumping to the sands of the river. Hadebe moved towards Dube, and as he spoke, he looked him in the eye.

"Now you hold yourself together, this is not fun. You think all these people are out of their senses but you? This is an important ritual we are doing here. Show some respect before we fine you a goat to skin and barbeque for the people on your own! Do you think all these people advising you are doing so because they love talking? Do you think we are happy to bury your children one after another, hii? If you continue ignoring this matter and it happens again, you will find yourself burying them alone!"

"With Sibanda by his side perhaps!" shouted an unidentified man from the group.

There was silence. The combing of the forests continued and the dogs followed, wiggling their tails, oblivious of the talk. The dogs were happy to be out hunting. That was all that it was to them. A sleeping duiker was startled by the movement of the men and bolted in the opposite direction. Motini, Zamani, Mpiyabo and Sabelo ran after the dogs, pursuing the unlucky animal. In no time, the dogs had caught the duiker. The catch added to an impala and three rabbits the other group had caught earlier. They had started their forest cleaning very early along the Marabi River until they reached the Kwanike hillocks from where they followed Simpathe until they came to the boundary with Chief Bidi. Finally, the men returned to the dance shrine where the women were singing and dancing the *amayile* dance.

The women ululated when the men arrived carrying game. They even sang louder when the men started skinning their catch. The younger boys plucked off the feathers from the birds they had caught. Others built huge fires on which to roast the meat.

* * *

Once they got home, Zanele and Nonceba began to iron their clothes. There was only Mpiyabo playing a sling game with Zamani in the yard. Thatha, nose on his toes, guarded the homestead like a crusader's dog. Nonceba was softly singing her favourite love songs by foreign artists. The songs prompted Zanele to think of Sipho. Was she in love with Sipho? Why was it that his presence affected her so much yet she knew there could be no future with him? The last encounter with him remained raw and sore in her heart and body. Thoughts buzzed, whirred and whizzed in her head like an old aeroplane. There was their family matter too. What if they met the mad aunt again? A week before Nonceba came to the village, as they moved about the grinding mill after cleaning the church, NakaThathabonke, the mad woman, had instantly appeared in front of them. She had paused, lowered her glance sullenly, then suddenly, without warning, started screaming.

"*Kuzothiwani ngalengane bantu! Wi... wi... wi... maye... maye ngomfoka Mahlathini! Umtaka MaMoyo ke yena bantu! Wiiii... wiiii... wiiii...*"

NakaThathabonke wailed like the Zulus when Nandi passed on. She rolled and rolled, holding the back of her head. She then rose and looked at Zanele. Khethiwe remained stupefied whilst Ntando and Zinzile giggled innocently. Zanele felt helpless and wanted to get away from this brazen display of madness, a display that she felt a part of because she knew who the woman was.

"Khethiwe, let's move fast!" Zanele said, feeling a little tense and defensive.

"I will take them all one by one. Nobody can get away with spilling my blood. Like flies they will all go. Very soon they are gathering to bury a young one. My family cannot be deprived because of them! NakaThathabonke, MaDube," Sipho's aunt said in a hoarse voice, a man's voice.

"Who do you want to take?" Khethiwe ignored Zanele and asked the mad woman directly.

"You are a child. These are adult matters." Then, looking at Zanele, she said, "Poor MaHadebe! Sorry my dear girl. But all will be well with you in the end."

Zanele's heart beat faster as MaDube surveyed her expansive waistline. Even though she managed to keep her courage before

120

her friends, she worried about what NakaThathabonke meant. She was afraid of an inevitable catastrophic mental breakdown should she fail to write her examinations. She felt like a commuter omnibus crammed with humanity. A lot of lives lived in her. Many voices spoke to her from within.

"Let's go to the shops. I want to buy you some drinks and buns." Ntando and Zinzile giggled more. Coca-Cola and buns were treats they were not ready to postpone just because they were coming from a mad woman.

But Khethiwe and Zanele were puzzled. A dirty mad woman buying them some drinks! Where did she get the money from? Khethiwe looked at the woman, puzzled, confused at how she seemed to sympathise with Zanele. Zanele just looked at the book she was carrying and pretended not to hear the mad woman.

"Men give me money at night, do not be fooled by them. They pretend not to notice me now just because it is daylight! Look, I have money!" she said turning around to show them her figure.

She was a well-built woman. Even then, in dirty clothes, she looked beautiful, her waistline and curves still in place. Sometimes, when her senses were working a little better, NakaThathabonke tried by all means to stay clean. She would brush her teeth with small pieces of wood she cut from a tree near the stream. Presently, she placed her hand in her brasserie and took out a dirty floral wallet. In it were all kinds of currencies: pulas, bearer cheques and rands. Ntando and Zinzile stopped laughing.

"Yes, you could buy us drinks if you want to," Khethiwe invited her.

NakaThathabonke smiled at them and together they walked towards the nearest store singing one of the Catholic hymns. She sometimes came to church on Sundays. Zanele's eyes welled with tears. She felt so sorry for her. They knew MaDube before she was mad. She remembered that she was a quiet and lovely woman.

121

Being a woman of few a words, she just smiled at her when they met during choir competitions around their small centres. When they entered the shop, the shop owner, who was also the keeper, grinned on noticing NakaThathabonke opening her wallet and taking out wads of notes. Khethiwe was amused. She had thought this money lover only turned heathen during Christmas time, when he took advantage of jovial crowds and inflated the prices of his goods.

"I still buy from your shop, but I know you have a goblin which sleeps with me on your verandah during the night!" NakaThathabonke said to the shopkeeper. Like a spirit, Khethiwe's imagination roamed the room. The shopkeeper did not answer MaDube but received her money before asking her what she wanted to buy. She told her to give the girls and her daughter-in-law MaHadebe whatever they wanted.

"Do not be fooled by these rich shopkeepers. Most of them are armed robbers across Limpopo. All this money and cars they show off are stolen," she uttered.

The shopkeeper did not look up. He worked quickly, taking drinks from the diesel-powered freezer and then some biscuits Ntando and Zinzile wanted. Khethiwe chose salted nuts. Zanele insisted a drink would be good for her, but NakaThathabonke asked the shopkeeper to give her a loaf of bread too. She received the change which she later gave to the younger girls.

For those moments, as they sat on the bench outside the shop, one would think MaDube had recovered from her mental illness. All of a sudden, she started screaming, two voices speaking in her.

"*Ubabhemi bantu, kambe!* One by one!" the hoarse voice in her spoke emphatically. She wailed, rolled on the verandah, removed her headscarf and ruffled her hair. They took that opportunity to leave, walking faster, almost running, afraid she would catch up with them and maybe demand her money back. She rose and, eyeing the shopkeeper like an infamous army general staring at his opponent, shouted, "Your big hairy bums!" The shopkeeper did not wait to hear more insults. He disappeared into a room behind the counter.

* * *

MaMoyo decided to take a bicycle and ride over to see Khethiwe before joining the other women at the dance shrine. She took along a parcel of sugar, tea, bread and some oranges her husband had brought from Bulawayo the previous night. She entered the Sibanda homestead almost at the same time as MaMpunzi who arrived carrying a medium-sized reed basket on her head. Inside the reed basket MaMpunzi had put bits of biltong, groundnuts and a kilogramme of coarse salt. The two women found Khethiwe sleeping in the shade of the gigantic tree that marked the Sibanda homestead. MaNtini was sitting beside her, shelling some groundnuts. Khethiwe's maternal aunt who had visited them to check on her was busy removing husks from corn while chatting with her sister. As they were still exchanging greetings, MaXaba, wife to Ndlovu, the Chief's police officer, alighted from a bicycle which she parked against the tree inside the yard. She unfastened a goatskin mat from the bicycle carrier and unrolled it before placing it on the ground. She then unfastened another parcel and held it like a woman holding a newly born baby. MaNtini met her and received the parcel in the same manner she was holding it. MaXaba then proceeded to sit on her mat. She was never known to sit on unfamiliar mats. Nobody took offence.

"I think we will receive sufficient rains this season, what with this scorching heat!" she clapped her hands, wiping them unnecessarily on her apron.

"I hope so too," MaMoyo said.

Meanwhile, Zinzile received MaXaba's parcel from her mother and disappeared into the kitchen to come out with a gourd of water.

"Has it rained yet in Mbembeswana? Your husband said you had gone there to check on the old woman," MaMoyo asked.

"It is the same as here – so dry that the cattle and donkeys are dying from hunger and thirst. The remaining donkeys are so skinny that I can't help wondering what they will use for the plough! The old woman is suffering from a horrible arthritis," MaXaba explained before receiving the gourd of water. She drank all the water without stopping before continuing. "It is worse because she does not walk anymore. She is a lot of work to her daughter-in-law who is such a responsible young woman."

"Umh... but how is she taking it, your daughter-in-law?" MaNkomo asked.

"I suggested that I wanted to bring her here but they both refused. She said she will manage. The big problem now is she's unable to take herself to the bathroom. Yet she is such a heavy woman!" MaXaba said.

"She was well-raised, your daughter-in-law. If it was one of these modern ones, she would since have left and followed her husband to Egoli with *omalayitsha*," MaMoyo said calmly.

They avoided Khethiwe's predicament and talked about the dance ceremony where they would all be going after lunch. They also talked about various village scuffles, scandals and hopes while drinking the tea Zinzile had made.

Chapter Eleven

It was a warm morning. The sky was a dry, harmless blue. The women, skirting gigantic anthills, arrived with the hollowed gourds sitting on their heads, coming forward in slow dignified steps. By midmorning, there was a great gathering at the rain dance shrine. From every path, more and more people kept pouring in. Everybody took it as their duty to sing for the rain god to be appeased so that rain could fall. The calving and lambing had been good, but water was needed to keep the little ones well fed from their mother's breasts. If the rains came, the grazing lands would be green with grass and shrubs that goats and sheep loved to feast on. Flowers of all kinds as well as pyrethrum daisies would start blooming.

MaMoyo, among other middle-aged women, fetched water from the well in one of Dube's fields. They made several trips so the people would have enough water to cushion themselves against the dehydrating sun. The spirit mediums, *iwosana*, who are also the rain dancers, wore *imisisi*, *indlukula*, and *amahlwayi*. They carried *amatshoba* and other paraphernalia that they normally used for the ceremony. The songs sung at the rain ceremony were sacred.

Dust clouded the shrine, provoked by the jumping feet of the dancers. The women clapped and ululated as the drummers beat the drums rhythmically. The drummers would bend systematically to dry their hands in the dust, careful not to miss the rhythm. The gathering moved backwards and forward in style, shuffling to the beat. The singing and dancing went on as the sun gradually became hotter. Urged on by the rhythm which sprang from the drumbeat, the dancers danced as if they were possessed. One male dancer, Makhosi, danced like someone with supernatural power. He particularly drew everyone's attention when he drew his neck in like a tortoise, then pulled it out like a duiker ready to spring, his feet tapping the ground lightly like someone leaping on live coals. Frisking like a colt, his gaunt shoulders shivering, he sprang up like a springbok, waving his *itshoba* in the air in rhythm with the drums and the clapping of the women. He did not seem to care about the blistering sun. A female dancer with very thin legs, whose stomach was divided into bowed corrugations, also displayed magnificent dancing prowess. She jumped up as if in a trance, mumbling several inaudible statements. Nevertheless, she was heard and understood by those who were supposed to hear her. Within a moment, they brought water in wooden bowls from which she drank without holding the bowls. She then spat out a fine spray of water from her mouth.

Sikhwehle kept watch over the beer which was in calabashes in the shade of a huge *muwawa* tree. During the break, people were given beer in small calabashes and clay basins. Those who customarily never drank beer were given a lighter drink called *amahewu*, made from fermented corn.

MaMpunzi had cantered away like a horse when the crowd was busy cheering on the solo dancer, Makhosi. No one noticed her surreptitious departure except MaNkomo. Even though MaNkomo saw her and had a very good idea where she was going, she would never let the matter escape from her trusted chest. MaMpunzi found Motini Nleya already waiting for her, crouching in the shadow of a huge boulder discreetly located near the banks of the Simpathe River. This was one of their secret love spots. There she showed him what a supressed lover she was and made him whisper words of manly content.

* * *

Zanele and Nonceba did their chores hurriedly before dashing off to see Khethiwe. They took along a few poetry books written in isiNdebele and English to read with her. Khethiwe was a natural arts pupil, even at primary school. She wrote short stories, performed poetry and was in the drama club. MaNtini was relieved to see the girls enter and she took the opportunity to go and show her face at the dance shrine. With each of her steps, the sound of the drums became nearer and nearer. The women already assembled there were happy but surprised to see her.

"*Livuka njani*, MaNtini? How is our girl doing today?"

"She is doing better, MaNleya. I left her with MaMoyo's girls. What would I have done without Zanele and Nonceba?" she said with the air of gratification.

"Thank you very much Mama MaMoyo. You raised well-mannered, responsible and loving girls," MaNtini said directly to her as soon as she came near.

"You can say that again. They are a disciplined pair of girls," echoed MaNkomo.

At the river, the illicit lovers promised each other heaven on earth. A cool breeze blew as the birds sang for them in their temporary but splendid isolation. As they lay there caressing each other's bodies, far away, Motini Nleya's wife was delivering a baby girl by Caesarean section.

"My sweetheart, why don't you leave this old man of yours and come with me to Egoli?" Motini asked, already, in the grip of sexual satisfaction.

"If you say anything more about the headman, I will report you tomorrow. You will pay a fine!" MaMpunzi giggled.

"So, you love him after all, don't you?" Motini teased.

"That is a bad joke. I am not happy. I have told you my relationship with that man has nothing to do with love. I am a replacement wife who came to make fire, cook, make more

127

children for him and provide conjugal satisfaction! That is what it's all about," MaMpunzi said in unfeigned anger.

"Sorry, my love. It must be tough for you in that place!" he said.

MaMpunzi remained quiet and pulled her arms from him. She pouted and folded her arms on her chest in the manner of someone seeking consolation. Tears trickled from her eyes. Motini was taken aback. However, he just looked at her.

"Tough is an understatement. Hell, on earth... And I do not care anymore. I am too frustrated to feel anything," MaMpunzi finally said in a hurt and desperate voice.

"I will talk to Njabu. I am friends with many of them. I will find you one who can take you to a better place where you and I can enjoy life without interruption," Motini said in a consoling tone.

"Who is Njabu?" she asked.

"*UMalayitsha*. He can take you to Egoli even without the necessary papers. Remember I did it once!"

"*Yeyi wena*, leave me alone! What will I do with my children? I don't want to solve a problem by creating another. What is done is done. Let me leave matters as they are!" MaMpunzi said seriously. She loved her children despite the fact that she bore them against her will.

"Listen, love, you can leave them with your mother. She will take good care of them, then we will send them money and whatever else they desire," Motini persuaded her while pulling her closer to him for another round. Motini's sexual hunger was hard to pacify, especially when he was with MaMpunzi. It was probably because stolen things taste like heaven.

"*Awu suka wena*! Money and material things do not look after children. Children are better raised by their own mother. Nobody can do a better job. No one can replace a mother. I will stay for their sake. The damage was done when I failed to escape from

Nkiwane on the very first night. You have a wife, after all," MaMpunzi said but did not resist Motini's advances. She also had a sexual desire that took long to pacify, and Motini was aware of that.

There was some silence after Tholakele Mpunzi's words disappeared in the romantic moment. Motini could not believe that he was really the one enjoying this beautiful woman. The moments were too precious for him. Yet for MaMpunzi, it was a matter of rebelling and just satisfying her desires at that moment. Before long, their bodies talked to each other. It was a matter of love on the rocks for lovers who did not care for anything else except for that moment. Afterwards, flashes of how she was made to be Nkiwane's wife played back in her mind. She regretted it all, but when she thought of her children, the regret seemed to fizzle away.

She remembered just how very clever she was at school, and how her friends and her younger sister cried when she gave them her books. She would not need them. She only needed pots and blankets then. It made her heart ache to think about how her teachers had come in a group to ask her father and his clansmen to let her complete her studies. Like Zanele, MaMpunzi was top of her class in all subjects. She had been the school head girl at primary school. She sometimes thought of poisoning Nkiwane and running away but she did not have the nerve to do it.

Perched up high in the branches of the trees that lined the banks of the river, the birds continued to sing their melodious songs, quite oblivious of what was happening below.

"What wife? She is packing her bags as soon as she arrives from hospital. I am sending her back to her people. I cannot waste my life living with a witch and a prostitute. I doubt if that child she is carrying is mine. She is lazy and dirty and I am tired of putting up with her smell and untidiness," Motini said. MaMpunzi was surprised that he had heard what she had said after all before their passionate lovemaking under the *muphafa* tree branches.

"Ha ha ha… *Hayi ah*… you men are something else. Maybe that is what the headman is saying about me to his girlfriends too!"

"No man can ever say that about you. He would have to be out of his mind!" Motini whispered, cupping one of her bulging breasts in his right hand.

A flurry of fluttering wings of red-breasted swallows startled them and they went quiet. The red amber eyes of a falcon caught their eyes. Mpiyabo, who had heard some voices somewhere in the foliage, hid behind the huge trunk of a *muphafa* tree, listening. The voices were clearly familiar. Since it was not a new scene in their eyes, Mpiyabo and Zamani continued tracking their cattle and donkeys whose bells they could hear from the distance. They ran in the direction of the sound, happy that they had found the donkeys they would need the following day.

Within moments, the horizon turned dark with heavy clouds, and the sky had suddenly changed from being a limpid blue to a heavily clouded blanket of impending rain. It was going to rain any moment. Thunder roared and lightning struck across the sky. The lovebirds ran in different directions, making sure they did not return to the rain dance shrine lest the spirit medium would shame them in public for their infidelity. Thick clouds of dust were sucked up by the fierce wind, the dust devil. Hail fell from the sky, tearing leaves, scattering them about, mingling with the foliage before dissolving and sinking into the dry earth. The thirsty land of Emlanjeni opened its mouth, sucking in the water to quench its thirst. Rain poured down, drenching the gathering crowds to their skins.

The first summer storm travelled with Siphamandla and Dingizulu on their way back home, in accordance with the traditional custom. If it had not rained, the community would have been worried sick because that meant something serious was going on or something had happened within the community which needed to be sniffed out and addressed. The previous days' footprints were supposed to be erased by the first rains before they arrived at the shrine. The good thing was that they managed to cross the Simpathe River before its banks had begun to burst with flood waters. They arrived drenched and were welcomed by the wild ululation of women. Their message had been heard by the rain god.

The rain had caught up with Zanele and Nonceba while they were reading some poetry with Khethiwe at the Sibanda homestead. They saw the clouds build up in front of their very eyes before a lacerating hailstorm began beating down upon the thirsty earth. They had to sit the storm out. It poured down from thick dark clouds that had been gathering since midafternoon. When at last they decided to leave, they found that the stream was already in flood. They stood around, waiting for it to subside. Simpathe River roared and rushed down, angry, wide and deep.

Chapter Twelve

The people of Emlanjeni talked in excited voices. The smell of the wet earth reached their nostrils with a richness that only the rain god could bestow upon the land. The smell of village life itself, the smell of smoke rising from wet thatch to mix with moist morning air, mixed with the smell of the wet earth. It had rained. The Njelele god had answered their request. Women, seeds in their pinafore pockets, some tied in their wrappers and head gears, greeted each other, exchanging this type of pumpkin seed or that type of cow-bean seed. Which were the ones that flowered early? No. Which ones spread their branches like pumpkin leaves? They talked and exchanged seeds in excitement. Simphathe and Marabi could be heard still flowing, carrying with them all the debris of winter. Nobody would dare cross these rivers. Those who wanted to cross Simphathe walked to Mahlasela Bridge. The Mopane and acacia trees welcomed the after-rain breeze and gave back fresh oxygen. Frogs and brightly coloured insects appeared along small streams which were still flowing with clear water. At night, the frogs would croak a nocturnal choir that would serenade the ears of the villagers who would be ruminating on the kind of planting they needed to do the following day. *Velabahleke*, a type of grass which blooms a day after the first rains opened its petals to the new breeze, smiling as it is expected to do. This grass is used by offenders who, when they are called to court for trial, pluck its bloom, put in their pockets, hoping that those sitting on trial benches would forget their offences as soon as they appear. Fathers called sons to check if all the harnesses and discs for the ploughs were in order, ready for ploughing. Oxen and donkeys were gathered and kept in their kraals, ready for the plough. Kraal gates were rebuilt to make sure wayward and libidinous bullocks would not escape in the night.

Men carrying knobkerries visited the homesteads of those with oxen and donkeys to ask for the plough. Once in, they walked hesitantly, with the humility of beggars, to be offered wooden stools to sit on timidly as if they were perching on spikey surfaces. Hadebe received many such visitors. A man of virtue in the community, he did not say many words. Sometimes he only nodded in agreement. The only day his voice was heard was the morning after his arrival from Bulawayo when he visited the kraal to inspect his cattle. After that, he then went into the goat and sheep pens to select the one to slaughter for the weekend. If it was not a goat then it was a sheep, but never an ewe. Once he was back from the kraal, he shouted Mpiyabo's name humorously, calling him to come from under the women's petticoats. He asked him a lot of questions pertaining to the calving of cows, matters concerning the scotch cart, the plough, his toolbox and any missing tools. Mpiyabo answered the questions in fear, often stammering. Sometimes he asked Mpiyabo questions in front of male, but in the end, they left together, walking towards the kraal with Mpiyabo carrying a rope.

Simphathe and Marabi usually flowed for days in those years when the rains were torrential. When this happened, herd boys abandoned cattle and goats to catch fish that would have been washed away from Mahlasela dam. They caught breams and catfish left up in ponds which would soon dry. Cows also calved during such a season. There was abundant milk in most homes. There were different kinds of milk: fresh, pasteurised or sometimes made into butter. Fresh vegetables from the fields were cooked in milk. They included *ulude, ibhobola* and many other types. Toddlers were seen with bulging stomachs ever full of finger millet *isitshwala* with their favourite relish. Those without cows did not have to worry because goats gave rich, thick milk too.

The late Khulu Hadebe, Zanele's grandfather, was a different man from those in the community. He did not drink beer, so he did not stay long when he attended beer parties. He did attend just to be with other village men. He took so much pride in his work as a blacksmith. There was a *mbondo* tree in front of the homestead. Behind the *mbondo* tree were several other trees to the west. A stone's throw away was a well dug by Khulu Hadebe when he came to build his home before Zanele's father was born.

Branches of the trees converged at the top to create a wide shade under which women pounded their grain. Khulu Hadebe's blacksmith workshop was on the western side, a bit further from the spot that women occupied. As he worked, hammering on red-hot metals, boys descended to the well with buckets to fetch water to cool the metals according to his instruction. That part fascinated the boys most, especially the "*fro-o-o-o-o… shwi-i-i-i… fro-o-o-o-o …*" sound as water landed on red hot metal. His hammer was heard falling on the anvil most afternoons, pounding on red hot metals as he made hoes, axes, sickles and whatever tools he could make. He taught his grandsons, Mpiyabo and Moya the trade, even though they could not pursue it further. Sometimes Zamani and other neighbouring boys came to pass the afternoon away, listening to his jokes and tales whilst they waited for the fire to burn the metals to be shaped. Villagers, mostly women, came to him with blunt hoes for sharpening. He did small jobs in exchange for chicken, and bigger jobs for goats and sheep. He never charged above that. Once, when a woman suggested to pay with a woven basket, he had refused bluntly. When the woman waited there desperately, he called MaMoyo and asked her if she would not be offended to receive the basket. MaMoyo treasured that basket very much. The villagers bought whatever they needed from each other mostly by batter trade. There were women renowned for moulding beer clay pots, weaving mats as well as baskets. On the other hand, men were vegetable gardeners, carvers of wooden dishes and spoons, and fish mongers, though some trades were seasonal. Morden builders and other artisans were also found in Emlanjeni.

* * *

Sunday morning, a day after the return of the rain messengers, the frogs in the rivers and streams bellowed and croaked. Multicoloured butterflies and dragonflies trembled in their flight as they sipped from the same wells with ebony maidens scooping water with their gourds from shallow wells. The young women had dug a few superficial wells on the surface of the riverbeds from which they were collecting clear water while singing and chattering. On such a day, the cicadas would be silent. They never made any noise if the sky was overcast. One could say that they drew their strength from the heat of the clear, bright sun. If it continued to rain, the veld would be carpeted with a profusion of wild blooms, mostly scarlet and pink or snow-white flowers that brightened the surroundings to make the insects and the bees thrill the air with their colourful wings.

Shawled old women plodded barefoot in the mud to the dance shrine, chattering happily, thinking and talking of what seeds to sow first after the ceremony of the seed-touching which was to be performed the following morning. In a few days' time, the lowlands and abandoned fields which were then grazing lands would be green with verdure. Nobody could say that the rain god had not answered the people's request for rain despite the fact that they were filthy rotten with mischief. People looked forward to the following month or two when the cattle would be fattened by summer greens. The sight of one's cattle, their skins shiny with life, brought pride to the men of Emlanjeni. The birds sang as if to answer the sounds of the castanets. Sweet-voiced girls giggled, as they played on the wet sands, while their young mothers filled their smaller containers with clear water which sizzled from the fountains in the sand.

Much later, MaMpunzi found herself being cross-examined by a curious audience.

"MaMpunzi, I did not see you yesterday afternoon. Who did you leave with?" asked a suspicious neighbour.

"With the great gathering that was here yesterday, it was so easy to miss each other!" MaNkomo attempted to shield MaMpunzi from the prying questions of some women.

"I left early before it started raining. I had stomach problems and I did not want to worry anyone. I walked slowly back home to make myself some *isihaqa* medicine. By end of day, I was feeling much better," MaMpunzi lied.

"*Isihaqa* is always the best for stomach ailments. It works so fast," said MaNkomo.

"Make it a habit to take aloe juice in warm water. It also helps to clean the system," MaMoyo said, pouring some beer into a smaller calabash for the older women who were sitting in the shade of a tree.

"Really? I did not know that the aloe works in human beings. I always use it for fowls!" said MaMpunzi.

"It is excellent. I have used it before," MaNleya echoed.

Simphiwe Dube's mother went past them and disappeared in the thick foliage whose leaves had survived the scorching heat. She saw at a distance, bulbuls and mouse birds twittering as they fed on ripe wild fruit, gorging themselves and drinking water in sips from the pond near the trees. Pigeons also fed on the green fruits carelessly. She looked from left to right to check if she was hidden enough from the prowling eyes of men and when she was satisfied, crouched behind some shrubs to relieve herself. Before she could do anything, she was startled to see MaSikhosana who immediately stood up, a bad omen by some traditions. A person was never supposed to leave such business when startled; if they did, it meant there was a spirit of death lingering in the family, ready to take a relative. Both women knew that. MaSikhosana moved away from her and waited. While crouching, Simphiwe's mother thought if she had manly authority, she would drive the remaining herd of cattle and pay the Ncubes silently. She finished her business and walked slowly back into the open, aware that MaSikhosana had waited for her in the shade of a *muwawa* tree.

"Truly, daughter of Sikhosana, I wonder what my son needs to see before he acknowledges and pays this avenging spirit. What do I live for when all my children and grandchildren are going down one by one? Like they say in the old proverb, if I do not give birth, my intestines go rotten instead. Surely five people buried within a space of eighteen months and one who has lost senses! How does an old woman live with that?"

"I hear you, mother of my mother. It is sad. Life can bring so much that one wonders what she can do about it. I really feel sorry for you. I feel your pain in my heart. But in all this, I do not blame anyone but the self-professed healer and child rapist, Sibanda!" MaSikhosana said.

"There's no need to blame Sibanda. I can say that my son is stubborn. Is it not better for him to pay the Ncubes with the same cattle he is paying Sibanda for the useless herbs and medicine?" The old women walked back to join the gathering in silence, each of them probably thinking painful thoughts.

The sound of drums and singing went far and wide that morning because of the wet soil and humid air. The dancers, drummers and the gathering were excited that it had rained and that the messengers had returned safely and without a message of reprimand from the rain god. It had continued to rain in the night, not ebullient like the hailstorm, but soft, calm, perfect rain which enters the earth without leaving a mark or any trace of a disturbance. The sun had come up with all its might, but still, the people did not stop. They went on dancing and stamping their feet on the ground until the soles of their feet looked like the underbellies of frogs, and until their *amahlwayi* went loose. Makhosi, who was profusely sweating, danced an erotic dance with another woman, *iwosana*, who had not been available since the rain dance started.

* * *

That Sunday morning, Zanele and Nonceba wore pretty dresses, wide brimmed hats and dark glasses to shield their eyes and faces from the scorching sun as they trudged with Ntando and other village girls to church. Zanele had a small jersey on despite the heat. They had managed to persuade Khethiwe to come to church with them. She could not bear to refuse people who had showered her with so much love that had the effect of temporarily making her forget her misery. Zinzile too was in a pretty Sunday dress and sandals. The feminine party walked purposefully but gaily, chatting incessantly and sometimes singing as they, with their palms, beat on their hymn books and Bibles as if they were drums. They got to St Joseph's Church early and managed to do all the necessary chores, assisted by the nun on duty, before the congregants arrived. The church was not as full as it usually would be on a normal Sunday since most people were attending the rain dance ceremony. It was mostly the youth and Sunday school children in church on that day. Zanele read both the first and second readings for the service. She had seen Mnqobi enter and sit next to Sipho as she stepped down from the pulpit. Khethiwe winked at Zanele when she saw Sipho sitting next to Mnqobi.

During offering time, Sipho walked proudly with an affected limp, casting his eyes furtively at where the girls sat. He wore a pair of blue jeans, a bright yellow, long-sleeved summer shirt with the image of a dragon on top of a printed vest on which was a picture of a leopard or cheetah. A huge silver chain hung from his neck. From inside his left pocket hung, like a holster in cowboy films, a bunch of keys, pen knives, nail cutters and some unidentifiable sharp objects whose use nobody could immediately imagine. Mnqobi, who was behind him, wore a black pair of shoes, a black suit, a purple shirt showing the collar and the cuffs, and a white tie with purple stripes. He had trimmed his hair. He went to sit where he had placed his big King James Version Bible which had luminous green, pink and yellow markers and a notebook in which he jotted down notes from the sermon. Sipho saw him and changed his sitting place.

Chapter Thirteen

Sibanda sat in the holding cell at Khezi Police Station waiting for his appearance in court on Monday. He thought of the day of *ijumo* where almost everybody except Dube was against him. Against his life. It was not his fault that Dube trusted his medicine. It was worth trusting. He would deal with every one of them as soon as he was set free from the cells. All of them, including the headman who thought he was a king because of his young and beautiful wife. After devising how he would sort those men out in his mind, he smiled. The only person who had visited him in that cell was Dube who had also brought him some food. He also brought him some herbs to chew and spit on his hands and smear on his face. He was also to put a small root under his tongue before his trial opened. He knew he would need some money to use for transport upon his release. They were both certain he would be released. Sibanda still had his bunch of an assortment of roots that his father had given him when he was still a little boy. That bunch was always in his pockets, the way devoted Catholics carry their rosaries. He moved it from one pair of trousers to the other that he would be wearing on that day. He did that after making sure that he was unobserved. When Nkiwane's boys had come for him, the pair of trousers he had been wearing had his charm in the little front pocket. He boasted that this was the charm that had drawn MaMpunzi close to him before Motini snatched her away. His grandfather had told him that married women of all classes would come crawling on their bellies towards him. That was a strong package for him which made him scale all walls of conflict, no matter how huge, and win. He believed that even the police dogs, with their strong sniffing powers, would put their tails between their legs and walk away from him. He would always have his way no matter what, be it plagues or persecutions. He trusted his charms the way the young ones of these days cannot do without their cellular phones. Sibanda peeped through the hole of the little cell to check if there were any eavesdroppers and straying eyes so he could perform his short ritual. He then inserted his two fingers into the deep pocket of his trousers and brought out the charm. The talisman was a small duiker horn filled with python fat, an assortment of red, white and black beads with a rabbit's skin woven around it. On the pointed end of the horn hung something from a hyena's tail. He looked at it, smiled and talked to it in a language that only he, and perhaps the sinister object, could understand.

"Hey, you scrounging rapist, who are you talking to in your hell hole?" someone asked.

The voice came from the door at his back.

"Do not dare call me a criminal! Have you put me on trial and found me guilty, hii? Be careful, you might find yourself in here without committing any crime!" he shouted at the invisible stranger.

"Do what you do, but do not forget that those herbs were created by God who made everything, living and non-living," the voice said.

"I have broken the jaws of people who poked their noses in my affairs before! You don't know me!" Sibanda cursed.

"Oh, is that so? Then this hell hole you are in right now is your place!"

The voice disappeared, followed by the thud of footsteps of someone excited or in a hurry. He knew that no one, even the policemen themselves and their superiors, would question or touch his charms. The community believed and feared such things. They did not need to prove anything because a word of mouth was enough evidence, or even a dream. It was said King Lobengula himself killed anyone that his *sangomas* claimed was a witch.

Sibanda sat down after a feeling of hatred for Headman Nkiwane overpowered him. How could he listen to MaNtini and then decide to get him arrested? He was going to teach him a lesson. He surely did not know him; he did not know the son of Mahlathini! He cursed, whizzed, and aimed his anger towards the old headman whom he believed had this stupid notion that he ruled the world. That Tholiwe would be his forever after the old man died. A sudden smile played upon his lips as he thought of the veritable queen, MaMpunzi. In his subconscious mind, he saw her gesticulating in front of him. Without knowing, he muttered, "That one will be mine and I must not waste time."

* * *

The sound of the drums at the dance shrine seemed to inspire Zanele and her choir at Roman Catholic Church to greater efforts. The rhythm of their own music became more frantic and insistent by the minute. The beat of the young Holy Sisters Guild Marimba Band had an irresistible air to it. The choir sang passionately and danced in appreciation of the rain.

* * *

At the dance shrine, MaNkomo served Sergeant Phakathi, who was not in uniform, a calabash of beer to share with Sikhwehle in the shade of an *amarula* tree. Sikhwehle sloshed at the brew with his pouting lips, splashing the opaque beer onto his beard. The visitor looked at him and MaNkomo with confusion. MaNkomo's eyes flashed in horror and shame, not knowing what action to take next. If she immediately brought another gourd, Sikhwehle would be offended and lash out at her. She looked at the visitor with pleading eyes whose message only the visitor understood.

Sikhwehle went on to mutter provocative scraps of commentary, his lips still drooling with beer at the corners. Sergeant Phakathi resolved that he would pretend he did not want the drink from the calabash yet and asked for water instead. Sikhwehle was not an inspiring companion to share beer with. Sergent Phakathi was off duty on that day, so he had planned to attend this ceremony and be part of this community whose ways of life fascinated him. He liked the way people related, helped and protected each other, besides honouring their traditional customs. He was not angered when the Chief's Council and elders of the land refused him permission to take pictures of the dances. He had respected their decision. They had moved with modernisation and yet still managed to respect and follow some of their traditions and customs. He thought he would take the opportunity to announce that those who wanted to be witnesses or just attend Sibanda's trial were welcome. Transport to and from Khezi would be available from the bus station at eight o'clock in the morning. He was well aware that there would be a ceremony of seed touching. He knew, however, that this was done clan by clan before sunrise and did not take time. The drummers thumped out a beat that echoed in the air as the dancers jumped and shook hysterically. They waved their *amatshoba*, with the women singing *amayile* tunes which symbolised the ending of the ceremony.

* * *

After the church service, Zanele and her party strolled towards the shopping centre from where MaNcube had asked them to bring her some snuff and candles. Girls from different schools chatted and giggled. Mnqobi was among the girls, pushing his bicycle, his jacket resting on the handles. Nonceba was perusing through Mnqobi's Bible.

Mnqobi lowered his voice and spoke to Khethiwe.

"You did well by coming to church. It is not good for you to spend all those hours alone at home."

"If it had not been for Sisi Nonceba, I would not have come. Did you not see how everybody's eyes were fixed on me? I do not want to be talked about like that," she said quietly.

"Khethiwe, it is all in your mind. Not all people know what happened. Even if they do, people sympathise. They feel what you are feeling right now. Those who were looking at you are probably admiring your beauty. You cannot exile yourself because of that," Mnqobi encouraged her.

"I have books, so I will be reading, and I will be fine."

"So you like reading too? That makes two of us! Which books do you have? We can swop," Mnqobi offered.

Mnqobi, who was all twitters about Nonceba, tried hard to show her that he belonged to her class. From the very first time he had seen her, he could not erase her image from his mind. He was aware that he would have to work hard to match up with her. Sipho was some distance behind them with the younger girls from Khethiwe's class. He had refused to join them when Zanele beckoned him to come close to them but kept on trying hard to eavesdrop on their conversation.

"Constable Mkhize, I can see you read your Bible! All the underlined verses and the markers!" Nonceba said.

"Leave me alone, girl. I am Mnqobi. Can't you see I am not in uniform!" he teased.

"Sure, she wants all these children to go tense and become afraid. Leave him alone!" Zanele supported Mnqobi.

"Actually, when I was younger, I thought policemen do not go to church," teased Nonceba again.

"Why would they not?" Khethiwe asked teasingly. Mnqobi smiled at that.

"Stop being mean, Nonceba! We are people too, and that is just a job. My grandparents who raised me are in the parish council. We went to church every Sunday at St Patrick's in Makokoba. I served Holy Mass since I was eight," Mnqobi said seriously.

"Wow, wow, Mnqobi!" Zanele mused.

At the shops, Zanele bought what they had been sent to buy by her grandmother. Mnqobi bought everybody some biscuits and soft drinks. As they sat down on the benches to rest and enjoy their refreshments, NakaThathabonke arrived cycling a bicycle. They had not realised that as they entered the shop, she had come by and taken Mnqobi's bicycle. She did not need permission because everything belonged to God as she would remind everyone who questioned her actions. She would take any bicycle to just enjoy cycling around the shops, greeting everyone she saw and remembered. As soon as she alighted from the bicycle, Zinzile and Ntando could not stop giggling. Zanele tried by all means not to laugh at Mnqobi who was furious at her. That day she was clean. Somebody had reminded her that it was Sunday. She had come to church and sat behind the choir from where she sang very loudly. She had a favourite bench on which she sat alone because people were afraid of sitting near her. Khethiwe warned Mnqobi not to ask her about it, otherwise he would risk insults in vulgar language. She could even remove her panties and throw them at him. She then joined them on the bench, sitting next to Zanele. She did not say much to her but just smiled. Mnqobi had moved away, afraid even to take his bicycle along.

As soon as they had finished their refreshments, Zanele offered her some biscuits which she happily accepted. Nonceba bought her a bottle of lemonade before they started off on their journey back home, Zinzile and Ntando taking turns to ride on Mnqobi's bicycle. Before they had gone far, a young man called to Khethiwe.

She had a sudden fright and stood still, her fingers tightening, her eyes searching for a cue from Nonceba.

"It is Mr. Mkandla, your English Literature teacher," said a girl who lived in the same neighbourhood with her.

"Go and see him Khethiwe. We will wait for you here," Nonceba assured her.

Teacher Mkandla moved closer so they could meet halfway. Khethiwe's heart beat erratically because she thought the teacher was going to ask her about her misfortune. Instead, he looked at her in a friendly way. He had heard through the grapevine about what had happened but made a resolution not to show that he knew. That way, she would be at ease with him. He liked her in class for her good use of isiNdebele and the English language. She used her words with cadence and a gripping imagery when describing or narrating things. She was the best student in the English Language, Literature in English and isiNdebele classes. As Khethiwe approached, he removed earphones from his ears and spoke with her in calm, dignified and measured tones, his voice lowered for just the two of them, and his spectacles on top of his wide-brimmed hat. Teacher Mkandla was wearing a pair of casual khaki trousers with countless pockets on the sides and black strings attached for decoration, as well as a striped, white golf shirt and a pair of sandals. His calm eyes were always hidden behind the screen of a pair of heavily lensed spectacles. He was the kind of teacher that young, naughty girls fantasised about. He again said something which made Khethiwe smile and then punched some numbers into his cellular phone and smiled at her. He restrained himself from patting Khethiwe for the valuable information she had given him. He remained standing there for a while, looking in the direction of the other girls but trying to conceal his gaze by punching letters on his gadget.

Khethiwe then joined others but blocked them from asking about her private meeting with her teacher.

"…National University of Science and Technology in Bulawayo!" Zanele was speaking as Khethiwe caught up with the conversation.

"Witwatersrand. I do not know much about its curriculum, but its name is derived from…" before she could finish what she wanted to say, Nonceba noticed Khethiwe joining them. She said, "Let's start then, but please do not walk too fast Zanele." She emphasised this for Khethiwe's sake.

"You were about to tell us the history of Witwatersrand University," Mnqobi encouraged.

"Before the university is a place where African waters divide. The Vaal and Orange rivers flow west into the Atlantic Ocean, and the Crocodile and our famous Limpopo flow east into the Indian Ocean."

"Still on the same subject, is it not the same university where Mandela studied at?" Zanele asked.

"Yes, it is. That is the reason why you want to study there, Za?" Khethiwe asked, smiling at her. She knew Zanele was Mandela's fan.

"Of course, I have so much respect for the world icon! I want to tread the same ground as him," she said before she started singing:

> *"Oliver Tambo thetha no Mbeki*
> *Ah khulul' uMandela*
> *Ah khulul' Mandela!"*

Mnqobi lifted his fist to salute the Nobel laureate. Nonceba playfully joined in the song also with her fist up.

"I am going to Witwatersrand, come rain, come sunshine! If I fail to get a place there, I will go to Fort Hare or even University of South Africa. I will be doing this for Madiba," Zanele said.

Sipho heard it and tightened his face in anger. He had been walking quietly behind them with his friends. He was not going to have a wife who read books and newspapers and gave speeches in front of men. Who was that Madiba? He knew Mandela, as everyone did but Madiba! Mkandla, who had been following them at a distance, on the other hand, smiled. He was amazed at the girls who, to him, were an embodiment of an intellectual power that did not match their age and environment. He blamed society for educating women to focus only on being mothers, house and husband keepers. He made plans in his head at once before taking another path which led to the secondary school gate.

"Tomorrow you are going, Sisi Nonceba? I will miss you," Khethiwe said sadly.

"Oh, won't we miss her!" echoed Zanele.

Nonceba made no answer or comment but acknowledged the statement by nodding. Her eyes glistened, indicating that she was sorry she was leaving. Nonceba's heart was as soft as butter. Everyone's step changed to resemble that of mourners taking their dearly beloved and departed's body to its final destination. They crawled on silently until Khethiwe asked when Nonceba would visit again.

"Maybe during Easter next year, since the December holidays are a nonstarter because we normally go *ekhaya* to Gogo and Khulu Godonga in Filabusi to help with ploughing, sowing, planting and weeding," she explained.

"*Ah!* Sisi Nonceba! Your father, a medical doctor, still troubles himself with village life?" exclaimed Zinzile.

"My father believes everybody should be accustomed to every kind of life in this dynamic world we live in," she replied. "We do all kinds of work which other people do. My brother, who is at university abroad, works for his upkeep there. My father pays only his tuition fees. We also eat all kinds of food at our house, *umfushwa, amacimbi, ibhobola* with peanut butter even if our deep freezer is full of meat!"

"What a good father you have, Nonceba! You should thank God and the universe for giving you such a handsome pair of parents!" Mnqobi said.

"*Awu suka*, Mnqobi, they are too strict! They should let them enjoy life instead of bringing them back to this village life we are trapped in."

"Zanele, I am surprised you talk like that. What is wrong with village life? I have observed that there are more people with good morals here than anywhere else I have lived. Except for a few problematic individuals, like any other community would have, people live in peace and harmony with each other, and children belong to everybody. *Kusalobuntu lapha.* You women and girls go to do your laundry at communal wells and you leave your water containers there and clothes hanging to dry on the trees! I was amazed that you actually go back and do your chores at home and come back to the well to find everything still the same as you left it. I want to live with people like you," Mnqobi said.

"What is surprising about that?" the village girls asked, surprised. Even Ntando and Zinzile were surprised at Mnqobi's remark. He did not reply but he just smiled, shaking his head.

"In town you cannot do that, especially in townships. People steal clothes from the washing lines. You don't share food and communal duties like you do here. You pay for everything. If a person asks you if you need help with your luggage at *renkini* terminus, you do not immediately agree. You will make them pay for their services," Mnqobi said seriously.

"And if I refuse?" asked Khethiwe.

"There will be trouble for you!" Nonceba said.

"Why should I pay when it is them who offered help?" Zinzile asked, confused too.

"True, Mnqobi. Talk about *ubuntu balapha*, you cannot let your goats and cattle roam the forests like they do here, even in other rural areas!" said Nonceba.

"It will be difficult with people migrating from their areas to start and run businesses here. They bring their cultures here which contaminate the place. There is a new butcher from another part of the country who was seen driving a herd of calves from *emlageni* at Tshatshe River! All those calves had not been branded yet, so nobody could prove who they belonged to!" Mnqobi said.

"What is *emlageni*?" Nonceba asked.

"Communal ranches for villagers near Tshatshe River. Cattle are driven there, left to feed on the abundant verdure, drinking from the river all year round. The paddocks are allocated chief by chief," explained Khethiwe.

"I hope things remain as they are for as long as it can be helped. That is the sad thing about change when people are allowed to come from wherever to start businesses here!" Zanele said.

"There is nothing wrong with that. What is wrong is those people who are given a chance to come here and then cause trouble with their behaviour. They also bring bad habits which destroy community peace," Khethiwe said.

"Let me tell you a story about what happened some time back. I had this friend I went to school with at Mzingwane when I was an A Level student. He was doing Ordinary Level when I was in Upper Six. He came from a rich family. Actually, when schools opened, he drove himself to school and then his sister who was at Girls College would drive the car back. Their father was too busy to even bring them to school. They had businesses across the country, but his mother's job was only to shop around the world.

150

Business language was Greek to her. She was not even lettered enough to know what mortgages were or where bills were paid. Everything was done by secretaries in her husband's office. On top of that, they lived a secluded life from their poor relatives who lived in the village. One day, my friend surprised us by telling us that it was his first time to see cows being milked in a village near Mzingwane Boys High."

"Ha ha ha! Liar!" teased Nonceba.

"Tell us *bhuti* Mnqobi, what happened then?" asked Ntando, curious to know how the story ended.

"Ntando, the way you love stories at your age, be careful when you grow up. You will make every householder's ear quiver with scandals!" mused Zanele.

"Ha ha ha!" all the girls laughed.

"Leave her alone. She is going to be a top journalist, lighting every paper with top stories!" Nonceba said light-heartedly.

"A terrible thing happened," Mnqobi continued. "His father died suddenly in a car accident at a time his company was not doing so well. Within three months, almost everything was gone, including the house they lived in. They had to move to occupy a wooden cabin which their father had built at their plot in Umguza. The plot survived because it was not in his name. The house he was building there was not complete yet. The girls refused to go with their mother."

"So where did they go instead?" Ntando asked again, giving Zanele a furtive glance.

"Oh, you would not want to know," Mnqobi said.

"They got married?" teased Khethiwe.

"It was going to be better if they did. They became fulltime prostitutes."

"Oh oh…" mourned Nonceba.

"What is a prostitute?" quizzed Ntando.

"We will tell you some other time when you grow up," answered Nonceba.

"The boys became robbers. That boy I am talking about is in jail in South Africa as we speak. The mother suffered extreme depression and almost lost her sanity."

"Tough story! Life changes for sure, and that makes it so scary," Khethiwe said.

"True, Khethiwe, but it would be better to rise from being poor to being rich than the other way round! My point is children must learn both types of life. They must do what their cousins in the village do in case of such events," Mnqobi emphasised.

"Umh umh…" Zanele doubted.

They had subconsciously increased their speed as they were engrossed in interesting stories. The beautiful weather gilded the afternoon. In no time, they parted ways and headed home.

Khethiwe was left with a sinking sensation when she thought about Nonceba's return to school. She wondered how she was ever going to feel better with Nonceba gone. However, her eyes were starry with gratitude. Nonceba had become her closest friend.

Mnqobi was puzzled by the power that Nonceba had over him. He had never met anyone as attractive as her before, and that endeared her to him to no end. Try as he could, Mnqobi could not get Nonceba out of his mind. He resolved to make sure that he made her his, body and soul, even though he had not yet dared reveal his feelings to her. But again, in moments of contradiction, Mnqobi told himself that he was not going to remain devoted to her memory, because Nonceba had given him the feeling that she was not quite his type of woman. Mnqobi suffered alone. After that Sunday, it became impossible for him not to think about her.

Nonceba was happy that Khethiwe had thawed gradually and hoped she would get better still.

Chapter Fourteen

Sikhwehle and Mpiyabo had just finished skinning a young ewe when the girls arrived back home. It was in honour of Nonceba who was returning to Bulawayo the following day. MaMoyo had just arrived home too, but MaNcube had remained at the rain dance shrine. MaMoyo had come home only because her husband had ordered her so that she could attend to Sikhwehle and Mpiyabo.

"*Dundu-ndu-ndu-ndu... dundu-ndu-ndu-ndu... dundu-ndu-ndu-ndu...*" sounded the drums at the dance shrine.

Birds abandoned their pecking every time the sound became louder. The sky, a fading strip of orange and blue, seemed to enjoy the drumbeat. Even nature, with its inexorable laws, seemed one with the sound. The wet soils carried the sound of the drums all over Emlanjeni, which was then sparkling in freshness.

Zanele and Nonceba had tea and sweet potatoes for lunch before hurrying off to fetch water for the second time. They had left their water buckets at the well on their way to church. They would need more water for the evening and the following morning. When they returned from the well, they found MaMoyo cleaning the intestines using an old enamel teapot. She poured water into it and carefully inserted the pout into the opening of the intestine before tilting the teapot to let water flow through, thus taking out the unwanted stuff, mostly half-digested grass, leaves and whatever else the ewe had fed on. She left the offal looking clean and transparent. Nonceba loved them, especially when they were cooked her grandmother's way, with no condiments other than salt.

MaMoyo had asked Sikhwehle to pour the ewe's blood in a wooden bowl. She would use it to make *ububende*, a delicacy made from stewing blood with overcooked lungs, kidneys and liver. Two pots glistened with fat on the hearth outside MaMoyo's kitchen. One had the remaining offal and the other had mixed cuts from the backbone, neck and thigh. When the girls returned, they found Sikhwehle ready with some roasted liver and ribs.

Those days Zanele did not like meat in general. She claimed that they did not cook it well at the mission school's kitchen. That was a convenient excuse which made her get away from anything that caused her discomfort without revealing her secret condition. Hadebe and his mother had no liking for offal either. While Nonceba and Ntando were enjoying the roast mutton, Zanele husked off the half-pounded finger millet with a winnowing basket. Mpiyabo and Sikhwehle stretched and nailed the ewe's hide to the ground. This, they did carefully with the inside of the hide facing the sun to make it dry quickly. MaMoyo preferred them to goatskin mats because of their fluffiness. She had carpeted her bedroom with them and kept some for her special visitors and friends.

They pounded jovially, encouraged by the relish for supper.

"My beautiful wife, I am so proud of you. You pound even better than your lazy mother, Zanele. Do you pound finger millet in Filabusi?" Sikhwehle asked, moving in rhythm with the faint drumbeat.

"Point of correction, Sikhwehle: first she is not your wife, and second, what do you mean when you ask whether beautiful women like her can also pound or not?"

"Ah, MaHadebe! Do I even need to explain myself? Pounding is for your type and MaNkomo, but not for this one!" he said, laughing so excessively at Zanele that Nonceba ended up laughing too.

"She is going tomorrow! You, MaNkomo and I are remaining!" Zanele said seriously.

"I would not even miss you two if you travelled to Masvingo today for two years," Sikhwehle said, sitting on the dusty ground, his hands stretched behind him. His gaze was on Nonceba who continued what she was doing without looking at him.

"Why would we go to Masvingo?" Zanele asked.

"To find men to marry you! Especially those Great Zimbabwe men," Sikhwehle said, sitting on a log facing Nonceba who did not know how to behave in his presence. She was surprised that he knew about Great Zimbabwe.

"I learnt to pound here, Jiyane. In Filabusi, we grind corn on stones. We even roast finger millet before grinding it, unlike what they do here," Nonceba answered him politely, unable to hide her fascination about the fact that a person whom everybody thought was mentally disoriented knew Masvingo and that Great Zimbabwe was situated there.

"Have you been to Great Zimbabwe, Jiyane?" Nonceba asked after a pause.

"No. Umdala Hadebe read to me in the newspaper that it was the town built by Zimbabweans with stone and no mortar before the arrival of the white settlers," he said, still grinning at her.

Sikhwehle was as mesmerised as he was happy that Nonceba had called him by his totemic name. It made him feel like a man among men. "You see, MaHadebe, she is mine. She has called me with my totem name, something you have never attempted! I can never marry your type, women who do not respect men," he said, grinning.

"Never! She has her own fiancé. I wonder when you will stop dreaming those wicked and misleading dreams of yours!"

"We will see about that," he said confidently as he rose and walked back to his fire. There, he prepared the ewe's head and its feet. He would cook all in a three-legged pot for the following day.

Nonceba was thinking about what she had read, how white historians had tried to deny that the Ancient City was built by Africans. It was even said that they sent their people to do some research on its origins, yet even Sikhwehle knew all this. She then realised that there was nothing wrong with Sikhwehle whom nobody could understand. She admired the sense of respect and dignity he gave to family life. She had felt disappointed by Zanele's interruption in their conversation. She had wished he could go on and on. MaMoyo came and carried away the smaller mortar and pestle they were not using and hurried back inside the yard. They finished pounding the finger millet, carried their powder in reed baskets and followed MaMoyo. That night, they cooked outside in front of the kitchen. They found hot air swishing off a three-legged pot which contained boiling water for *isitshwala*. It looked like the water had been boiling for quite a while.

MaMoyo washed the inside of the mortar with water, preparing to pound the boiled lungs, liver and kidneys which were cooling in a wooden basin. She poured the water she had washed the mortar with into a waste liquid container in which they stored water for pigs. Nonceba then pounded the cooked meat so carefully that it did not turn to a paste. MaMoyo scooped the contents with her clean hands into the original bowl and then placed a small earthen pot onto the hearth, poured the thickened blood into it and asked Nonceba to beat the mixture with a wooden sauce stirrer. She emptied the pounded stuff into the blood pot and left it to cook slowly as she stirred it continually. MaMoyo cut some fat from the meat hanging in the kitchen hut and put it in the simmering pot before adding some salt. Little Ntando who was fascinated by Nonceba's stirring perhaps forgot to keep watch of the dogs to protect the drying hide. Thatha tore away little pieces of meat which had remained attached to the skin, making holes on it. Sikhwehle threw some little stones at Thatha, cursing it for its mischief. Thatha winced and limped away, its tail tucked neatly between its legs.

"Ntando, what were you doing? You let Thatha chew my mat!" shouted MaMoyo, missing her with the sandal which she had thrown at her.

"I was... I wa..." she stammered.

"Shut up. Don't dare talk back!"

* * *

Back at the dance shrine, Headman Nkiwane announced that Dube and Mxotshwa's case would open for hearing and deliberations the following Saturday at the chief's court. The great gathering began to melt away before sunset. The crowd murmured their agreement as they discussed it, walking in pairs, threes and in slightly bigger groups while others cycled away from the shrine. MaNcube walked with MaNdlovu and MaMlotshwa, each of them carrying two empty beer calabashes. The clouds brooded heavily that one doubted if those who had to walk long distances were going to get to their homes without being drenched. People had an air of satisfaction with the rains despite other pending matters awaiting deliberation such as Dube's case.

* * *

"MaGodonga, when are you visiting us again?" MaNcube asked Nonceba, while picking little pieces of meat stuck between her irregularly spaced teeth with tooth picks that Sikhwehle had carved for her from a small twig. The family sat chatting after supper.

"Next year, probably during the Easter holidays."

"That is a long time away, MaGodonga. We enjoy having you around," Mpiyabo complained, joined by MaNcube.

"Then visit me in Bulawayo instead. I will buy you pizza and ice-cream," Nonceba said, speaking softly.

"Ice-cream is too cold for my teeth. You buy me those sweets that look like cooked ox liver!" MaNcube said.

"Ha, ha ha!" laughed Ntando.

"You mean chocolates, Gogo?" Nonceba asked.

"Ha ha ha."

"He he he."

Ntando laughed her heart out, a sudden change of mood from the pouting that had taken over after being scolded earlier on.

"What else did you say you will buy me?" MaNcube asked Nonceba, ignoring the laughing Ntando.

"I will buy you pizza," Nonceba said.

"What is pizza?" Sikhwehle shouted as he passed by, going to where the sheepskin was.

"Pizza is some round and flat bread baked with different ingredients like meat, fruits, vegetables and sometimes even cheese on top. I read somewhere that it was brought from China and India to Italy by their famous traveller and explorer Marco Polo, way back before Christopher Columbus travelled the world. That was between 1254 and 1296."

"Nonceba! Who tells you all these things?" Mpiyabo remarked as Sikhwehle marvelled at her. Hadebe looked at her with pride. He enjoyed sitting around the fire in the evening with his larger family whilst at home. He just listened to them and asked questions. Sometimes he shared with them his experiences at work, the people he met and other places he had been to.

"No, *malume*. I do not know much. It is because I try and read a lot," Nonceba said, smiling.

"So Marco Polo was a traveller?" asked Hadebe.

"Yes. He was an explorer, travelling the world, learning new things and bringing them back to his own people," explained Nonceba.

"I see now!" Zanele exclaimed.

"I can see that you, like me, thought that Marco Polo was a bus," mocked Sikhwehle. Indeed, Asian companies had branded their buses by that name.

Everyone burst into laughter.

"Umh, everything has meaning in this life," MaMoyo said after the laughter had subsided.

"You can buy me that one. I am sure it is soft since it is bread, but you will have to come with it for me because I am afraid of cars and white people in the ci–" MaNcube said.

"And me too!" shouted Sikhwehle before MaNcube could finish speaking.

Siphamandla and MaNkomo brought a chicken and some groundnuts for Nonceba to take to her father, their son-in-law too. They also brought some dried wild vegetables for her mother, *ulude, ibhobola* and okra. Siphamandla put down little Farai whom he had been carrying in his muscular arms whilst MaNkomo carried the little girl on her back strapped tightly with a baby sling. They talked about village triumphs and tribulations late into the night. Zanele was in her own world with discomfort so that she could not even participate in the chatting. She secretly wished everyone would go and sleep so that she could be on her own in her dark bedroom hut. She vowed that she was not going to see Sipho that night. He would have to wait for her till morning if he wished. And what's more, what would she talk about with an uneducated Sipho instead of making plans about going to university where she belonged?

Chapter Fifteen

Sibanda sat in his cell thinking of his previous triumphs to encourage and prepare himself for the approaching trial. His smelly clothes were in serious need of washing. He had not had a bath for days.

"That day I made a fool out of all of them," he thought as he jumped up and down, then stopped to prance around, boasting. "What will they do to me? I am untouchable, he he he! Let me hear your laughter son of Mahlathini!"

He was startled when he heard something hit the door of the cell. He immediately sat down, thinking it could be someone eavesdropping on him again. The fear inside him faded as images of his previous trial flashed in his mind. The memories excited him. The same charm had worked, surely it *must* work again.

The incident had happened two years back. The morning was sunny but soon, the clouds had rolled to cover it, making the day a tedious one for those who had plans to travel. As he came from his usual spot with the headman's wife late in the afternoon of that day, dark clouds had threateningly hung low. He saw a hyena chasing a flock of sheep near the Marabi River Bridge. Knowing that sheep die silently, he let the hyena catch one and waited till it had killed it. Khulumani Sibanda chased the hyena away and went to pick up the dead sheep. He cut off its ears before he drove the other sheep away. As darkness fell upon the land, he was satisfied that there was nobody in the vicinity watching him and carried his catch home. He walked with so much confidence that even when he met old Sikhukhula, he complained about hyenas killing domestic animals day after day. The village healer did not suspect a thing since he was in a hurry to assist a sick man further away. He went straight to skin his catch in MaNtini's kitchen hut. When

160

she asked where he had got the ewe from, she suffered a fist blow. She knew they only had one brown-headed ewe in their kraal.

The matter came to light when he beat his wife one night after a beer drinking binge. She cried for help while threatening to report him for stealing Hlabangana's ewe. That night, Sikhwehle and Dingizulu were passing by when they heard MaNtini shouting at her husband that she would report him for theft at the village court. Sikhwehle and Dingizulu then entered their homestead to enquire about what they had just heard. Upon their enquiry, she dished out all the details.

He became excited again as he thought about how he fooled them at the village court.

"Did you steal and slaughter Hlabangana's ewe, Sibanda?" asked Headman Nkiwane.

"I did not steal Hlabangana's ewe. I skinned my own ewe after finding it half dead, almost eaten alive by a hyena," he lied.

"How did you know it was yours since you said the hyena had devoured its ear and destroyed the branding?" the headman asked with some formality in his tone.

Sibanda had kept quiet for a while and looked at some doves cooing up in a tree nearby.

Ndlovu looked at him. "Sibanda, answer the question. We do not have the whole day to discuss your matter," he urged calmly.

"*Badala*, do not forget that I also lost a brown-headed ewe that time. Hlabangana is not the only one with sheep in this community. Mine had a brown head and a patch on its left hind leg. The one I picked had that same mark. I do not deny that Hlabangana may have lost his, but he should go and find mine, then I will replace the one I skinned if it was his as you say."

"Liar and deep designing guttersnipe! You never had a brown-headed ewe. It was Hlabangana's which you slaughtered. You even beat me when I as…"

He charged ferociously at his wife, quivering like a dog sniffing a hare. MaNtini jumped and hid behind MaMoyo and MaXaba.

"Do your misdemeanour again and you will risk spending the day tied to that acacia tree. How many times should you be told to respect this court?" Ndlovu lifted the rope as he emphasised his threat. Dingizulu and Sikhwehle stood guard, ready to pull him back if he tried to be violent again. Headman Nkiwane indicated that everybody had to sit still for the trial to continue.

"Why did you not report the matter when you saw the ewe after it was killed by the hyena?" asked another man from the village.

"Why should I have reported when it was mine and I was the first to pick it?" retorted Sibanda.

"So, you picked it? MaNleya shouted.

"If it was any of you who saw the ewe first, would you have reported it? There is no case here, and now you are listening to this woman liar!"

"She is telling the truth. I want my ewe!" shouted MaNleya from where she was sitting.

"Since when did a woman have a say about issues to do with domestic animals? Go and bring mine and then I will surely give your ewe back. After all, it may be that I made a mistake and skinned yours. But I am not a thief!" Sibanda retorted.

"I feel you should consider what Sibanda is saying. He also lost an ewe. Hlabangana's ewe can be found," Dube suggested calmly.

It was Simphiwe Dube who had defended him with that statement which he uttered while looking at the headman with respectful reverence. People whispered, complained and yet the day ended without a solution to the matter. He, thus, escaped without punishment.

On the day of that trial, MaNtini came with her own people. After escaping her husband's beating, she had run to her aunt who then escorted her back to her matrimonial home. With the help of a neighbour, the two women encouraged her to stay strong and not to abandon her children because of such a trivial matter. Sibanda would come round after they talked with him themselves. They did talk to Sibanda the following morning. He seemed to agree with them about maintaining peace at their home. However, as soon as the negotiating pair were out of sight and hearing, Sibanda descended on the defenceless woman like a wounded leopard taking revenge. He beat her to a paste. When she fainted, he poured water on her and raped her. Zinzile had come to her rescue by calling their neighbours, Siphamandla and MaNkomo, who arrived to find him still with her inside the bolted kitchen. Siphamandla had to break the door for them to gain entry. Sibanda attacked, but when Siphamandla sent him reeling across the room with a huge blow to the face, he retreated. MaNtini reported the matter to the police, but it was treated as domestic violence. Rape was completely dismissed even by the villagers themselves because no woman could claim to have been raped by her husband. With all these issues in his mind, Sibanda smiled at the dark walls of his hell hole as he began to fantasise about the headman's wife.

* * *

After the bus had left with Nonceba and her father, Zanele walked back home alone, thinking seriously about her future. It was early in the morning. The bus had come at exactly 7 o'clock, its usual time. Sipho, sizzling with anger and jealousy, waited for Zanele who was coming towards his hiding spot. *I will teach her a lesson today*, he thought. She was about to pass by when he sprang for her.

"Where is your boyfriend?"

Zanele was frightened by the voice from the thick foliage on the banks of the Simpathe River. Sipho had made it his habit to follow Zanele and Nonceba wherever they went without them suspecting anything. He had overheard Nonceba and MaNkomo persuading Zanele to leave him. He had seen them visiting Khethiwe twice and had also sneaked behind them as they walked with Mnqobi from the church. He had spent a day hiding near the well and eavesdropping on their conversation when they talked with Mnqobi.

"Are you now dumb? I asked you a question, where is your boyfriend?"

"I did not know that you gave me a boyfriend. You tell me!" Zanele replied angrily.

"Today, you will learn something. Your father and that whore cousin of yours are gone with her boyfriend. Your policeman boyfriend will find you in pieces today and we will see what he will do to me!" he charged at her with determined ferocity.

He lashed at her with his cattle whip before throwing it away to use clenched fists.

"You leave me alone, you unlettered boy! That is all you know, you son of a murderer!" she tried to free herself, but Sipho would not stop. Like a mindless monster, he punched her breast even as he punched her head. Sipho pounded Zanele and sent her crashing to the ground with one last devastating blow. She lost consciousness and flopped to the ground helplessly. As if the dusty earth had whispered to her to come down, she lay still on the ground. Some women who saw what was happening from the windmill-driven borehole situated a short distance away came running, shouting at Sipho to stop beating her. When they saw the state she was in, they ran back to fetch for some water to pour on her. A group of women going to Khezi for Sibanda's trial also came running. In a moment, there was a crowd around Zanele. Sipho

164

had fled into the thick forest. MaNkomo who was going to the mobile baby clinic appeared on the scene. She quickly and carefully unbuttoned Zanele's blouse then they splashed water on her, calling her name slowly. Two women knelt down and prayed. Some were so frightened that tears flowed down their cheeks.

"The Chief should chase these people away before we see what we have never seen before!" shouted a woman from another village.

"Now they want to kill Hadebe's daughter!" echoed another from among the women who had brought some water.

"They should be chased away together with their chickens, cats and dogs," cursed another.

The cursing and talking stopped. The frightened women stared at the girl as she lay motionless on a piece of hard ground just before the bank of the Simphathe River. MaNkomo kept calling out Zanele's name even as she muttered a desperate prayer.

"Zanele! Please Za, do not do this to us! Please Za wake up, MaHadebe. Please wake up!"

MaNkomo asked people to move away a bit so that she could get more fresh air. After what seemed like an eternity, Zanele twitched, opened her eyes and tried to sit up but failed. A woman in a blue *isishweshwe* and MaNkomo helped her up and gave her some water to wash her mouth first and then drink. The woman was continually saying a prayer in her mother tongue.

"*Kiyareboha Modimo o aka,*" cried a Sotho woman from among the crowd.

Zanele was swollen all over and blood trickled from some of her wounds. MaNkomo thought about how often she had warned her to stop making contact with that heathen Sipho who only came to church because he wanted her. All the while, the crowd was heaping insults on Sipho and his clansmen. A man who was coming from the shops offered to carry Zanele on his bicycle carrier. MaNleya cycled behind them after cancelling her trip to attend Sibanda's trial in order to keep watch on Zanele with her mother who had remained at home. MaNkomo proceeded to the baby clinic, but would, however, come straight to Hadebe's homestead to check on her. MaNcube had gone to the court with the rest of the women who had used a shorter route. She only knew about Zanele's beating later in the lorry. The rest of the women proceeded to Khezi, cursing the Dube clan all the way.

* * *

"Khulumani Sibanda, you are accused of raping your daughter, Khethiwe Sibanda on the night of 20 August 2004, at your homestead, Headman Nkiwane's area under Chief Mlotshwa. Take on your Bible and promise to tell the truth, nothing but the truth to this Honourable Court."

"Your Worship, I know nothing about the case levelled against me," he said with astounding calmness.

"The accused is denying the charges. May the plaintiff go into the witness box and tell this Honourable Court what she saw the accused do and swear before God that what she shall say is nothing but truth."

The public prosecutor led MaNtini to the witness box and handed her the Bible.

"Say everything MaNtini, we are behind you!" the women in the grand arena murmured, encouraging her. They had come out in their numbers, some pregnant, others with children strapped on their backs.

"Sshssh!" the policeman who had brought Sibanda in silenced them, placing his forefinger across his lips. The magistrate looked on and listened quietly.

"Your Worship, it was on the night of 20 September 2004, before the cock had crowed for the first time, when I heard

Khethiwe and her sister Zinzile screaming in their bedroom hut. I ran out to investigate. Zinzile bumped into me as I entered their room carrying my lamp. I saw my husband, Sibanda, holding Khethiwe who was naked down with one hand while the other one was holding his knife. I asked him what he was doing to the girl. Still holding her, he lifted his knife, ready to cut me. I retreated and he pushed me out and bolted the door from inside. Khethiwe screamed until she was…" The woman suddenly paused to gather her emotions together before continuing. "I called Zinzile who had run into the night. I was still standing outside the door with the lamp."

A police officer moved to give MaNtini a handkerchief to wipe her tears away. Sobs were heard from the audience.

"Khethiwe screamed until she was quiet. I tried to open the door from outside in vain. I looked for something to bring it down but couldn't find anything. It was Khethiwe herself who opened it carefully much later and we ran away to take refuge in the goat kraal until we were sure he was fast asleep. We then sought refuge at our neighbours' place, at the Dubes'."

"Wizard!" a woman cursed from the audience.

"Wife batterer and rapist!" shouted another.

MaMlotshwa and MaSikhosana stood up as if they would tear Sibanda apart with their eyes. Zinzile covered her face with her hands. MaNtini's tears flowed silently. More women murmured their complaints.

"Silence in Court!" shouted the attendant.

"Now Sibanda, what do you say for yourself?"

"Your Worship, I never raped my child. I don't even know she was raped. Maybe it was one of her mother's many boyfriends who did it. I was surprised to see Ndlovu and his men coming for me as I slept peacefully. This woman I call my wife is an ignoramus and a simple-minded liar."

"And the men who came with Ndlovu found you in your girls' bedroom. Did the goblins take you there?" shouted MaNtini, with roars of support from the audience.

"Shut up woman! It is my home, I can sleep in any hut I want," Sibanda shouted back.

"Mrs Sibanda, you will be given your time to speak," the Public Prosecutor assured her accusingly.

"You raped your daughter Sibanda. We saw she was raped, and she can even speak for herself!" screamed an old woman who had checked on Khethiwe after the rape. MaMpunzi echoed the old woman as tears trickled down her cheeks.

"We are witnesses! He raped his own daughter. Miserable bastard!" screamed women in unison, shouting all kinds of obscenities.

"Were you there?" Sibanda asked fiercely and threateningly.

"Silence in Court!" the magistrate hit again on his desk.

Khethiwe was brought to the dock to narrate what happened to her. Sibanda denied everything she said. He just said he was in the girl's room because he came home drunk and did not remember his bedroom hut. He knew nothing about Khethiwe's rape.

Since there was no tangible evidence presented yet, the case was postponed and Sibanda was ordered to pay $20 bail.

"We will settle your account!" the women promised him before they started to sing their song:

> Inzima impilo
> Inzima impilo
> Kithi bomama
>
> Life is tough
> Life is tough
> For us women

Ngapha ngizithwele,
ngapha ngibelethe,
ngapha ngiyawonga
Abagulayo!

I may be pregnant
At the same time
Carrying a baby on my back
But still expected
To care for the sick
To do all house chores

Ngapha ngizithwele,
ngapha ngibelethe,
ngapha ngiyawonga
Abakhulayo!

The women sang the sad song, dancing outside the courtroom, some with tears flowing down their cheeks. Old MaNxumalo was very disappointed and angry, not only with Sibanda, but also with the judicial system. She remembered a previous case involving her neighbour whose children starved because their father was in jail, sentenced for ten years for a crime he did not commit. The true story was that the father had been sent by a butcher he worked for to drive an ox he claimed he had bought the previous day from a villager. The ox due for slaughter was in another neighbour's field, driven there by the butcher himself in the thickness of the night. As that man, just a worker following orders from his boss, drove the beast in the early hours of the morning, the son of the owner of the beast saw him. The man was caught, tied to a tree, beaten and held as the villagers called the police. The police did not listen to his explanation that he was simply acting on superior instruction. Poor as he was, he could not afford a lawyer. Now as the women sang at Khezi after Sibanda had been granted bail, the man was rotting in Gwanda prison after the butcher closed shop and disappeared.

Sibanda walked triumphantly towards the bus stop, thanking his medicine and ancestors. He planned to visit his *sangoma* near the Simukhwe River to get more medicine ahead of the next trial. He made sure to use a bus than be with that pack of old and lousy women. At Khezi, Simphiwe Dube melted as he saw him approach the bus stop with a smile.

The sad women gathered at Headman Nkiwane's homestead as soon as they had arrived home. A few men, including Ndlovu, were asked to escort MaNtini and her friends so she could collect her belongings and go to her people. Everybody was afraid that if she went alone, Sibanda would harm her. Khethiwe had vowed never to set foot in that place they called home. She would rather die in the bush and be eaten by wild animals. MaMpunzi kept watch over her as the party of women went to collect some clothes, blankets and Khethiwe's books. MaNtini and her daughters were to go and stay with her family *emkhonyeni* along the Mbome road and attend school from there.

Sipho had disappeared without trace like rain drops on the vast Simphathe sands, after beating Zanele before the eyes of the women who saw it. The thought of running to his maternal relatives' home in Sihayi Communal lands along the Simukhwe River had come to him. He had hidden in the bushes to check on her progress. He was aware that his father had killed someone and the dead man's spirit could be possessing him too. He would commit suicide if Zanele failed to come round. Strange voices spoke in his mind, telling him he was doomed and would die in prison. He prayed and cried, remembering his mother who had

170

died when he was still very young. After what seemed like a century, he was relieved that she had recovered and then proceeded with his journey. When he got there, he told his grandmother and uncles that he was visiting them indefinitely. Even though they saw in his temperament that there was something amiss, they did not immediately show him that they were aware that something was wrong. His sister who lived there let him be, thus giving them enough time to bond.

On the Friday of the end of the month, Sipho's uncle and aunt cycled with him back to his father to understand what had happened. They were well aware of the talk about an avenging spirit said to be haunting their late daughter's family. Nobody had even the slightest idea about the story that Sipho had knit for them.

It was a tradition that on the day of the new moon, or every Wednesday, or a day after an angry storm, nobody was allowed to work in the fields or do any hard work. People who defied the laws of the land were fined or risked serious penalties. The paramount deity, the god of Ematojeni, proclaimed these laws through the rain messengers who only heard his voice from above the cave.

* * *

That Wednesday, the men set to rebuild their common well. The logs protecting it were hanging loose because of the moist soil such that if donkeys pushed them, the logs would fall in. The well itself was full, almost overflowing. The rains had not stopped since the rain dance.

"You know, gentlemen, sometimes I think the god of the white man could be the same as ours at Njelele!" Sikhwehle remarked, pulling a huge log away from near the well as he took a shovel to deepen the hole into which he would fit a new pole.

"*Hayi bo*! Jiyane, you are always full of mysteries!" said a man who was a leader of a new church. He and his wife were pastors, and they rented an old storeroom at the township for their services and meetings where they preached the good news of prosperity.

"You may say so, but I too concur with Sikhwehle," Sabelo, MaNleya's husband, asserted. "There is a similarity in the way that the god of Matojeni and God Almighty communicate with their people. The messengers they both choose are not rich people. Look at Moses in the Bible; he was just a shepherd. Look at Elijah and Elisha the great prophets; they were simple peasants with nothing to their name. God in the Bible spoke with Moses through a burning bush. He told him to remove his shoes because the place he was standing on was holy. God gave His laws for transmission by Moses from a mountain. No one ever saw His face. They only heard His voice."

"You see! Thank you, Hlabangana. At least you agree with me!" Sikhwehle said, beating his chest.

"We did not say we disagree. We just do not know. Nobody could look at them. Both Gods spoke and it happened," echoed Dlodlo as he fastened a log.

"My grandfather told me that a long time ago there was a Khabo man who doubted our rain god. He told me that this man was always complaining about and mocking the rain dance ceremony," said Dlodlo with a faraway look in his eyes.

"What happened to the man?" Dingizulu interrupted.

"You listen quietly! Learn to listen and understand first!" Dlodlo said seriously, weaving a flexible branch between the logs.

"This Khabo man was a naughty, wealthy little man who had one wife. He had not received the white man's education but was so wise that he was in the Chief's Council. The man was so determined to see the face of the god at eMatojeni that he talked about this every time the messengers were set to go. He questioned

172

everything. The other thing he disputed was the possibility that the rain god could be female."

"The god cannot be a woman!"

"Stop interrupting, Sikhwehle, we want to hear this story! Are you a woman?" teased Siphamandla.

"Are you not the one who is seen pounding sorghum with a baby strapped on your back? I am sure you are mixed up in the head!" Sibanda said.

"Leave Siphamandla alone! He is a modern, loving man. You should see the white man! He even changes the baby's nappies. I sometimes admire the ways of that race. The white man's mind moves very swiftly even when he is looking at things that lie far ahead," Hadebe said solemnly.

"The white man's mind – never trust it! Planning to cheat Lobengula of his cattle, his land together with everything in it, while he sat in his office in the Cape." said Hlabangana.

"…Cecil John Rhodes, *uMlamlankunzi!*" Sabelo interrupted.

"It is as if you salute him!" Dlodlo mocked.

"We shall come back to that matter later. Now let us hear what this inquisitive Khabo man did," Siphamandla said, bending to lift a thick log from the ground.

"The messengers set off and after they had done their business as usual, the god asked them to go and call Khabo to come to the cave since he wanted to see 'him' face to face. The messengers went back home and told Khabo the message. The elders of the land were worried and their worries were most sincere, but Khabo himself jumped up in excitement. It was arranged that those who knew the way were going to escort him. They walked for four days but he did not worry about that since he was as strong as an ox. They carried the necessary offerings and gifts, those normally carried by the messengers."

"You see, even in the Bible people carried offerings!" Sabelo said.

"Do not take us back! We all know that!" shouted Sibanda.

"Some people who do not read the Bible do not know, *mdala, sitshele*!" Siphamandla said, inserting a log into a hole.

At that moment, they finished their task and went to sit in the shade of a *mswingwa* tree. Dingizulu brought the beer calabash that MaNleya had left for them together with the lunch brought by the other village women. Dingizulu had earlier placed the calabash on wet soil near the well where they were working to keep the beer cool. He put the calabash down carefully. Next, he cut a twig from a tree with his sharp knife and stripped it bare of its bark. When he was happy with what he had done, he used it to remove insects that had drowned in the potent brew and now lay floating in the froth. He then stirred the beer with the twig. Sikhukhula was first to join Dingizulu. He sat down and took a long drink from the calabash. The rest of the men came and took turns to quench their thirst.

"Khabo entered the cave barefoot. Afterwards, when he talked about what had happened, he confessed that when he entered the cave, he did not find it easy to look up and that a voice had spoken from somewhere inside the cave, saying, 'Khabo, my child, I have heard that you want to see my eyes. You may look up now.' Khabo began to look up and as he did, an unknown powder showered down upon him and he was immediately struck blind. He had to be led home, now blind as a mole. The whole kingdom was left in awe by this wondrous occurrence. Thereafter, the rain god appointed him the next rain messenger. He gained his sight back when he went to Njelele with the people's message."

"Just like the biblical Paul," exclaimed Sabelo.

"Since then, those who were in the habit of defying the customs followed them religiously again."

As the story about Khabo ended, coincidentally, the men finished drinking the beer, picked their tools and returned to their homes.

Chapter Sixteen

The matter between the Dubes and the Ncubes was of grave concern to the community. According to the laws of the land, a communal response was necessary, as was an intervention. People started coming in from the villages. They arrived at the Chief's court as soon as the sun had risen. They left their freshly tilled fields to be there to see and hear for themselves. Women carrying rolled goatskin and sheepskin mats to sit on arrived in small, lively groups, talking animatedly about the matter at hand, an unusually high-profile case for a chief's court. The men too arrived, some cycling on their bicycles, others with knobkerries across their shoulders. Some people were from as far as Sigangatsha, Beula, Nsewula and Mbome in the south-west. Others were from the east up to the Tshatshane River. Some men cycled while others came in scotch-carts.

Sergeant Phakathi and Constable Mkhize walked over to hear the most talked about case in the history of Chief Mlotshwa's jurisdiction. Within an hour, the mud and thatch courthouse were filled. The overseer then asked everyone to move out of the courthouse and sit in the shades of the *mopane, muwawa* and *marula* trees. The trees stood in a row, their shades converging in the centre to create a spacious shade for people to comfortably sit in as they followed the proceedings. The women sat separately from the men, leaving a gap between them as well as space at the front for the Chief's Council and those whose matter was before the Chief.

While waiting for the Chief and his council to come in, the women talked about what to plant and which seeds germinated faster on which type of soil. They exchanged quite a variety of seeds while the men busied themselves with manly issues in which beer parties, the cattle and the dip tank had pride of place. Some were exchanging tobacco, crumpled newspapers to roll the tobacco in and matches. The din from the gathering was like the sound of thousands of buzzing wild bees hovering above the yellow blooms of the acacia forests.

"*Amahole* are always a nuisance in a society," said Old Dlodlo to Ndiweni and Hlabangana with no attempt at subtlety. Ndiweni and Hlabangana were lighting their pipes. Soon, wisps of tobacco smoke began to rise from them, the aroma invading the surrounding air.

"*Amahole* are people too Mpangazitha!" said Sibanda as he took the bait.

"Yes, they are but the difference is that the *amahole* beat and stab their women with knives and rape their own children. They also make their wives do manly chores and refuse them the right to eat meat."

"Gluttons!" added Sikhwehle. "And they steal their neighbours' sheep!"

Even as Sibanda remained quiet, his facial expression promised Sikhwehle that they had unfinished business.

"One of these days the fake charms you worship like a god will leave you in the open and drive you mad, I tell you!" warned Hlabangana.

Sibanda could only glare helplessly at the three elderly men. The grey of their hair and their beards rendered them well beyond the ridicule of younger men, at least not openly. All that Sibanda could do was to look studiously at the pair of tough leather boots that his *baas* had given him during his time in Mzansi. His eyes glistened in the sunlight.

Suddenly, there was an almost palpable silence. The cacophony of voices from the crowd ceased, and the people stood up and the men removed their hats. In that short interval, the only discernible sound was that of feet shuffling in the dirt. The Chief walked in behind his aides and the members of his council. Dlodlo and Hlabangana stood opposite each other. As soon as the Chief had passed, they joined the procession to be part of the Council of Elders.

The Chief was a large man whose equally large arms hung loosely at his sides. His build and posture gave him the look of ancient authority. He walked in a slow but menacing manner. He had a straggling and unkempt beard that was accentuated by a wide, heavily furrowed brow. A man of few words and brooding thought, he stood in front of his leopard skin cushioned chair facing the gathering as if to approve of them. His aides stood on either side of him. The members of the council took their positions. The Chief's presence compelled silence and respect. Women kept their eyes on some spot in front of them as a sign of respect. Chief Mlotshwa took his seat and the people followed suit. However, his aides stood at attention on either side, facing the people.

Mzingaye Ntuli, the chief's spokesperson, stepped forward. He looked at the crowd, searching for the accused and those who had brought charges against him. After failing to locate them he spoke, "Our honourable Chief Mlotshwa, advisors, the service council and all who are gathered here, I greet you all."

The gathering responded to his greetings.

"Is the Dube clan here yet? I ask you to come to the front. Please open the way for them. Simphiwe Dube, remain standing. The rest of you may sit down."

There was a bit of shuffling and adjusting as people made way for the Dubes and the Ncubes.

"Our Chief, Baba Mlotshwa, advisors, service council and all those gathered here, this is Simphiwe Dube, accused by his clansmen. Now I will ask his brother Buhe Dube to give an

178

account of the case they are bringing against their brother. You who are gathered here, you were called by His Honour, our chief, to come and hear this case so that we can try it together and come up with a solution for the family and the community to live in peace. Thank you once again for coming in your numbers. I now ask Buhe Dube to stand and tell us what the matter is."

Buhe, who normally did not say much in such gatherings, speaking only when required to do so by the Chief's spokesperson, stood up, licked wet his lips, observed the expected protocol and started, "It all started last year on the fifth of February, early on a Wednesday morning. I was fixing the goat kraal when I heard the sounds of an axe chopping wood. When I looked up, I saw my brother Simphiwe working in his shed with his blacksmith tools. I wondered then who was cutting the tree but ignored the matter and continued building the kraal. Moments later, I heard my brother talking with someone. I could still hear the axe on the wood as the person I had not yet identified went on with his cutting. Sensing that trouble was brewing, I decided to go and investigate. I saw Mxotshwa Ncube, may his soul rest in peace, cutting down the giant *marula* tree just outside the boundary of my brother's homestead. I saw Mxotshwa Ncube raise his axe, aiming it at Simphiwe's head. My brother Simphiwe ducked and moved to the side. The axe missed him by a few inches. Ncube cursed furiously in the foulest language I had ever heard. Just then, a scotch cart was passing by on the main road. The people in the scotch cart heard and saw everything. These people can be my witnesses. At this point my brother was holding a sharp rod he had been working on in his shed. Simphiwe then held Mxotshwa's axe in one hand and tried to wrestle it from him, but Mxotshwa overpowered Simphiwe, pushing him to the ground. Simphiwe fell on his back still holding the rod which was facing up when he fell. Mxotshwa bent down, his axe raised high, aiming for Simphiwe's neck. Simphiwe tried to rise to evade the axe but as he did so, he accidentally pierced Mxotshwa in the chest with the iron rod. Mxotshwa fell, dead."

There was some muttering and several murmurs of disapproval from some among the gathering. Crying, Mxotshwa's mother made sounds like those of a whining horse. Buhe took a breath as he waited for the murmuring to go down before continuing.

"The accident was reported to the police who took Simphiwe to the holding cells. Thereafter, the matter was tried at the High Court in Bulawayo. Simphiwe came out a free man according to modern laws, as you can all see him today. Be that as it may, we believe that we, as the Dube clan, should appease the deceased's family and apologise for the accident, loss of life and spilt blood. As it is, we have lost five members of the family since that misfortune happened. Our sister has lost her mind after being sent away by her husband's family under unclear circumstances. Our Honourable Chief, Service Council and all gathered here, we have come to seek your opinion and to ask that you help us persuade our brother to do the honourable thing, apologise and appease the Ncubes for spilling their blood before we all perish. Without exaggeration, my chief, that is the truth upon my word of honour. I thank you."

"Oh! Poor Simphiwe! What a misfortune!"

"Mxotshwa was wrong. Death was calling him!"

"Simphiwe was not supposed to kill him still."

"*Yeyi wena*, it was an accident what cou…"

Silence returned after Mzingaye lifted his arms. In that silence the people's minds were in overdrive. It was obvious that some people sympathised with the Dubes while others felt sorry for the Ncubes and the loss they had suffered.

"Now, let Simphiwe give his own account about this matter," said the Chief's spokesperson.

He came forward. He was so thin that if someone hugged him it would feel like embracing a bag of bones. His skin was dark and pale, almost grey. His watery eyes were red balls in deep sockets. His protruding nose was in competition with his teeth, which appeared longer than normal when he spoke. His hair and beard could be counted as tufts that stood inches apart, unkempt. The striped pair of blue and white trousers he wore made him look even taller. The women looked at him with sympathy, hoping Mzingaye, the spokesperson, would give him a highchair to sit on as he spoke. They feared he could be easily blown away by the wind. Nobody expected Simphiwe to have the strength to stand. He cleared his throat, observed the expected protocol and began to speak, "I sincerely apologise for spilling blood on your soil. I am ready to pay what this honourable court of justice fines me. I am very sorry and sincerely apologise to the Ncube family for what happened. However, I do not agree with this issue brought by my family which says that it is the dead man's spirit killing our family members. How do they know that it is an avenging spirit that is causing the deaths? My late father had gout and high blood pressure in his lifetime. Before the incident, he had been sick. We often hear that someone has been shot in Johannesburg. My nephew was shot and died there. I mean, such a thing has happened many times before. You cannot blame me. I have never used a gun in my life. Women die too in childbirth, which is why people carry gifts to say *amhlophe* to the mother and family when the deliverance has been successful. My daughter was swept away by a flooded river. That was an accident, you all know it. People die of different causes. As for my sister, she has always been lazy. That is why her husband sent her away. She has stress. She is not mad. Actually, I feel the Ncubes should apologise to me because they made me shed blood. I was proven innocent by Government Law itself which saw and reasoned that I acted in self-defence without the intention of killing anyone. The late Mxotshwa is the one who wanted to cut me to pieces in my own space with his axe which everyone saw! Now you say I should pay! No, I am not going to pay the Ncubes."

With those words Simphiwe Dube concluded his defence and waited for the spokesperson to tell him to sit down. Drops of sweat glistened on his face, and the sinewy veins on his neck and hands looked taut, as if the effort that he had used to speak had made his blood rush. The murmuring began. Dube's family surrendered the matter non-verbally. Simphiwe's mother echoed the late Mxotshwa's mother with mourning. She cried with a pain that radiated and touched the members of his family.

"There is the matter to you all. You have heard from both sides. Now it is our duty as a people to arbitrate for these families. You have heard their grievances about their son's unfortunate doing. They are truly going through a difficult time and living in fear and uncertainty, never knowing what is going to happen next. It is our duty, as the community at large, to restore peace to them as we are also not spared in this pain of burying children from the same womb one after another. Now it is over to the floor."

Mzingaye Ntuli, the spokesperson, took a deep breath and drank water from an earthen pot with a gourd. The Chief listened with calmness and dignity. The first to be given a chance to talk was Motini Nleya who boldly stood up. Sibanda looked at him contemptuously as if he had been sprayed with the undying odour of a civet cat.

"Our Honourable Chief Mlotshwa, Service Council and all who are gathered here, I greet you all. Thank you very much our spokesperson for this opportunity. I will not waste time but get to my point." Turning to Simphiwe, he said, "Without beating about the bush, let me say I am sorry to my brother Dube on the matter of the misfortune that befell you. You accidentally took a life, and yes, the court of law found you not guilty. Their ruling could be justified, but we, as a people in Emlanjeni, cannot let you hide behind the finger of modern law. Our dear brother, be man enough to apologise and pay because you are fighting with a spirit here and not with the living Ncubes. Are you not pained by losing your family members morning and evening? Well, if you are not, then as the community, we are and our hearts are bleeding. Save your family. Apologise and appease the deceased. Those, my Chief, are my few words. Thank you once again, Mr. Spokesperson."

There was an overwhelming clapping of hands in support of Nleya.

"I, Khulumani Sibanda, respect the modern court as I always stand for justice! And please, do not speak for everyone, you do not represent Emlanjeni villagers!" said Sibanda after observing the protocol. Insults were shouted, especially from people from his village.

"You may clap your hands and even go as far as ululating, but I feel we should be fair to this man. Simphiwe, to me, is the victim who should be paid by the Ncubes, and since you strongly believe it is the avenging spirit causing deaths, fair enough. The Ncubes should pay for the time Dube spent in the cells, his travelling to and from the High Court and all these deaths. We are talking of five and they lost one soul. How can a man continue to suffer as if he is the one who called Mxotshwa to come and offend him in his own space?"

Sibanda sat down after thanking the court for the opportunity to speak. Some frowned and cursed silently, while others mumbled disgruntlements. Most men remained calm even though they were surprised.

"Son of Mahlathini, stop misleading people! This is not a laughing matter. The Dubes are perishing and the sad thing about an avenging spirit is that it destroys the whole family, innocent people included, saving the perpetrator for last. We sympathise with Dube, but the noble thing to do right now is to apologise and appease the deceased for the sake of his family. I thank you Mr. Spokesperson," Dlodlo, affectionately known as Mpangazitha, his totem name, said as he sat down to great applause.

"I also agree with *ubabu'*Mpangazitha. Dube must not be misled by the rapist, thief and wife-batterer's empty words! He should just apologise and –"

Dingizulu, who had begun speaking without being given a chance, did not finish his words. Sibanda ferociously charged at him but was apprehended by Ndlovu who always sat next to him in all gatherings with his ropes ready. The spokesperson reprimanded and cautioned Sibanda, telling him that if he ever did it again, he would be fined three goats which he would slaughter alone and cook for the people. Dingizulu was also cautioned for speaking without being given a chance.

"*Hayi amahole la azasibonisa okunye*! There was no proper upbringing for this upstart. He and his people could not have survived if it were in King Mzilikazi's era," Dlodlo whispered to Sabelo in the heat of the moment, making sure that the spokesperson did not hear them.

The spokesperson then gave the Ncube family time to speak. Their representative stood up and expressed respect to the system.

"We, as the Ncube family, are sincerely saddened by what is going on with the Dube family. If we could stop it alone, we would, for the sake of the other family members, the children and their next generation. We all know that these deaths are caused by the angry spirit of our deceased brother. We cannot force Dube to come and pay but if he can, then we will accept anything to save his clan. Sibanda asked about who should be paid. Let me say it is the family of the deceased, the widow and the children, who must be compensated as per our custom. With these words I thank you, our spokesperson, for the chance."

"Do not be so rude when it is you who caused all this trouble," Sibanda mumbled from where he was sitting.

"And yours is the most unbiased opinion in this chiefdom?" another man answered him in a whisper.

"You are saying that because you want to protect your client who brings you herds of cattle every day to get your worthless medicine to shield him from death. You are a cruel, deceitful man, Sibanda. Stop it at once! If people listen to his mad sister's words, they would think it is Mxotshwa himself speaking through her!" Sikhwehle fired his opinion from where he was sitting, folding some crumpled piece of paper with tobacco in it. Sibanda glared at him with threatening eyes, but Sikhwehle did not even look in his direction. Instead, he lit a cigarette and began to inhale, blowing coils of smoke into the air. When Ndlovu stared at Sikhwehle reproachfully, he quickly put out his cigarette and sat up straight. Sibanda would not dare attack him because the punishment for such action was uncomfortable and painful. Strong men would tie such offenders to a *gagu* and pour heavily salted meat soup on them to attract ants that would feast on their skins the whole day.

Some people mumbled their agreement with Sikhwehle but could not openly show it for fear of being sued or bewitched by Sibanda. It was a serious crime to say that someone was a witch without proving it. Only the likes of Dingizulu and Sikhwehle could freely say such things because people assumed that they were not balanced mentally. Sergeant Phakathi and his young colleague listened and observed everything quietly, with Mkhize showing signs of admiration and fascination. Gangeni, a man who drooled pathetically, was next to be given a chance to speak. He kept wiping his mouth constantly. This man had never been married, was childless and still lived with his old mother and nephews. In other gatherings, nobody would bother to hear what he said because of his physical challenges and status in life, but at Chief Mlotshwa's court, everybody was given a chance and their views were respected. He observed protocol and shared his opinion.

"Son of Mthembo, I heard you say there was nothing unusual about these deaths, that they are natural. Have you ever heard what your sister, or whatever is speaking through her, says? I doubt that very much. And I would be ashamed if you have not yet found time to listen to her. You are saying she lost her senses because she was stressed? Stress is a foreign illness. We do not know it in our ways of life because we share problems. No one ever lives alone, unless they are greedy and do not want to share their food with others. You say she is lazy, really? Lazy now because of this accident? Can someone who has been married for ten years be sent away now for laziness? Is that normal? Maybe to you, yes! Only on Monday, your son almost killed someone's daughter over a trivial issue. Please do not tell this court that you do not see anything wrong in all this. I challenge you to give this court a satisfactory solution to all this so that our community finds a way forward. I thank you, my chief for the opportunity to speak."

The man's words struck everyone's soul. Dube was given the opportunity to speak and answer the man's question. "Sipho is a child who is going to be punished as a child. You cannot link him to this sto –"

"How about the girl who was swept away by the Marabi River, was she not a child?" Dingizulu interrupted. The spokesperson silenced him with his hand, but the words had escaped his mouth and were acknowledged by the gathering.

Dube continued his defence, "If my church allowed me to consult *sangomas*, I could go and find the cause and solution to all this," Simphiwe said solemnly.

"Liar! You consult your *sangoma*, Sibanda, and go on to do your useless evil rituals in broad daylight!" shouted Sikhwehle. There was a murmur from the gathering. Mzingaye tried hard to silence the people who eventually went silent. Mzingaye motioned to Buhe to explain what they had done as a family.

"We went to five different spiritual people for consultation over the issue and they said the same things: it is obviously an avenging spirit. What frightened us more is that three of the *sangomas* we consulted said somebody young is dying in this planting season if the matter is ignored," his brother clarified to the listening villagers.

Buhe sat down, wiping sweat from his brow. Judah, a man who was a self-confessed prophet and healer, stood up. He had his own church just outside his homestead where barren women gathered every day for holy water. It was said that some women who were not from his church never returned after an encounter with him but would not say the reason. Some of those who conceived were whispered to have given birth to children of suspicious likeness to the bishop. Their husbands never questioned because it was said that the prophet's Holy Spirit worked in mysterious ways. He observed protocol and took to the stand.

"I am surprised that everybody thinks Dube is supposed to pay for all this, yet the Bible says vengeance is the Lord's. It was a mistake that the late Mxotshwa died in Dube's hands, but that is not to say he is a murderer. The courts proved it. Life belongs to God – his time had come to die and it was written that he would die that way. Spare Dube this agony and leave all this to God. I thank you, Baba Spokesperson, for affording me the time!" Mpostoli Judah said and sat down.

"Amen, Amen!" Sibanda joined the group of women from that man's church to applaud their prophet.

"Prophet of Baal! The most incorrigible thief! God what? Prophet of barren women! You know what they give you when you visit them in the pretext of selling them petticoats and..." Sikhwehle ridiculed the prophet, loud enough for everybody to hear. Murmurs of shock mingled with embarrassment rose from the crowds.

"*Mfundisi*, I wonder how you read your Bible. Have you ever read the Ten Commandments which were given to our father Moses? I plead with you to go and read your Bible and understand it better. Dube, pay the Ncubes and save us from this painful experience. We are not going to wrap you up in flattery because we want peace restored to our community. With those words I thank you," MaXaba, Ndlovu's wife, said and immediately sat down.

"Pay with the same cattle you are wasting away on this self-proclaimed and useless healer, Sibanda!" Dingizulu screamed from where he was sitting. It was as if Dingizulu and Sikwehle knew more about the matter than the rest of the villagers.

The debate went on hot and heavy until there were no more facts to be adduced and the spokesperson closed the meeting after ordering Dube to pay in order to appease and ask the spirits of the land to forgive him. The next trial date was set for the following Saturday. The gathering melted away late that afternoon. Some were planning to plough their land in the gathering twilight.

* * *

Zamani and Mpiyabo were walking around the thick forests of Kwanike hillocks, shooting at birds with their catapults while listening for their cows' bells. Different sounds and echoes punctuated the afternoon air. Zamani stood cocking his head to listen, sometimes tossing it impatiently with annoyance if he did not hear his cattle's bells. The pair also checked their bird snares to see if there was any catch.

Mpiyabo was fascinated by the glorious clouds of butterflies, winged insects fluttering their wings, diving, toppling, swerving, wobbling down and alighting on fresh flowers. They could hear some girls' unrestrained laughter from the east on the riverbed of the Simphathe River which fed the Kwanike Dam. The girls were probably fetching water or doing some laundry. Zamani continued to listen, straining his ears as he tried to filter cattle bells from all these sounds. Suddenly, his eyes fell on a dove which met his gaze and pulsed its wings softly, almost ready to take off. When the bird hesitated, he took a stone from his short trouser pocket and made ready to shoot with his catapult, but before he could aim, it flipped its wings and took off, leaving him disappointed but with hope. Its flapping made the insects which were sucking nectar from some flowers fly away in the same instant, making a swirling cloud, their wings undulating. Large birds with curved claws and feathers of variegated colours launched into an instant flight as the boys approached the pond they were drinking from. The vultures which laid their eggs in shaggy nests on the Kwanike cliffs took flight at the boys' approach. The boys pressed on, occasionally stopping to listen for their cattle bells.

They eavesdropped on the delightful conversations of the giggling and laughing bigger girls. For some moments, hiding behind a rock boulder, they peeped at the younger girls' small but fully standing breasts and smooth legs as they scooped water, splashing it on each other's fresh bodies. The girls had fresh flowers nicely tucked into their hair. They stood for some time, marvelling at the young unsuspecting girls and creating impossible sexual fantasies with what they were seeing. A bit further from them, older women were doing laundry with their tops bare. The two boys walked on quietly as there was nothing to ogle at there. Older women's breasts were something natural in their culture and did not invite gazes of fascination from young boys. A stream with the clearest water that anyone could imagine came out of the Kwanike boulders, pouring out its precious load that quickly disappeared into the sands of the Simpathe river. Green pigeons swarming on branches of trees alighted one by one to take a sip from the clear water. After enjoying the feed of sage and other wild herbs, corkscrew honed antelopes stepped on the erosion raked riverbed and headed for the dam. Mpiyabo warned Zamani not to frighten a duiker which was dancing gracefully across the ravine under acacia and *mphafa* trees. They observed with fascination the harmony of nature and life in the wild.

As they approached the dam, they startled flocks of birds which fell into a vivacious hysteria, honking as they rose. The boys plunged into a pond of clear water where the birds had been drinking from. Mpiyabo's dog, Thatha plunged himself in too, but his master caught him and threw him out of water, coming himself out of the pool. Listening carefully, he thought he heard the bells of their cattle. Thatha shook a gale of water drops as if to complain about the denied pleasure. Mpiyabo listened again and when they were both sure they ran in the direction of the sounds. As they were running up the rocks and cliffs that they normally climbed on days such as this one, the pair was startled by the sound of voices and the smell of a fire. They moved quietly with their eyes searching their vicinity.

In the short distance was Dube, naked to the bone, his body half smeared with ashes, and his skin looking like the colour of a week-old corpse. Sibanda moved forward to cover him with a red and black cloth and commanded him to squat facing the fire into which he kept throwing herbs. Dube muttered something to the fire after being instructed to do so. Sibanda's body was as dark and shiny as the wild honey he had smeared. Zamani coughed. Sibanda raised his eyes, shivering like a dog scenting blood in its nostrils as fury smoked in his brains. He shouted that whoever was sneaking on them would meet death if he ever told anyone. The boys moved as lithely as monkeys in the maze of the Kwanike hillocks, fleeing the pair in the cave. By the time they arrived back home, they were panting like dogs that had just been chasing a hare. In the hurry to escape, the two boys forgot about the cattle they were looking for.

* * *

"You know what Za, this matter between your in-laws and the Ncubes could end badly. Siphamandla told me that Dube refused to pay at the Chief's court and that he was supported by Sibanda, the one who gives him fake medicine. What makes me sad is that the *sangomas* are saying the next victim will be a young person from the family who will die during this planting season!"

"MaNkomo!"

Zanele had her arms across her stomach, and her heart was pounding so furiously she almost missed her breath. It was Wednesday afternoon, and they were on their last trip to collect firewood before Zanele returned to school the following Saturday. The schools were going to open on Tuesday. She normally took the bus to Bulawayo first on a Saturday to stay with her aunt, Nonceba's mother, as she prepared to board the school bus on Monday with the rest of the boarders. She felt something was going to happen and wished she could turn back the hands of time.

* * *

The previous March during the Easter holidays, Sipho had called her out of the church and persuaded her into the darkness. As the

191

birds of the night were singing their nocturnal songs, Sipho had led her to a point of no return somewhere near the classrooms but far away from the singing choir. That had been her first sexual encounter with him. Looking back now, she regretted the whole misadventure. The whole thing had been a let-down, an ordeal for her. She had not experienced any fun from it. After that first incident, Sipho would visit her at night and together, they would escape into the darkness, unnoticed. On seeing that she had missed her menstruation, Zanele asked her mother for permission to visit Nonceba. Nonceba's parents were away on holiday in Italy. Sensing trouble, she went to a local clinic and lied that she was a married woman and wanted to know if she was pregnant at last. Her heart nearly fell at her feet when the nurse confirmed her suspicion. Somehow, she managed to keep it a secret for quite a while. When Nonceba asked her what was wrong, she said it was nothing and told her that she had always suffered from stomach aches and vomiting. Even though the maid suspected something, she felt it was not proper to mention it as it would appear like she was intruding.

* * *

"Mpiyabo and Zamani told us that they saw Dube with Sibanda at the hillocks in a cave, talking to a strange fire while dressed in red and black cloaks with their faces painted with ashes," Ntando gesticulated as she told MaNkomo the strange story.

"Ntando! Which hillocks?"

"Kwanike. I was there when they came running home to tell Gogo," she said.

"If they are not careful and forget that we have a tough Chief, they will find themselves living in the bush with animals like what happened to these!" she pointed her finger at Sithwala's ruins which they were passing.

"What happened to them?" Ntando asked.

"They were forced to leave their homestead and crops. They do not know Chief Mlotshwa! He does not want such nonsense in his chiefdom."

"I remember they had a deaf and dumb daughter-in-law and it was a strange old couple, Sithwala and wife."

"Tired of complaints from the neighbours, the Chief chased the family away. Their daughters had run away from home claiming that some strange, short men raped them at night. The whole ordeal started in their dreams but as time went by, they would wake up wet on their private parts as if they had slept with men. As time went on, they saw a human hand taking food from pots in the hearth and later they were beaten by the nocturnal creatures for salting the meat. The strange invisible creatures became a menace in the community, blocking certain roads and stealing money from people's pockets. The matter was reported to the Chief and villagers were called to hear the case and deliberate on it. As they sat down for the proceedings, a voice warned them that it was listening on them. People did not see it but heard it from a tree. A moment later, the thing without a body hurled stones and missiles at those who spoke against it during the court session. It was serious, Za. The Chief's advisors called in the police who were also beaten for questioning the old couple!"

"How were they chased away then?"

"That deaf and dumb daughter–in–law delivered a baby alone with the old woman. They took advantage of her disabilities, took the baby away, mutilated its body and buried it by the riverbank. The Chief chased them off to live in a community with no people."

"Umh!"

They made bundles out of their firewood and walked quietly home. The girls kept glancing back at the ruins of Sithwala. MaNkomo sensed that they were afraid and tried very hard to cheer them up. She regretted having given them the full account of the eviction of Sithwala from Chief Mlotshwa's chiefdom.

Back home, she found her husband bathing the babies, the beans for supper's relish already cooked in an earthen pot. She quickly cooked the sorghum *isitshwala* and fed the baby before eating her share. Zanele found her mother almost done with her cooking and they sat on the reed mat to eat.

"We ran for dear life this afternoon at Kwanike hillocks near the dam!" Mpiyabo said to her mother.

"*Oh maye,* you saw the leopard Sikhwehle was talking about?" she asked surprised.

"No! Ma, they saw SekaSipho and Sibanda doing rituals wearing…"

"Ntando, my sister you are a true *mamgobozi*. Nothing ever misses your ears! You talk as if you were there," exclaimed Zanele.

Mpiyabo narrated the incident. MaMpunzi listened in shock. She had also come to collect a tablecloth to darn from MaMoyo.

Everyone was horrified at Dube and Sibanda's boldness in practising their witchcraft in broad day light.

The moon and the stars continued to shine later that evening, making it even easier for Ntando and Farai to play games under the stars while the elders chatted incessantly. Their childish voices reached far and wide to compete with laughing hyenas, whining jackals and other nocturnal sounds. MaNkomo passed her endless endearments to Zanele whom she thought she would not be able to see before she left for school. The villagers had started ploughing and planting. The chores of the season lessened socialisation between the villagers.

Chapter Seventeen

Zanele woke up to a gray, desolate dawn, feeling worse than miserable to be leaving her mother, Ntando, Mpiyabo and MaNcube to go back to school and face the unknown. She was afraid too that if her pregnancy was discovered, she would not be allowed to return to school. What would she be without writing her exams? She decided that she would leave a week earlier, on the day of the second trial of Dube's case. She badly wanted to be at university with Nonceba the following year. Her heart pounded in a different way as if warning her that there would be no peace where she was going. Her body too seemed to freeze with her thoughts. She seemed to be smouldering with unexpressed, concealed fear and grief. She felt as though something was ravaging her inner being. Her mother observed this but did not think there was anything serious troubling her daughter. Perhaps it was just exam fear, she told herself and dismissed the thought from her mind. There were examinations in two weeks after the opening of schools and many students, even intelligent ones like her daughter, feared them.

Zanele smiled and laughed nearly to tears when MaNcube gave her an old bead necklace for her to keep as a souvenir. She always thought of how her friends described her closet as a museum because of the trinkets and presents given to her by MaNcube. She could not think of throwing them away, afraid it would be a gesture of gross ingratitude. Her mother had taught her and others never to refuse a present because what was important was the act of giving being demonstrated and not necessarily the present itself. She also taught them never to ask visitors if they are hungry but always to bring food to them and let them refuse it on their own.

The bus came and she stepped aboard with supressed elation. The party which had helped her with her luggage walked back home with Ntando sniffling and sucking her thumb behind Mpiyabo.

At Renkini, Zanele was met by Nonceba and Mandla, Nonceba's boyfriend who was on vacation from the Aviation School. They went to the house with Mandla, much to Zanele's surprise. Nonceba's parents did not approve of clandestine relationships with boys and insisted on openness. They wanted to know what sort of boys she was dating. Dr. Mahlangu, Nonceba's father, encouraged the girls to be open about their relationships. His family prided itself in being adherents of modern ways, yet kept and observed some of the traditional ones as well. Mandla and Nonceba made breakfast for Zanele while she freshened up and changed clothes. She opted for a pedal pusher and a big shirt. After breakfast, they watched a movie, after which they did a round to the shops for her school tuck. After shopping and meeting a few friends, they went to see Nonceba's father. Mandla did not run away or hide but came up to greet the old man.

"How are your studies going, son?" Dr. Mahlangu asked as he shook his hand firmly like a golfer.

"I am fine Doc, thank you. I have started practical flying lessons, but I have only covered fifty thousand miles."

"How many should you cover before they test you?" Doctor Mahlangu asked nodding his head, looking him straight in the eye.

"A minimum of one hundred and fifty thousand miles."

"Just fight on. You'll make it."

"Thank you, Doc. I'll try my very best, sir."

"Alright, my boy."

Turning to Nonceba and Zanele, he said, "My angels, hurry up and let's go. I need to calm down a bit before returning to the hospital. I will be operating on a patient at eight o'clock. I do not want God to charge me with negligence."

"Goodbye Doc, and all the best with your patient." Mandla waved at them, speaking in his British-laced accent which fascinated Zanele.

"Thank you!"

* * *

As the bus whined away to Empandeni Mission with Zanele the following morning, she was mulling over the humiliation she had brought upon herself by associating with the eavesdropping coward called Sipho. The memory of their last encounter wounded her and she felt her guilt like a knife deep inside her body. Even though she sometimes felt her heart mellowing towards him, she knew that she could easily have broken it off. Instead, she had foolishly led him on and was now reaping the harvest of her waywardness. Her regret became more painful when she thought of Nonceba and Mandla and how they looked perfect together. But what was done was done! The only thing left for her to do was to follow where her world was going. The bus arrived at the mission school without her noticing the passage of time. She had been very quiet on the bus. She even feigned sleep so that she would not have to talk to anyone.

On the second day of the trial of Dube's case, as early as eight in the morning, the paths started filling with villagers walking towards Chief Mlotshwa's court. Some people chose not to work on their fields while others had done some ploughing after having woken up as early as three in the morning. Sipho came to the Chief's court with his uncles, Buhe and another, driving his father's ox which would be used to pay the Chief's court for spilling blood in his territory. They secured the beast in the communal kraal used to keep animals brought as fines. Sipho quickly went back home, avoiding the scandalmongers who would have pointed fingers at him and updated those who did not know him and his recent crime.

"Our great Chief, the Service Council and all those who are gathered here, I greet you all," the spokesperson started.

"Greetings to you too, Baba Ntuli," the gathering answered.

"We are continuing with the case between Simphiwe Dube, his clansmen and the Ncubes. Right now, I would like Dube to stand and tell this honourable court what he has decided to do."

"Great one, Baba Mlotshwa, your advisors, Service Council and all of you gathered here, I sincerely apologise for staining your chiefdom with blood. I have brought the ox as appeasement for soiling the Chief's community with human blood. There it is in the kraal," Dube spoke humbly as he pointed at the strong ox that stood in the kraal chewing lazily on some cud.

Clap, clap, clap!

"Now you are a man!" said an unidentified voice.

"Why don't you wait for him to finish, *amawala ngawani?*" sighed Dlodlo.

"...Apologising to the Ncubes, I did last week here, but paying them... umh! I have seriously thought about it. Who has proof that the deaths are caused by the avenging spirit? I say, I will not pay the Ncubes for that!"

Another Dube, not a relative of the Dube standing trial, but just someone with the same surname and totem who came from another clan along the Tshatshane River east of Chief Mlotshwa's court, stood up, observed the protocol and adjusted his leg. This Dube walked with a limp and must have been a victim of polio in his childhood.

"My brother, I sincerely ask you to be a total man and move forward with solving this case. I feel sad when I hear that you won't pay. Then what shall become of your family, my dear son of Mthembo? Do not swallow the green bile of a crocodile on behalf of your family. An avenging spirit's thirst to kill can only be assuaged by appeasing it. It is unlike the white man's hunger when he came to take our land and everything in its stomach and on its surface, the living and non-living, wanting us to abandon our *uMlimu* and worship his God. Avenging spirits want only one thing: appeasement in the form of cattle and an apology. That is all. Compensate the Ncubes and we shall have peace." With affected modesty, Simphiwe Dube's namesake thanked the spokesperson and the Chief before sitting down.

"How does the white man's guns and stealing of land fit in this matter? Are you saying their modern system of trying crimes is unfair? That they judged unfairly at their High Court and the Ncubes are thieves? If yes, I will not second you on that one. First, the Ncubes crossed streams and rivers to chop down a *marula* tree in someone's territory. They got what they were looking for, and now Dube has to pay? How unfair!"

"Sibanda, stop feigning incomprehension. We do not take pleasure in discussing this without coming to a solution. As the old saying goes, 'Always ask for the way from those ahead of you'. Truly speaking, none of us here are fools. The white man's judicial system is fair because it has suited you on your crimes and interests!" said MaDlomo, a headmistress from Nseula Primary School. She was married in that village.

"You do not apologise to the Ncubes standing here, for this is not their ancestral home. You must make an appointment to go and see them, talk with them and hear what they would want as compensation. Then, move from there! I thank you," a man from Mzila communal lands asserted.

"I feel that the last speaker is imposing his opinion on my brother in Christ by suggesting that my brother should pay whether he likes it or not and whether he wants to or not. There is no blame ascribable to anyone here. Death is God's decision. It is disturbing that my son here should be blamed for this death," Judah spoke with an air of superiority. He addressed every member of his church as his son or daughter.

"We-e Mfundisi, your Dube was seen naked performing rituals with Sibanda, his body smeared with ashes while talking to a strange fire. Was that God's fire? Is he the same god who does not want you to consult *sangomas*?" Sikhwehle asked, scoffing at the man who was rumoured to be the next bishopric candidate of his church. "Were you making your own burning bush? Our own Moses, heh?"

The Chief allowed himself a slight smile, but the spokesperson laughed with the rest. Suddenly, there seemed to be less tension and debate began in earnest. It was nip and tuck, with no holds barred.

Dube still refused to pay.

As the sun became brilliantly warmer, a heat wave threatened to melt people's brains. A young man came stepping up like greased lighting. At first, he rushed forward as if to relieve himself of the burden he was carrying. Then he suddenly stopped, seemingly overcome with grief and fear. Kneeling, he whispered his errand to a man who was sitting at the edge of the gathering. The man was startled and asked him to say it again. Afterwards, he motioned the boy to follow him to the spokesperson. The people stopped murmuring and looked at the pair walking towards the spokesperson. The man whispered into Mzingaye Ntuli's ear and beckoned the boy to move closer, but the boy was then sweating, probably out of fear of being so close to the Chief. The halo shaped *induna* ring around his head, a symbol of ancient wisdom, could have frightened the boy. The gathering went quiet, anxious to know what news the boy had brought. The Chief and his council put their heads together and deliberated a little. Finally, Mzingaye Ntuli stepped away from the council, stood still before the crowd and puffed up his cheeks. After sucking in some air, he blew it out remorsefully, speaking with a voice of controlled calm but audibly enough for everyone to hear.

"The boy whom you all see has brought sad news. I am sorry to have to tell it to you at this moment that there has been a terrible accident, a fatal accident at Mahlasela Dam a few minutes ago. The boy you saw driving that ox over there is no more. Sipho, Dube's son, has died. He was kicked by his donkey around his groin and died on the spot. Dube's son, the same Dube with the case we are arbitrating, has just died."

The silence that followed lasted about five seconds but felt like a decade. Then a palpable air of tension and remorse surrounded the Chief's court.

"I will repeat. The messenger is saying Simphiwe Dube's son Sipho is lying dead at Mahlasela Dam as we speak. He was kicked by his own donkey. Those who came early saw him driving the ox into the kraal. Simphiwe Dube, your son is no more!"

All eyes shifted to Simphiwe Dube who felt as powerless as a log floating away in a wildly rushing river. The Chief's eyes glinted fiercely as they locked with Sibanda's, who fidgeted and quickly looked down, feeling the Chief's anger on his nerves. Sipho's grandmother fainted. Some women took turns to fan her while others brought water, pouring it on her. The Chief rose, and the people rose with him and then sat down again, such being the custom.

"My people, I am hurt beyond feeling by this incident. I convey my sincere condolences to the Dube family and all of you at large. It is sad to note that there is someone who can be as mean as Simphiwe Dube. It is sad indeed. There you are now! From here you are going to the dam alone, to take the body and bury it with

Sibanda, your advisor and lawyer! As soon as you throw the last mound of soil on the grave you will go and apologise to the Ncubes, pay ten heads of cattle before you round up your belongings to find somewhere to live, far away from my people. Do not delay and force me to burn down your huts. Both of you!"

The Chief sat down, his body heavy with tragedy and stateliness. The taste in his mouth was like the taste of dust and ash, but his eyes had a ferocity like that of a predator. The women wailed and mourned as the atmosphere became sombre. MaNkomo felt a pang of pity for Sipho and experienced various emotions. Her tears rolled down her cheeks and dampened her blouse as the secret she was harbouring almost overpowered her. She managed to hold herself together. People cursed Sibanda and all those who were supporting him, including *uMfundisi*. Old Sikhukhula knelt as he sang Chief Mlotshwa's praise songs, moving slowly towards the council. People opened the way for him, encouraging him with their nodding.

"Great One, the soil has punished your stubborn child. Please, Baba, at least let your people bury the poor boy's body and let his soul depart in peace. The land has beaten him already, please, Baba. I plead for your child, not that I agree with him!"

"Let him bury the body alone. Surely, the boy I saw this morning! Let him bury him with Sibanda and none of my family will participate. I will make sure of that!"

Sipho's maternal uncle wailed as tears trickled down his cheek.

"I should have let the boy stay with me. It is my fault. We should not have brought him back to his evil father. What is my sister saying in her grave? Forgive me my sister!" Sipho's maternal aunt mourned sorrowfully as other women joined in the wailing. People stood and surged up and down like cattle and goats confined in a pen as if they were afraid of facing Sipho's death.

"Great One, I am very sorry about this, but let us bury the boy with dignity. Let him go peacefully. Dube will go and die and be eaten by vultures alone. This is painful for everyone now. Misfortunes and obstacles such as these always happen in life. Most of us have learnt from this," pleaded Mpangazitha, kneeling.

Hlabangana too came kneeling, pleading with the Chief. The glare that was in the Chief's eyes spoke of an anger aimed at Sibanda and all those who were supporting Dube's decision not to pay the Ncubes. His advisors and the Service Council said nothing but looked at him with pleading eyes. Most people in the gathering stayed where they were, heads bowed and faces downcast. When they heard Dlodlo speaking, they lifted their faces up, appealing to the Chief with their eyes. Much to their relief, Dlodlo's pleading melted the Chief's heart. Chief Mlotshwa did not immediately give an answer, and the elders let him be. He motioned to the old men to rise and take their seats. The people rose with him.

"My people, this is indeed a difficult time. May I ask that some Dube family members kindly go and organise a scotch cart as we all either go to the dam or the Dube homestead for the funeral. I will be there at the dam myself to see on my own this unfortunate incident that has befallen us. Since the men of the law are here with us, they will come with their books, do their work and clear us to remove the body. Such a death is treated as an accident, and you know the body is not allowed inside the homestead. Do we understand each other?" he intoned, authority in his voice.

"Oh, Great One, thank you for your understanding and for forgiving your child," said Dlodlo as he clasped his hands together in a polite gesture. The people clapped their hands together, thanking the Chief for his long-suffering kindness.

Sipho's grandmother had to wait for the scotch cart to carry her to the dam. The funeral procession took almost an hour to get to the scene of the accident. The trip to the dam felt like a decade of walking. Many felt a weakening in their limbs and were unable to carry their bodies. The procession sang a funeral dirge as it made its way slowly but steadily. Some women wept in their singing. MaMoyo's heart beat in an abnormal way and often her stomach contracted as if she was suffering labour pains.

A small group was guarding the body. Nobody had thought of covering Sipho's body. He was foaming from the nose and mouth, his eyes wide open. The area around his groin was swollen and his pair of short trousers were drawn up. An elderly man stood there chasing away the flies that had already sensed a feast with a swat from a tree branch, too bewildered to say anything. MaMoyo removed her wrapper and covered the body which had turned greenish and was blackened by the sun. Looking at the corpse made invisible things crawl on one's flesh. The women sat apart, wrapped in their grief. Dube, Sibanda and close relatives of the Dubes sat close to the body. Dube looked as if he was afraid to cry, but pain had almost disoriented his mind and senses. Those who had insulted him earlier sympathised with him and directed their silent insults at his friend whose mouth and lips were dry and cracking.

The Chief and his entourage arrived before the scotch cart. Sibanda, with a pervading sense of guilt, lifted the wrapper off the body for the Chief and his counsel to see the deceased's face. The Chief peered and then looked away, hurt written all over his forehead. Sibanda's lordly superiority which he always used to reinforce dominion over weaklings had evaporated from him. The police talked to the boys who were with Sipho before he died and wrote something down in their notebooks. They told the Chief and his council that this kind of death required a post-mortem before the body was buried. One of the policemen cycled back to the camp to make a call to Khezi so a defender truck and a metal coffin could be brought. The villagers sat waiting.

Though Simphiwe's mother was forlorn and frail, she felt something like pity for the boys that had been with Sipho. They looked even frailer than she did. Perhaps it was their fear of the police as well as the dead body and the growing number of people arriving at the scene. MaMoyo and other Catholic women sang a funeral song and said a prayer. The villagers waited all night. Some women with homes nearby went home to cook and brought food which was shared by the villagers, far away from the body, behind the dam wall. The police truck only arrived the following day in the afternoon because, as the police said, there had been no diesel for the truck.

Buhe brought a branch of a tree they used in a ritual meant to take the spirit of the dead back home with its body. He uttered something to the soil which the body had laid on, sweeping the air above it in a slow motion with the branches he had made to look like a hands broom. Then he carried the branches carefully in his arms to give them to Sipho's grandmother who was lifted into the cart after the body had been placed in the metal coffin. Buhe walked ahead of the scotch cart.

The mourners followed the donkey-drawn scotch cart. It was as if the donkeys knew that they were carrying a body, separated from its spirit by one of their own, because nobody used a whip on them. The women followed behind, wailing and singing funeral songs. Other women from the Dube clan, MaMlotshwa and MaNcube, joined Sipho's grandmother in the scotch cart with his maternal aunt who just stared into space emotionlessly. She had stopped crying.

At the Dube homestead, they found those who had gone straight ahead making a makeshift shelter of tree branches outside the homestead where the body was going to spend the night before burial the following morning. Nobody had warned them about the post-mortem.

Sipho's father and other close relatives had gone to the hospital where the body would be kept awaiting a pathologist. Unbeknown to villagers, and with the system's legendary inefficiency, they would go on to wait all week for the body. In Chief Mlotshwa's jurisdiction, no ploughing or planting could be done until a dead body was buried. This again irritated and annoyed MaNxumalo. On Wednesday, she tried talking to her son to let people go on with their normal life because they risked starvation. The matter was discussed among the Chief's council which felt that it would be an abomination. So, the villagers continued to wait for the body which was finally brought on Friday night.

Sikhwehle and several other men brought sand in wheelbarrows to prepare a wet bed for the body. This, they did so that it would not decompose quickly from the heat. The customs of the land did not allow the bodies of people who died from accidents and suicide to be placed inside the homesteads. The people believed that if they did, the spirits of the deceased would remain to torment those on earth. Dube, who appeared as if he was a dry leaf to be blown away by the wind, behaved like someone who had lost his mind. He walked about, came and checked the body, knelt beside it, mumbling inaudible things as tears trickled down his face. Some elderly women brought warm water in a dish and asked the rest of the people to move away from the makeshift shade which was closed on three sides. With a little swab they closed the eyes, the mouth and wiped the body before dressing it in the departed soul's best clothes. They awaited a coffin from St Joseph's Mission's carpentry shop. Dube was a member of the village burial society. The society supplied the coffin, food and money to a grieving member. People sat in a sombre mood as the sun cast its rays directly upon their eyes, paying vigil to the breathless body.

"*He madoda, umfana wami* uSipho is gone, life is cruel," Buhe said tearfully, whilst sitting with other men.

"Life is not cruel. If it was not for this hindmost pig, this could have been prevented a long time ago. We would not be here at all!"

"Dingizulu, who are you calling a hindmost pig?" Sibanda charged at him.

"You, who else? You think we are having fun here? Actually, you are the one who is supposed to be chased away, not Dube. Remember you have many other crimes, including mooning at other men's wives!" Sikhwehle taunted him.

Buhe looked at Sibanda with tearful eyes, tears that were an accusation. In response, Sibanda looked sideways, without bothering to towel away his forehead which was oiled in his own sweat and closed his mouth with a handkerchief. Many a person had smouldering anger in them, an anger that found vent in the comments they passed with their hearts, and not lips. Dube's new wife, Sipho's stepmother, sat with the other women without tears or traces of mourning. She just sat there. She was of a difficult temperament and had a secret liking for cruelty. She hardly ever smiled. Nobody had ever heard her laugh out aloud. She never attended other women's activities and if she attended any social and communal events, she never helped with anything, but just sat there like a stranger.

* * *

The women met at the well and took the opportunity to say what they thought about the recent tragedy that had befallen the village.

"Today is my second time to step foot in that homestead."

"Ah MaNleya, you did not come to these other funerals?" asked MaNkomo.

"I could not, I do not know why. My feet just felt heavy each time I decided to attend!" MaNleya answered still in a sombre mood.

"You are not the only one who feels that way. It is that woman who could not even shed a tear at her own daughter's funeral. I do not even want to sit next to her. She has an impenetrable aura, so heavy it is like she is carrying the devil himself in her chest," MaMpunzi said while removing the logs from the well.

"Poor Sipho! Your mother dies leaving you with your infant sister, and before you see life to its fullest, you depart too. This is sad," MaNleya said, shaking her head slowly.

"Sipho has a sister? Where is she?" MaNkomo, who seemed genuinely surprised, asked. It was her habit to pretend not to know anything, especially when it came to prickly matters.

"Her mother died when she was a week old and she was immediately adopted by her maternal aunt who raised her as her own. She might come tomorrow for the funeral and I will show her to you. Sipho used to visit her every fortnight at Sihayi where she lives," explained MaNleya.

"Oh, is that so?" asked MaNkomo with concern.

"If you think that this is sad, it is nothing compared to someone who commits suicide by hanging themself on a tree!" MaNleya said.

"I have never attended the funeral of a person who commited suicide," said MaNkomo truthfully.

"Normally, if a person commits suicide, they are buried right where they died."

"MaNleya!"

"Some years back, before you came to this area, MaSikhosana's granddaughter was rumoured to be having a sexual liaison with

Sibanda. It is said she fell pregnant by him. Her husband worked across the Limpopo in South Africa. When she heard that her husband was coming the following week, she decided to end her life. She cooked the evening meal for her two small children, fed them and put them to bed. She then took a rope and went far away from home towards the Simpathe River. She was discovered by old Sikhukhula in the morning as he was looking for his donkeys for the plough."

"MaNleya!"

"It happened," MaMpunzi affirmed.

"So, when the death message went around, people gathered outside their homestead waiting for the police to confirm her death. Just to confirm, not to pull the body down and take it to a mortuary because it is against our tradition. We all walked to the scene of the suicide silently because in suicide cases, no singing is allowed. When we got there, we gathered around the tree in a half-moon shape and started cursing the evil spirit which had made her commit suicide, leaving her children, friends and relatives, crying. The police did what they had to do as the cursing went on. The men dug the grave right under the hanging body. After the grave was deep and ready, the men helped each other to cut down the rope such that the body fell directly into the grave. There was no singing, but the cursing continued with everyone saying out aloud what they were feeling. As soon as the body fell into the grave people turned to face the way they had come. While some men were filling the grave with soil, others were cutting the branches of the tree and digging up its roots after which they burned it, all the while cursing the evil spirit on the tree. From that accursed place, the people walked home silently to wash their hands with herbs which are believed to chase away the evil spirit which causes suicides."

"MaNleya, that is cruel and mean!" exclaimed MaNkomo.

"Yes, it is. We believe that people must not commit suicide whatever problem they meet in life. We live as a people. If you are chased away from home you can go to an aunt, brother, sister or even a neighbour. Suicide is the attitude of selfish people who think only of themselves and not of other people. How about the children she left behind, who would look after them? Do suicide victims ever think about anything else besides the problem they might be facing at the time? I support that kind of burial for everybody who commits suicide!" MaMpunzi said emphatically as she lifted her water container onto her head. She was thinking of her own situation, especially when she failed to escape from the headman before he could sleep in the same blankets with her.

"She died because of fear of her husband!" MaNkomo said.

"So, the fear of her husband was more important than her two children who were both below ten years at the time?" MaNleya asked with an air of annoyance.

"I was practically saddened by her selfish attitude, especially when I looked at the children asking us and the grandmother if we had seen their mother. Umh, it was sad. The husband could have chased her away, but the children still needed her. She could have gone back to her people to give birth and work for her children than die. Children need a mother, not money!"

"Did her husband come?" MaNkomo asked.

"He did but he found her body already buried. He was so heartbroken and told her parents that he would not have sent her away. He said that it was his fault because he had left her for too long without sending her any money and groceries!" MaMpunzi said.

"What happened to his children?" MaNkomo asked.

"The children are being looked after by their paternal grandmother. After the funeral, there was a time when people could not cross near Sibanda's homestead at night. Some claimed they saw a fire going up and down his yard. Others even claimed the moving flames were the ghost of MaSikhosana's late granddaughter. While all that was being said, Sibanda disappeared from his home," MaNleya explained.

"Where did he run to?" MaNkomo asked still perturbed.

"He was rumoured to be in Binga and some claimed that he had gone to Chipinge to see a *sangoma* who gives him strong medicine. When he came back, the ghost disappeared," MaNleya said.

Chapter Eighteen

Since arriving at school from vacation, Zanele started experiencing tormenting nightmares. One night, she dreamt that she was walking with MaNkomo to fetch firewood and they came across mushrooms on an anthill. Even though the dream was believed to mean the death of someone close, she chose to ignore it. Another dream came in which she saw Sipho being swept away by a flooded river in a basket. She woke up with sweat all over her body and was almost sick. That morning, she did not attend her class discussions but washed her uniform and ironed it to occupy her mind and body.

* * *

Women in sober, conservative clothing followed behind the men who carried Sipho's body to its final resting place. It was early on a Saturday morning. They sang solemnly. Most women wept as they sang. The wailing of the women swept across the land towards the hillocks of Emlanjeni, awakening the land from its brooding tranquillity.

> *"Amagugu alomhlaba*
> *Ayosala emathuneni."*

The headman refused that Dube be part of the pallbearers even if he wanted to, for he seemed so weak and shaken that they did not trust he would reach the graveyard which was a distance away without falling. Preachers from different churches had preached during the night about loving and forgiving one another. The whole vigil was about forgiveness. At the graveside, the Catholics led the burial service because Sipho and his maternal relatives were

Catholics. His body was lowered into his grave next to his grandfather's. They would forever lie side by side. His father put up the headstone while his maternal aunt put another stone at his feet. Close relatives then followed suit, lifting the stones that were collected by old women together with the grass they were sitting on. Women sang him away with his favourite song as recollected by old schoolmates:

"Ngingowakho
Ngingowakho,
Jesu wami ngingowakho njalo
Ngingehlukaniswa lawe noma
Noma sengisifa
Angilaku nikomunye inhliziyo yami
NgekaJesu yena yedwa kuye ezulwini!"

It was the Chief himself who spoke after the laying of the last stone. He was obviously very angry and spoke with grave authority. "My people, my words will be few as I can see you are all tired and grieving. It is regrettable that we have to bury such innocent souls, tomorrow's leaders, because someone does not want to apologise. Last night, I was thinking about the need to revisit this new judicial system which I have discovered to have many loopholes. Next time in parliament I promise you, I will raise this matter for debate. I strongly feel that the traditional judicial system must be given a chance. This so-called modern law should leave us with a choice when it comes to such matters. I encourage you also to live together in peace. Do not be greedy and stubborn. Never mislead each other but live in truth and fairness. This boy was taken from us in broad daylight, with our eyes open. You can never fight an angry spirit seeking revenge. I am sure you have all learnt something from this. Let us protect our future, our children's future, because there can be no tomorrow without them. Avoid fighting at all costs, for there is no mourning and grieving in the home of a coward, as goes the old saying."

"That is so," the mourners agreed in unison.

The people washed hands with water mixed with herbs and ate roasted, unsalted meat that they took from acacia trees where Sikhwehle and his crew had hung it. It was to be eaten and left outside the homestead for those who were coming from far and wide. People departed one by one, leaving Dube as if to let him face his pain and misery alone.

Chapter Nineteen

Things were not well for Zanele. Apart from the superstitious chill that kept harassing her spirit, melancholy pangs seized her. Fear did not leave her alone either. The company of many people suffocated her and the smell of cooking beans and beef invoked nausea in her. In the bathroom, various smells of different bathing soaps tormented her too. Afternoon lessons became cumbersome. She did not go to most lessons during the first week. Her nightmares got worse.

On the Saturday of Sipho's burial, as the girls lined up for their cleaning duties around the school, Zanele remained in her dormitory lying on her friend's bunk bed, covered in heaps of clothes and books. Next day, on a Sunday, she was absent during the morning mass. She had dreamt of Sipho again. In that dream, she was alone at the village well. Sipho appeared from the gate of the well, scaring her. She skirted the boundary of the well but suddenly Sipho rose in the air, carrying his favourite knobkerrie.

"My dear Zanele, daughter of Hadebe," Sipho spoke. "I am sorry I beat you up for unfounded suspicion driven by jealousy. I have left you a son and his name will be Nkanyiso. He will be your source of light. Do not be afraid of what is going to happen today, everything shall be well. I will be with you in spirit. I will be with you. We shall be together."

After saying these words, Sipho floated away and his clothes changed into a crisp white robe.

Zanele woke up in a welter of sweat and horror. She desperately decided to hide her face from her friends till she was feeling better. Her constant urge to visit the toilet also made her uncomfortable. It became obvious to her dorm mates that something was amiss with her but every time they asked, she would say it was either a headache or a stomach ache or both.

At church, the school head instructed everyone to go to the school hall for a roll call. Since the boarding mistress had locked the main entrance and had the keys with her at church, there was no need for her to go to the girls' hostels.

* * *

Meanwhile, Khethiwe too did not last a week at school. Rumours of her ordeal were whispered around on the very first day and by break time, some girls could be seen talking about it behind the ablution block and all around the school grounds. What made things particularly difficult for Khethiwe was the fact that everyone knew her. She was a star when it came to the arts. And she was an all-rounder, brilliant in other subjects too. Even though nobody came directly to her, she knew she was the subject of discussion. The hallucinations and nightmares which had subsided ever since they moved to their maternal grandparent's home resurfaced, and when they became worse, she left school.

MaMoyo, MaNkomo and MaNleya visited her and her mother when they heard that she had dropped out of school. They took her to the mission to see Father Mzila who took the matter to the nearest mission where there was a convent. By the end of the week, the Sisters had taken her in for counselling while she stayed at the Convent with them. They would enrol her for school the following year as a boarder with the hope that she would have recovered. She would work in the kitchen during her holidays for her tuition fees until she finished her academic studies.

* * *

At Zanele's school, the girls filed into the school hall silently after church. Form ones and twos sat in the front row and form threes to six sat randomly. The prefects lined up along the sides of the hall. The matrons for both the senior and junior hostels sat at the back, watching for noisemakers. After prayers and the rituals associated with the roll call, the school head, Sister Monica, walked up to the stage and started calling out names:

"Zanele Hadebe!"

Silence.

"Zanele Hadebe!"

Silence.

The school head stopped calling and looked at the senior girls' matron, Mrs. Nkomazana who panicked and walked to the front, looking for the Upper Six girls. She failed to locate them since they had sat randomly and not in their normal assembly order. She stammered and called out, "Girls from St Anna Hostel, prefects, where is Zanele? I saw her in the morning and she didn't sign a sick form on my book."

The girls looked at one another before gazing down at their feet. The school head instructed the matron, the head girl and Sister Feluna who was in charge of the hostels section of the school to go and look for her. She continued calling out names. After the rollcall, the rest of the girls were dismissed for the day.

At the hostels, Zanele felt thunderous palpitations at the sight of the trio coming towards the senior hostels. Since there was not much to do, she decided she would wait for them and hear what they had to say. She had not even done her ablutions and her hair stood up in wild strands. Her arms and feet were weak. Her stomach protruded for everyone to see in her short and skimpy night dress. Mrs. Nkomazana looked at Sister Feluna who only shrugged. The head girl looked at her, shaking with horror. The humiliation of that moment was to linger on for the rest of her life.

Without wasting time, Zanele quickly changed into her tunic and tied her hair into a ponytail. Moments later, the team which now included her, filed into the school head's office. Even though Hadebe's daughter was wearing her sports tunic, her stomach bulged for the blind to see. The burden of her secret was off her chest.

"*Okulempondo akufihlwa emgodleni*. That which has horns cannot be hidden in a sack," laughed Sinqobile once they got to their hostel.

"We have a saying too that goes, '*inxeba lendoda alihlekwa*, a man's wound is not to be laughed at,' so do not laugh at Zanele who has been the Maths and Economics teacher that you never paid!" said one of the girls.

"Pregnancy has become a wound now?" Sinqobile replied.

"I hope they will let her write her examinations," a girl in a sports tunic answered her.

"I hope so too, Thembeka."

"Let mothers go to maternity leave. Let her go and get married to Sipho. What examinations? Do you want us to lose sleep and fail because of her baby?"

"Sinqobile! Do not be so mean!"

"That is what these rural girls know only – having sex with their boyfriends and falling pregnant. Zanele is so intelligent academically, yet so foolish when it comes to social issues."

"We did not know she was so foolish!" shouted Thembeka.

"Who are you to judge her? It was just a mistake!"

"In some developed societies, schoolgirls are allowed to fall pregnant."

"It's not allowed here and that is right!"

"I would love to be in that society and see if there are as many pregnant girls as you imply!"

"The problem with some of us is that we copy other cultures and then try and overdo things we do not know. What rights are there for children who fall pregnant when they still need care themselves?"

"It's true. You will find that the problems created by those rights affect us negatively and we do not even see it!"

"I call them rights without responsibility!"

"Do not blame Zanele, please. It is her environment. The people you spend time with have so much influence on your character development. People do it in the villages and get married to the herd boys. It is not an unusual scenario!"

"There you go again, Thembeka, with your preaching. She was not supposed to date Sipho in the first place! What could she talk about with this Sipho, the herd boy and bird snarer?" Sinqobile retorted.

"Are you now the matchmaker? And his likes are not supposed to be loved? Sipho was probably Zanele's first boyfriend and maybe they did it once. You should forgive her. Mistakes do happen," a voice came from somewhere under the blankets. That particular girl loved sleeping after removing her uniform.

"There can be no excuse for a girl of Zanele's intellect to fall in love with a village boy like Sipho and worse still, allow him to sleep with her and make her pregnant. It is her choice." Sinqobile shook her head, letting loose the strands of her braids which had escaped the bunch she had tied to hang with wild abandon.

"Now listen, especially you, Sinqobile, you might not be pregnant like Zanele, but your morals cannot be compared with anyone else's in this room. It is just that you are clever enough to sometimes use protection with your numerous boyfriends. How many times have you had abortions? Just look at your sagging and flabby breasts. My grandmother who lives in the village whom you despise so much, has breasts firmer than yours!" Zanele's friend Hanani lashed at her.

"Sinqobile has a herd of boyfriends! She must be the last to comment on Zanele," Thembeka said.

"It is my life, leave me alone!" Sinqobile retorted.

"Why should we leave you alone when you make fun of our friend whom you academically depended on? Shame on you! She kept her baby and you killed maybe ten so far, who knows!" shouted Cynthia, a bookworm who never commented on social matters.

"All along I was listening, and I'm surprised by her remarks, let alone her holier-than-thou indignation! Sinqobile dates old men, actually any man who can take her to places of fun in the outskirts of Bulawayo where they roast meat, drink and dance and then book a night in a lodge with her," another girl said tying her shoelaces.

"*Kotshisanyama!*"

"She nearly died doing a backyard abortion in Makokoba!"

"You lie, Batsirai!"

"It is true and you know it! Do you want me to tell them Sisi Sinqobile? And Broe Dumi, your sugar daddy with an old Mercedes Benz, who has lost four wives to HIV and AIDS already!"

"Remove the log in your eye before you remove the speck in…"

"…In another's eye!" the girls chorused the verse and roared in laughter.

* * *

Zanele had earlier on felt a corrosive rush of hatred at the thought of Sipho. She felt her adrenalin squirting into her bloodstream and her heart seemed to bounce against her ribs in such a wild lunge that the baby moved in her womb as she followed the party led by Sister Feluna to the office. She knew the sun had now set upon her. She did not waste time and admitted to the school head that she was pregnant. The anxiety and great serpentine coils of fear which she had lived with disappeared. When she looked at the other girls and thought of Sinqobile who had confided in her about her escapades with older men, she felt like a terrible and daring regular whore. Yet it was just a careless and impulsive association with Sipho which had taken her virginity away, leaving her scandalised.

She was dismissed on the spot and an arrangement was made that she would be sent home to her mother the following day. Zanele, Sister Feluna, Mrs Nkomazana, the senior matron, and Mrs Hlongwane, the senior teacher, were going to be driven by Fuyana the driver early the following morning. Her dormmates did not stress her at all, but sympathised. They prayed there would be a way she could be given a chance to write examinations in the next fortnight. Some cried for her as they wrote little encouraging farewell notes to her. They agreed they would continue to pray collectively three times a day for her. Surprisingly, it was Sinqobile who came up with that idea. The other thing they agreed on before supper time was nobody was going to entertain questions from the girls from the other hostels. They would not entertain visitors till she had departed the following morning. Scandalmongers were not going to get a chance. Hanani brought her supper from the dining hall and they helped her pack her things. Schools would be closed soon anyway. Much to her delight, she had an appetite for lunch that day. For the first time, she slept through the night peacefully and was not haunted by dreams of Sipho.

* * *

Zanele, Sister Feluna, Mrs Hlongwane and Mrs Nkomazana arrived at the Hadebe homestead just after lunch. MaMoyo and MaMpunzi were startled to see them coming out of a car whose arrival they had not heard. At once, MaMoyo felt something in her stomach but was happy to see Zanele come out of the car in a tunic, moving slowly. She wondered why her feet were swollen. She met the visitors and welcomed them into the homestead. MaMpunzi excused herself but MaMoyo motioned to her to stay. Understanding the situation, MaMpunzi went into the kitchen and brought a stool and reed mats for the women. Zanele's stomach protruded so visibly as if it was a statement to say, "Do not ask me why I am here." She did not bother concealing it.

After the greetings, niceties, and introductions said by Zanele, Mrs Hlongwane spoke, "Mama MaMoyo, MaMpunzi and my mother MaNcube, we are here as messengers from the mission sent to bring our girl home."

"What is the problem my mother?" MaMoyo asked just for politeness and clarity.

"She made a mistake. We plead with you to accept her and not chase her away. She is eight months pregnant," Mrs Hlongwane said.

MaMoyo looked down and saw a vision of Sipho dressed in white, crying, kneeling down as if pleading with her. She saw again in a flash, his body lying in the sun at Mahlasela dam. She looked first at MaNcube and then MaMpunzi, lifted her eyes to face the visitors and spoke, "We hear you, Mama Hlongwane, Sister Feluna and…" she paused. Mrs Hlongwane corrected her before she proceeded. "We have heard the message and thank you for bringing her home because you never know what could have happened if she had come on her own."

"Thank you too for your understanding," they all said in turn.

"Zanele, it is Sipho, is it not?" MaNcube asked calmly.

Her look killed Zanele's words. She had already suffered humiliation, guilt and shame beyond measure. Zanele did not answer her but fixed her gaze on the ground. After a moment, she mumbled a few inaudible sounds without looking up and scratched the dry earth with a little stick. At last, the intimidating uncertainties of their arrival were over. She had managed to contain and conceal her fear all the way, speaking only when she had to give Fuyana directions.

"Mistakes do happen, my mother. If this Sipho is a responsible boy, he can look after the baby while Zanele pursues her studies. She is an intelligent girl. Our elders say *lingalahli imbeleko ngokufelwai*. Do not throw away a baby sling because the first child has died," Fuyana said solemnly.

MaMpunzi looked at MaMoyo and wiped a tear. Her eyes were curtly stinging too. MaMpunzi remembered the whole Saturday scene, the boy arriving with the message, the Chief's anger, the dam where the body lay uncovered, the night of the vigil and finally the Chief laying the last stone on Sipho's grave as if to say that was the last time such a funeral was to be held. She sniffled and looked at MaMoyo.

"MaHadebe, take your things and go and wait for us in my hut. We will call you later," MaNcube said.

Zanele did as she was told, stepping lightly on her swollen feet like a barefoot ploughman walking on the edges of his uncultivated, thorny land. When Zanele was out of earshot, MaNcube spoke in a low voice for everyone there to hear what had happened to Sipho. As MaMpunzi told the visitors about the whole avenging spirit saga, Mrs Hlongwane stared up at the clear sky like someone dreaming or making serious decisions in her heart.

MaMpunzi offered the visitors *amahewu* prepared by MaNcube the previous day and they each politely took a gulp.

Their throats were too dry with the sad news. Mrs Hlongwane called MaMoyo aside for a private conversation as the rest discussed other matters, then the visitors left, feeling more than miserable.

The three women decided and agreed that they should find a way of informing Zanele before Ntando arrived from school. Slowly, they filed into MaNcube's room where they found Zanele lying on a sheepskin mat. She was startled when they entered. She rose and sat up, leaning on the bed, relieved when she saw that her mother was not alone and that she was with MaNcube and MaMpunzi. MaMoyo did not think she had the strength to face her daughter alone, for Zanele had indeed shamed her in the community.

"MaHadebe, I did not know that you had a mother at school. What a well-cultured and good woman your lady teacher is!" MaMpunzi started, trying to make the atmosphere a bit lighter.

"Fruits of education! I really admire these learned people. If I had the chance, I would register too for a night school and get more education," MaNcube said light-heartedly.

Zanele was confused. She had expected her mother to descend on her with a log or even chase her away before her father had heard of it. The three women then checked on each other's eyes.

"Zanele, we have heard about your matter, and we thank you for not attempting an abortion. It is well. We shall see what to do!" MaMoyo's words confused Zanele even more. It was as if her falling pregnant was being glorified. Sipho's vision came again, this time blinding her eyes. It looked so real. Zanele felt awkward.

"We are still confused by what happened on Saturday..." MaNcube skirted around the matter but continued, knowing fully well that divulging the sensitive news was inevitable.

"Your father-in-law's matter with the Ncubes has left this community in tears and stiff with shock."

A quick shiver of anxiety cut through Zanele. She experienced a fey sensation about it all. Why were they beating about the bush?

"When do you start writing your examinations?" MaMpunzi asked, cajolingly.

"The week... actually next week."

"Tomorrow we will start for Bulawayo early in the morning. Your teacher, Mrs Hlongwane, promised to negotiate with the school head to let you write. She said she will let you stay at her house till you finish writing," MaMoyo said seriously.

A smile flashed on Zanele's face, and a joyful tear trickled down her face.

"Please, I suggest you go to Zanele's aunt first. She is the best person to talk to your father, and if you go alone, he will crush you to a stain!" MaMpunzi said encouragingly.

"True, MaMpunzi, men are always difficult in such matters. If a child makes a mistake, the mother is to blame or they take after their maternal relatives. Worse still, they can even deny that they ever fathered the child. If they excel, then they are theirs!"

Zanele thawed and her body relaxed.

Then her grandmother spoke. "Sipho's matter is a tough one. You just have to be strong especially in the condition you are in."

"First, I am very sorry I disappointed you. I promise to work hard and correct my mistakes. I do not care if Sipho was arrested or what, as long as I can write my examinations. I will have a bright future with this baby," Zanele felt the tension vanishing from her. She felt free.

Her words were followed by an uncomfortable and confusing silence.

"I know you will pass and get a good job so you can buy me the sweets that I like so much," MaNcube said with difficulty.

"They are called chocolates, Gogo. Sure, I will buy you some." She smiled.

MaMoyo and MaMpunzi looked at each other, fidgeting, still strained and remorseful.

"The thing is Za… MaHadebe… Sipho. The thing is Sipho… Sipho…"

"Gogo, what is it that you cannot say? You are frightening me by delaying what you need to tell me."

"Sipho is no more, Zanele. He passed away on the Saturday you left, and we buried him the day before yesterday," MaMpunzi courageously let the words out.

"It is true, Zanele, but please, be strong. He was kicked by his donkey in the groin and died on the spot on Saturday," MaNcube said, deep in a sorrow she could no longer hide.

How aptly her dream had described the present reality, Zanele thought. She stretched her legs and leaned on her grandmother, her eyes closed. Her stomach protruded so her baby moved visibly. Palpitating with different emotions over Sipho's death, sadness as well her own humiliation and shame, the tears flowed down her cheeks, tears she did not understand. Sipho had beaten her, and now he was dead before they had talked. Fate seemed to be bearing down upon her from all sides. The dreams, the premonitions at school that Saturday, her mad aunt saying her baby was not going to see its father… Zanele could manage being expelled from school. She could try again but could not support the agony of Sipho's death and its vindictive presence. She felt as if someone had performed surgery on her soul. In the anguish of her heart, Zanele cried until she fell asleep on her grandmother's lap.

The three women stayed, all quiet. MaNcube's eyes flicked each time her granddaughter moved on her lap. When she woke up, Zanele did not feel restful at all. MaMpunzi had rolled the drum and gone after Zanele had woken up without saying much except that it was going to be well with her. Both MaMoyo and MaNcube felt cheated by Zanele but they did not know what to do about it.

They had lived with her for the past three weeks without noticing anything. How strange! They wondered how she had managed to conceal a pregnancy for that long and concluded that she wanted to write her examinations. She was not someone who gave up that easily. What a show of strength of character!

* * *

As villagers broke the clods of earth in their fields with cow bean and pumpkin leaves flapping free and spreading wide, MaMoyo and Zanele walked silently to the bus stop as if they were cross with each other. It was still dark, before sunrise. They stepped on the path they had used over and over again, not realising that the canvas shoes on their feet were being plastered with mud. It was as if they were wearing shoes of mud on their feet if one observed them from a distance. Zanele was thinking of Sipho, especially the fact that she had accepted him without qualification. Still, she thought, in the wilderness of her humiliation, her Form Four results gave her the energy. As they were descending on the Simphathe River, Siphamandla greeted them with bantering humour, whistling a song as he drove a donkey-span in the opposite direction, happy it had rained peacefully the previous night. Some of their richly green crops had flowers blossoming profusely. MaMoyo's early finger millet and sorghum crops greeted the groundnuts and cow beans in the morning sun, outshining each other with their liveliness, happy with the sufficient moisture and the sunlight that they enjoyed.

They did not have to wait long at the bus stop. The bus arrived just after they had finished removing mud from their canvas shoes. They went aboard and found seats even as the conductor was banging the side of the bus with his fist and whistling to the driver to resume the journey. By eight o'clock, they had alighted at Renkini bus terminus and boarded a local bus to Matshaemhlophe where Nonceba's parents lived.

Chapter Twenty

"*Sethule, sethule,*" Mrs Mahlangu opened her arms wide as she welcomed and greeted them with much cheer. She had been on duty at Mpilo General Hospital the previous night where she worked. She paused and smiled at MaMoyo.

"That is why my right eye was twitching. It was a sign that I was going to see a person I last saw a long time ago. My hand was itchy too!"

MaMoyo forced a smiled and handed her the bags and the live chicken she had brought for her brother-in-law.

"My sister-in-law, is it the school fees which make you look so gloomy? Please do not remove your shoes, the kitchen floor is cold. We will clean it," Mrs Mahlangu said cheerfully.

"No, aunty, let us remove them. It was drizzling when we left and our shoes are covered with mud. We do not want to leave mud tracks on your beautiful carpet," MaMoyo said light-heartedly.

They exchanged pleasantries over breakfast.

"*Naka* Nonceba, you must be surprised to see me at your doorstep this time of the year when others are planting, ploughing and weeding. I do not bring good news. Your niece here, Zanele, would get your brother to axe me."

Zanele's aunt listened without interruption. Zanele herself sat still and stiff. She wore a flared dress and the huge load was not showing.

"What has the Doctor's wife done? What have you done, Za?" Mrs Mahlangu asked, but Zanele lowered her gaze.

"I received unexpected visitors from her school yesterday afternoon. They brought her home. She has been expelled from school. She is pregnant and we buried the responsible boy, Sipho last Sunday. He is Simphiwe Dube's son. He was the sixth Dube we have buried in the last two years since that incident occurred."

"Yo yo yo! What a misfortune to start with, Za! I am so sorry!" Mrs Mahlangu exclaimed.

There was a moment of silence as Nonceba's mother went into serious thought mingled with pain. She found it difficult to understand the matter and she could not even look at Zanele. After a while, she lightened up and said, "I know someone at her school, Lethiwe Mkhwananzi, who is Mandla's aunt. You know Mandla, Nonceba's friend? I went to school with Lethiwe. I am sure we can talk to the school head and allow her to write her examinations. She is there, isn't it Zanele? She teaches Maths and Science, right?"

"Yes, she is there. Her name is Mrs Hlongwane," Zanele said with some energy.

"Yesterday, she asked me to come to school and she will help speak with the authorities herself!" MaMoyo said with relief too.

Mrs Mahlangu showed some signs of relief. There was some silence as each one of them sat there grappling with their silent thoughts. While that was happening, Zanele fell asleep on the couch. Her aunt smiled and woke her up. She sent her to sleep in Nonceba's bedroom. The two women talked till late afternoon. She then picked the phone and dialled Hadebe's company for him to pass through their house after work. Hadebe lived in Gwabalanda. After waking up, Zanele went to the study where she took all the past examination papers filed there and decided to ask her aunt if she could borrow them. She hoped and prayed.

Doctor Mahlangu was the first to arrive from work and was given the full details of Zanele's ordeal. Even though he was disappointed, he understood and promised to talk to Hadebe on their behalf.

* * *

"Did Zanele come to pay condolences to the Dubes?" MaNkomo asked MaNleya as they scooped water into washing basins at the stream on a Tuesday afternoon.

"I do not think so. She cannot be allowed to do that. The school does not allow them to have boyfriends in the first place!"

"Then why did she come home when schools have just opened and they are sitting for their examinations soon?" MaNkomo wondered aloud without directing her question to anyone in particular.

"Did you see her?" MaNleya asked, directly looking at MaNkomo.

"No, but Siphamandla did. He met her and MaMoyo rushing for the bus near Simphathe River. Maybe it is the school fees, maybe they haven't paid yet."

"I doubt that. The Chief's advisor has always paid Zanele's school fees on time. I wonder what could have happened," MaNleya said, concerned.

MaNkomo knew and was happy that at least no one had suspected Zanele of anything. They talked about other village matters while doing their laundry at the stream which separated their homes. River water washed clothes better than the water from the shallow wells that the people of Emlanjeni dug in vlei areas. Borehole water was worse, they claimed. It was hard on their clothes and therefore required more washing soap and stronger detergents.

* * *

MaMpunzi was seen at her favourite spot on the banks of the Simpathe with Motini Nleya by Siphamandla who had often denied the possibility of that affair when MaNkomo whispered to him about it. He was most surprised since he only knew about

Sibanda. He then secretly thought he would try his luck too, but then his wife's remarks of threatening to chop his thing off to feed to the dogs scared him and he dropped the idea. He told himself that he did not want a woman who was everybody's lover.

Chapter Twenty-One

Men arrived at Headman Nkiwane's field wearing overalls and work suits, ready to cut *mopane* branches and weave them around the bigger logs to make a security fence. Many of them had farmer's hats on their heads to shield them from the scorching sun. Sikhwehle wore a Dunlop overcoat that Hadebe had given him some time back and a threadbare cap which still had its capping intact. Headman Nkiwane's field was near his homestead. They were going to start with the eastern boundary. If they did not do it now, the goats would have a feast on the young crops which had sprouted luxuriantly, especially the finger millet which caressed women's legs when they went weeding. The women came to assist too, pulling the chopped branches to hand them over to the men who received them and got on with the weaving.

Headman Nkiwane's home boasted of six round huts and three granaries. There was MaMpunzi's kitchen hut on the far left, the brewery hut and Nkiwane's mother's hut in the second row from the granaries. In front of MaMpunzi's kitchen was the bedroom, the girls' bedroom and the boys' at the end of the row. Just inside the gate was *ikhutha*, an enclave dug and fitted with dry logs that formed an arch. Men and boys sat and took their meals there in the mornings and evenings while discussing men's matters. The fencing of the homestead was done with logs placed closely together. Near the main gate, to the right, was a huge *safice* tree with a generous canopy of branches which made a big cool shade. That was where village courts and meetings were held. To the right of the homestead were the cattle and goat kraals while to the far left stood MaMpunzi's hog kraal. The sow in there had just produced thirteen piglets which were all ready for sale either by batter trade or cash, which was how women traded amongst themselves to raise money or anything they needed.

Far outside the Nkiwane homestead was a dense forest on muddy dark clay soils with a little stream cutting across it, flowing from a natural pond somewhere to the east. The dense forest of mostly *mopane, mswantsha, umtewa, amarula* trees and other shrubs stretched further and further away as it curved and encircled an old, abandoned field which would have been laid bare were it not for the acacia trees dotted around it here and there. A path used by children when going to school ran between their field and the homestead only to disappear into the thick, dense forest. Scandalmongers claimed that the forest was the lovers' nest for MaMpunzi and her multiple men.

MaMpunzi, MaNkomo and MaNleya left the other women who were pulling branches. They went home to prepare lunch for the men and women at work. Dingizulu joined them since he was of no use in the field. He had been drinking opaque beer since morning, waiting as they strained the beer while telling them the latest village news. MaMpunzi slaughtered a rooster for relish and placed huge pots of *isitshwala* prepared from finger millet flour on the fire stands. As the pots and their contents were heating up, she took her wicker trays and began winnowing some pounded sorghum. As soon as they had finished cooking, Nkiwane and Sikhwehle walked in and asked them to wait for them. They were going to slaughter a young he-goat for relish. People had come in their numbers to help. The women then reduced the heat on their pots and waited for the fresh goat meat.

"MaNleya, is MaMoyo back from Bulawayo yet?" MaMpunzi asked as they cleaned the insides of the goat.

"I am not quite sure. I spent the past week guarding the field against stray goats. If she is back, it would mean she came back last night with the late-night bus."

"Talk of guarding the fields against stray animals, our communal field is a problem also. Our field needs some mending, especially on Sibanda's side. He is not bothered as he has not even started ploughing this season!" complained MaNkomo.

"Who will help him? Besides, his friend Dube is still in mourning," MaNleya observed.

Back in the field, Hlabangana, Sibanda, Ndlovu, Siphamandla, Dlodlo and Motini Nleya wove the fence as other men were cutting branches off the trees. The women sang an old village ditty as they pulled branches, their voices competing with the birds' soft voices twittering from the nearby trees. On this day, nobody mentioned the misfortune of the Dubes although the incident was still fresh in their hearts and minds. Nobody wanted to stir ashes when embers were still hot.

* * *

Khethiwe had slowly become used to convent life. Besides praying and Bible study, she helped with the cooking, sewing, cleaning and other home economics duties. Not only did that heal her emotional scars, but she learnt a lot in the process. The school head also arranged with the hospital to send counsellors twice a week for her. Her trauma eased with time. MaNtini visited her one day and was pleased with her progress, more so when she saw that Khethiwe had even put on weight. She thanked the authorities with tears streaming down her cheeks.

"But how is everybody at home, Mama?"

"People are ploughing, planting and weeding. It is still raining. However, everyone is still scared about the Dube matter and its developments!" MaNtini said solemnly.

"What happened?"

"Kunzima *mtanami*. Sipho died."

Khethiwe held her mouth as her mother narrated the whole sad story to her. She did not ask her mother if Zanele knew yet. She decided she was going to write to Nonceba and ask her instead.

"How is Father? Where is he now?"

"He is at home alone. Zinzile and I are still at your grandmother's. She and everybody conveyed their greetings. Zinny says you should write her, here is her letter. Sorry, I was almost going to return with it."

"Thank you, I shall write to her. Does he know that I am here? Father, I mean?"

"MaNkomo says he tells people you are at Macheke, to some he says you are at Empandeni, and to others he says you are in Rome, in Italy training to be a Catholic nun. He does not really know."

Khethiwe laughed till it hurt. Her mother was impressed and relieved that whatever the nuns were doing to her was truly working. Khethiwe could now talk about her father so freely!

"Who would want to live with an old man with as bad a reputation as his?" Khethiwe later asked after a bout of laughter.

"You are laughing, but many would choose to live with him. He is a man and always has the upper hand in these matters. He is rich now with Dube's cattle and goats, and his medicine and charms could work for him!"

"It does not work. He is just a conman. What a father I have!"

Khethiwe's words hurt her mother. She felt guilty for having allowed herself to marry him and bear children with him.

"Let me go, my child. We should thank *malume*. He and his wife loaned Zinny their bicycle. She cycles to school and appears to be happy with her new friends. Hold strong because you never know what the future holds for you!"

"Bye, Mama!"

Khethiwe waved but avoided looking at her mother. Both of them were trying to hold back tears. It was sad for them to get used to the idea that they would never have a normal life as a family.

Back at the convent, Khethiwe sat in her room, thinking. She thought about her own predicament. What was she going to become in life? Nursing. Yes! She had already concluded on that. Sometimes she imagined herself wearing a veil but decided against it because convent life required a calling. She was not going to train to be a nun because she wanted freedom in her life. She did not, however, want any involvement with men, not now, and never! She imagined herself working with victims of rape and abuse and decided that she would open a centre for them after she had graduated as a nurse. She would learn all the skills required there. With these thoughts on her mind, she smiled and fell asleep across her single bed. She dreamt of herself walking with brisk energy in a centre for disabled and abused women and girls. Strangely though, in this dream she had a veil on and was a nun running the centre from a big office and a small clinic within. She was awakened by a woman who helped in the kitchen for them to prepare dinner for the priest and his guests.

Chapter Twenty-Two

The people finished building the fence around Headman Nkiwane's field in the afternoon. There was quite a din as they spoke about a variety of things. The men sat in two groups. The elders who were of Hlabangana and Dlodlo's age chose to sit in the shade of a *muwawa* tree while the younger ones sat under a *mbondo* tree inside the yard. The women sat in groups in places where the huts cast shadows that then became useful shades for the occasion. They waited for lunch to be served as they talked about the crops, asking each other general questions and exchanging pumpkin seeds, watermelon seeds and other things.

MaNkomo, MaNleya and the girls who had come to help with the cooking started serving the old men in the shade of the *muwawa* tree. MaMpunzi and MaMoyo served the younger men until they each had a share. The offals, as usual, were served in a separate dish. Motini Nleya sat with others but did not eat what he was served. MaNleya remembered that he did not eat finger millet *isitshwala* as he claimed it tightened his stomach and blocked his digestion. MaMpunzi and MaNkomo then quickly prepared maize meal *isitshwala* for him. Done with eating themselves and after collecting the empty dishes for the younger girls and women to wash, the women called Motini to come and eat in the kitchen where they were sitting.

"Are you now a woman that you eat in the beer hut?" Sikhwehle teased Motini after lifting the beer calabash MaNkomo had filled for the men outside the yard.

A few moments later, Sibanda came into the hut to light his cigarette on the hearth and greet the women he had not seen in the field or outside. His gaze landed on Motini's secluded lunch. He grunted a greeting, his heart gone hard from just looking at Motini.

"The headman himself is eating outside, yet you sit in here like King Lobengula, enjoying the soft meal, he-e!"

Sibanda's words unsettled Motini.

"He does not eat finger millet *isitshwala* and the cooked goat meat was finished," MaMoyo, who had just arrived, answered Sibanda.

"Mama MaMoyo, why bother answering him? If you did not eat your fill, why don't you join me? Is it not that you are now a bache –"

"Hold your stinking mouth!" Sibanda barked ferociously at Motini.

"Who has a stinking mouth?" Motini asked, charged with anger.

"*Wena*, who else am I talking to? You seem to have forgotten who I am!" charged Sibanda.

"Who does not know you and what you are capable of? Raping your own child, stealing, mislea –"

"Shut up, you two! What do you think you are doing? Huh? What do you really think you are doing? You think we do not know what you are fighting for? *Nxa!* Shame on you both!" lashed Sikhwehle, sounding incensed.

MaMpunzi and MaNkomo looked at their skirts. MaNleya and MaMoyo remained puzzled. MaMoyo sat up and helped Sikhwehle by filling the calabash for the older women who had just arrived outside to spend the afternoon with others. After filling the calabash for Sikhwehle, MaMoyo scooped some beer from the large beer pots and drank before returning to the sheepskin mat she had brought along with her. Motini thanked the women and left the food he had almost finished. There was some silence after the three men left the hut. Such occurrences were a usual spectacle, especially when Sibanda was around.

"Thank you very much, daughter of Mpunzi for being at my house that day," MaMoyo spoke. "Truly, I do not know how I would have handled my unexpected visitors on Monday!"

Everyone listened since they did not know how to ask such a sensitive and stressful matter in the first place.

"Thank you, Mama, but I did not do anything. I had just come to ask for a drum to boil water for this *ilima*."

"Being there was good enough for me."

"How did it go?" MaMpunzi asked.

"We would not have made it without Nonceba's mother. Hadebe was so angry. He nearly cracked my skull with a knobkerrie had it not been for Nonceba's father!"

"Ah Mama MaMoyo, what happened? Why?" MaNleya asked, puzzled and concerned.

"MaNleya, start preparing for a new baby, your daughter is eight months pregnant. Hadebe thought I knew, and that all along I was pretending not to so that he could continue spending money on a useless girl who wants to bring death to his family!"

"Poor Za… Where is she now?" MaNkomo asked, faking ignorance.

"Back at school," MaMoyo said calmly.

"That is better. Did you try and negotiate that she writes her examinations?" MaNkomo asked again.

"Yes, I did. Many thanks to that woman, her teacher and her aunt, who drove us back to school. The other thing that made Sister Monica, the school head, sympathetic is the fact that Sipho, the boy responsible, is no more."

On hearing that Zanele had been allowed to write the examinations, MaNkomo could not hide her joy and relief. She had prayed silently for Zanele's matter to be solved amicably.

"It is him? Oh shame, oh pity!" MaNleya held her stomach.

"Had I not hidden and locked myself in Nonceba's room, he would have killed me. Zanele fainted in fear. Then the Doctor had to come in as well. Calm as he is, his quick, hawk-like speed of mind saved us as he spoke encouraging and comforting words. He said, '*Babazala* calm down, we have to plan ahead with a positive and clear mind. Let's allow our minds to go further than this situation. Everyone makes mistakes. Zanele deserves a second chance in life. We should thank God that she did not think of harmful backyard abortions which could lead to death. We must think of the way forward. Give her a chance; she is intelligent enough to pass her examinations even in her condition. The responsible boy is dead.'"

"*Umh hayi bo amadoda*!" MaNleya said, lifting her hands up.

"Zanele's aunt played a major role in the arbitration, if I may call it that. She urged her husband on as he took it upon himself to convince Hadebe to see things from another angle. In the end, Hadebe thawed and allowed us to proceed."

"We thank God!" MaNkomo said smiling, happy for her friend.

"You did well by taking the bull by its horns. Zanele will make it. She is a brave girl," MaMpunzi spoke.

"I was surprised at the size of the stomach when she came. She is so strong. What about those trips to the well, firewood, chores at home... and I never saw anything! It registered in my mind when I remembered that she had refused to eat meat claiming that at school this and that!" MaMoyo said.

"I was surprised at the size of the stomach too. How did she conceal it?" MaMpunzi wondered.

"MaNkomo, you must have known something. She spent hours each day with you!" MaMoyo said, looking at MaNkomo directly with questioning eyes.

"Nothing, Mama, nothing," MaNkomo said looking down.

Even though MaNkomo knew it all, she never told anyone. She was a Manyika and the Manyika are renowned for keeping secrets. That was hers and Zanele's secret. She was disappointed when Zanele involved herself with Sipho and had often accused her of the most heinous form of treachery, falling in love with a truant and a failure like him. Nobody could say MaNkomo was garrulous and prying but still she did not seem to miss anything. She observed and listened. MaNcube, who had an eagle eye and an earthly instinct, had noticed the change in Zanele within two weeks of conception. Her eyes had an uncanny accuracy on such matters. She had kept the matter to herself to avoid worrying MaMoyo who was a dragon which crushed the bones of her children if they misbehaved, breathing fire in the process.

* * *

Sibanda and Motini continued with their little fights as they drank millet beer while sitting with the other men in the shade of the *mbondo* tree. Dube was not among them as custom did not allow him to be. He was still in mourning.

"Just because MaMpunzi served you lunch exclusively, you now see yourself as a bull!" Sibanda started.

"As a bull? What have I done? If there is something bothering you, why don't you say it?"

"You forget that I see!" Sibanda said, looking at him with ferocious eyes.

"Stop giving yourself airs and making complaints without any foundation," Motini said calmly, with an air of someone who had conquered.

Angered by the response, Sibanda charged at Motini who remained seated. Taken by surprise, Motini subconsciously clenched his hands into fists and blocked Sibanda's blow. Sibanda tripped in the process and kicked the beer calabash with so much force that it broke to pieces, spilling the contents.

"*Nxa!* What do you think you are doing, you scrounging scoundrel?" Dingizulu complained, walking the strut of deformed people from behind the cattle kraal where he and some men were taking turns visiting for a few minutes each. Sibanda turned to charge at Dingizulu. He struck him with a blow that made him stumble off balance and fall on his back. Sibanda pinned him down and punched him on his head and ears. Then he turned and punched Motini's head, sending him crawling in the dirt. With maniacal zeal, he turned to beat Dingizulu again but Sabelo jumped to block the deadly fist.

With closed eyes, Dingizulu screamed and waved his hands wildly. Sikhwehle came by and in a flash, gave Sibanda a blow which sent him down in a heavy thud. Sibanda tried to scramble to his feet but was met by another of Sikhwehle's ferocious fists which sent him spiralling on top of the grey heads' beer calabash. Ndlovu came running from behind the kraals and caught Sibanda, assisted by Sikhwehle and other men who were drinking together with them. Headman Nkiwane emerged from behind the granaries where he had gone to get a chisel. His nostrils quivered with anger. Without wasting time, he instructed that Sibanda be tied to a *gagu* tree where he would spend the rest of the afternoon.

People went back to doing what they had been doing before the scuffle. MaMoyo and friends sat down to shell the groundnuts that they would sow in their fields while the old women wove reed mats and beer strainers, chatting. MaMpunzi secretly felt stupefied as if the whole world's shame was upon her. Motini had risen earlier as if he was going to relieve himself behind the cattle kraals and disappeared for good.

"Whoever touched me is going to face danger. You don't play games with me! I, son of Mahlathini," Sibanda barked from his confinement. He cursed, panting, as efforts to untie himself failed. He shouted from the tree, his frantic voice competing with MaMpunzi's sow and piglets, until Ndlovu threatened to bring him some 'sweetener'. Sibanda then apologised profusely, imagining millions of ants feasting on him once the sweetener was applied on him. He remained as still as the flame of a candle in a closed room.

* * *

"This matter between your brother and Sibanda can bring another disaster to this community, I tell you!"

"MaNkomo what are you talking about?"

"Open your eyes and ears woman! Truly, this ancient custom of marrying young girls to older men without their consent should be stopped," MaNkomo answered her carelessly.

"You mean my brother is cheating on his wife?" MaNleya asked.

"I did not say that. By the way, has his wife given birth yet?"

"Yes, a baby boy, two weeks ago on the Saturday of the rain dance."

"*Asengamhlophe amahle.* Congratulations!" said MaNkomo.

"*Aseyiwo.* Thank you."

"MaMoyo is a brave woman, volunteering such information about Zanele's disgrace. I admire you people!" MaNkomo said, suddenly changing the subject.

"MaNkomo, how do you hide a human being? It is off everybody's chest and shoulders now. They did a good thing by allowing her to write her examinations!" MaNleya said.

"Please, let's go back to school! I heard that evening lessons for adults will be starting soon at Nyashongwe Primary School?"

"Surely, let's."

MaNleya thought of Sipho's death with pain. No ritual was to be performed in memory of his life, yet the way he died did not point to a fault of his own. If he had committed suicide, it could have been understood. Still, people were to pretend that he never existed.

Chapter Twenty-Three

As MaNleya walked on after parting with MaNkomo, a flood of thoughts came to her mind. In particular, she thought about her husband's brother who had died of "the disease." Before he died, he had started losing weight, his hair thinning, his eyes getting whiter and brighter, and his lips crimson as if blood had welled from them. He had refused to take his medication, believing a neighbour and a couple of relatives had bewitched him. His wife got tested and was found infected with HIV. She accepted the situation and religiously took her medication. She was still alive, fit and working, even managing to send their children to school.

MaNleya remembered how frail her brother's wife had been on the day of the funeral when she helped her to her husband's grave. It was quite an effort for her to push the soil into his grave using the heel of her left foot. Part of her face was covered and revealed only her downcast eyes which avoided facing the grave. She did it before anyone had thrown in a handful of soil into the grave as custom demanded. Once she had done her part, MaNleya and *umzukulu wekhaya* led her away to sit in the shade of a tree, covered in a blanket, her face cast down, until the burial was complete. Later, the father of the deceased placed the headstone and the mother or her representative from her relatives' side did her part in placing a stone at the foot of the grave. The morning after his burial, close relatives lined the unswept hut where the body had lain in state and the mourners had kept vigil through the night. An uncle of the deceased brought a flaming piece of cattle fat greased *isihaqa* or *umlembelembe* tree branch and shone a flash of light at each and everyone in the hut. That is known as the dark-cleansing ritual, with the light cleansing the darkness associated with death and keeping a vigil with the dead body before it was buried. Those inside the hut for this ritual stepped out one by one. MaNleya was the last to be cleansed through *ukukhanyiswa* after which she swept the hut and the area surrounding it. Together, with the same uncle who was performing the ritual, they collected the litter into an old disused reed basket together with the ashes which had been accumulating since the start of the funeral wake.

MaNleya's father then took one of the logs they had removed from the fence of the yard to create *intuba* with which the deceased body had been taken out to its final resting place. He led the party to the nearest place where village paths crossed. Next in the row was the uncle carrying the heavy litter basket, helped by another uncle of the deceased. MaNleya followed them, hitting together a pair of disused hoes to make a clicking sound, officially telling her daughter-in-law that her husband was dead and buried. The daughter-in-law blew red melon seeds to her ears.

The party of close relatives and community members followed from behind them. The children of the deceased tottered behind the elders, torn pieces of their father's shirts dangling on their shoulders. The party arrived at the crossroads and waited for everyone to arrive. As soon as they did, the uncles emptied the ashes and litter and at the same time the children ran off, bumping themselves on trees until the clothes fell away. They then came back to join everyone else and await their turns as MaNleya shaved off everyone's hair. The widow then changed into clean clothes which she wore inside out while waiting for the hoe washing ritual.

MaNleya did not realise that tears were trickling down her cheeks. She felt a burning ache for Sipho who had died such a painful death at so young an age. She also thought about Zanele and the baby that was coming and was never going to see its father.

Back at the headman's homestead, the men had moved to sit around the bonfire *ekhutheni* as soon as dusk fell. The women sat around a huge fire built in front of the beer hut. The younger women had left to cook for their husbands and families and to breastfeed their babies. Sibanda had been released too. He sat drinking with other men, talking as if nothing had happened. The elders were cautious enough to give him his own beer gourd to drink from since he had been threatening those who had touched him. Besides their fear of the consequences of having humiliated Sibanda, the elders feared he could poison them since he carried all sorts of medicine in his pockets. He could not be trusted though some people knew that his medicine was fake. The headman stood up to thank his community for coming in their numbers to help him rebuild his fence and encouraged them to do the same for everyone else. He also announced that there would be a finger millet festival at the Hlabanganas the following Wednesday. There would be no hoe washing ritual at the Dubes as was the custom since such deaths had no rituals honouring them.

Sikhwehle and Dingizulu roasted the goat ribs which the men ate as they drank into the night. Had it not been that the village was still mourning Sipho's death, Hlabangana and Dlodlo would have sung their ancient ditty and danced.

Later that night, Sibanda lay on his bed, his thoughts warming his blood. Even though the beer had numbed the pain of being tied to a tree all afternoon, it could not numb the pain caused by what he had seen in the beer hut. He ploughed a whole field and weeded it in his brain. He had to do something about Motini's attitude towards him. All along, he had suspected that something was going on, but this time, everything was so obvious.

He saw Motini enjoying the meat and the attention. He did not, however, give up on his wishes on having MaMpunzi sweeping his yard, cooking and cleaning for him. She would be his for life. They just had to wait and see. He thought about it all until he had a sound plan and knew what he was going to do. He slept until the sun had ascended and was well up in the sky.

Chapter Twenty-Four

"*Ekuhle,* Baba Hlabangana!"

Dube, his brother Buhe and their uncle, arrived and called out greetings to the people from outside Hlabangana's gate early on a Sunday morning. Zamani's dog barked ferociously at them. They ignored it as they stood motionless before crouching outside the main gate. Buhe repeated the greeting-cum-calling, but no one appeared from inside the yard. A few moments later, Hlabangana, wearing a vest with an animal imprint at the front, walked from behind the kraals. The cattle kraals were empty, but the calves could be heard mooing for their mothers from the goat pen. Zamani had taken the cows to graze on the morning dew dripping grass so that they could have sufficient milk. Old Hlabangana answered the greeting, his limbs weak from a huge hangover for he had been drinking the previous night with Sikhukhula at his shrine. Sikhukhula's son-in-law had sent the beer. They drank with Dlodlo and the headman too, happy that the son-in-law appreciated his knowledge of medicine for he had cured his dying mother of cervical cancer.

"Men from the south, come in, come in!" Hlabangana yawned and apologised, citing his hangover as the problem affecting his hearing. He continued, "Please, go straight *ekhutheni.* I am sure there are enough stools for you to sit on. I will be coming to join you soon."

They made their way in a single file to the appointed place, their knobkerries in their left hands. They found a couple of stools on which they sat in a circle with the fire which Zamani had built at the centre. Zamani had placed his grandfather's *incukuthu,* a metal piercing rod used to bore holes on hoe handles, cooking sticks and other wooden utensils which needed piercing.

Hlabangana came out of his bedroom hut dressed up, a pipe between his lips. He bent down to add charcoal to the pipe and then sat on his stool which was slightly elevated above the others.

"Did the last rains do much damage in your area as it did here?"

"We did not see any damage, but it was fierce, with violent winds and lightning," answered Dube's brother, Buhe.

"See that *umkhaya* tree fallen over there? It was brought down by the storm last night. We have to burn it down before the women use it for firewood!" Hlabangana said pointing at the gigantic tree which lay on the ground.

"Umh! It was quite a storm indeed, but this season will be better if it continues to rain like this. Nobody will starve as was the case in previous years!" added Buhe after taking a quick survey of the fallen tree.

"We just pray and hope the devil won't send locusts, birds or whatever to destroy our crops before they ripen and are ready for harvesting," Dube said, his voice solemn.

"I don't think it is the devil who does that. God punishes us for our sins, but we do not want to repent. We are now a very greedy and selfish people who do not even think of our own children's future..." Hlabangana said before being interrupted by Zamani who was greeting the three men. Before they could answer, Zamani was off to his grandmother's kitchen.

"Boys of these days will never become men. They spend most of their time clinging to their mothers' petticoats and grandmothers' skirts, *hayi man*..." Hlabangana complained without noticing his wife, MaMlotshwa, kneeling behind him, ready to greet the visitors.

MaNleya also entered through the small gate, balancing a water container on her head, her right hand pulling some branches to use as firewood, and the left carrying a basket with fresh pumpkin leaves. She wanted to prepare a breakfast of *isitshwala* with leftovers of chicken stew for her husband and father-in-law before going to church.

An older man who was an uncle to Dube and Buhe, that is, their late father's younger brother, cleared his throat and spoke, "We apologise for coming unannounced. We come to you with our humble request, Baba. We request that you give us your ears. As our elders say, *umntwana ongakhaliyo ufela embelekweni,* a child that does not cry dies, suffocated in its mother's shawl. We are your children, and we are crying."

There was a moment of silence before Hlabangana answered Simphiwe's uncle who was sweating in the cool morning.

"You did the right thing to look for advice. Let's hear the request," said Hlabangana, paying attention.

"We do not know if this will be acceptable, but we are just trying, Baba. It's about the banishment of Dube, my son here. In other words, the decision made last time that he should move away from this community."

Pause.

"Alright, how do you want me to help you? It was the Chief himself who banished him."

"Yes, we understand the decree, and why he was banished from this community. It is with that understanding that we could not go to the Chief directly. Our elders say, to reach the summit of a big mountain, you have to meander up the slopes. Therefore, we seek your advice in this matter. We have been thinking that you could... you, eh, could... eh, plead for us that he should be pardoned, considering the punishment he has received already."

Smoke escaped from Hlabangana's nostrils as he listened meditatively. Heavily shrivelled skin clothed his bones so loosely that one could easily remove it and replace it with another. His beard, white and wispy, spoke of many years of arduous experience. Under the thicket of his eyebrows were small clever eyes, which, despite his age, never seemed to miss a thing. He pulled the red-hot rod from the fire and used it to pierce hard into a hoe handle.

"I hear you, but the right procedure would be to go to the headman first, bring the matter to his attention and then we proceed from there."

"Thank you very much, Baba. We know your word is wisdom. We will wait to hear from you!" said the older Dube.

Afterwards, they talked about the rain and the sun and left Hlabangana to do his work.

For the first time since burying Sipho and paying Mxotshwa Ncube's people the ten heads of cattle the Chief had ordered, Dube felt some life. Of the ten cattle, two cows were each donated by his uncle and Buhe. Dube had seriously considered his unknown destiny and cried for nights in his bed. It was being said that the Mxotshwa family wanted to negotiate with the Chief that they return five of the cattle and take goats instead, considering the pain the family was already going through.

They walked abreast of each other, silently. Somewhere along the way, next to MaNleya's field, they saw a scotch cart. Its team of donkeys, still tied in pairs, was grazing on the green grass nearby. It seemed the scotch cart had a puncture because one of the wheels was removed from its place. One of the boys guarding the contents of the scotch cart and donkeys was playing nearby, watching some birds singing melodiously and playfully up the trees. The boy aimed his catapult at a dove which was perched up a *mbondo* tree near the path, let it off and hit the dove's left wing, maiming it horribly. The bird of peace streamed a trail of feathers as it tumbled onto a branch of shrubs where it lay fluttering its wings. The boy ran after it, but it gained balance despite flying on one wing. The dove tottered from tree to tree until the boy lost sight of it.

On the left side of the path, scattered thorns, green bush weed twigs and veld grass were motionless, shimmering with the dew on them. Simphiwe Dube felt a refreshing breeze fan his face as he stood there like a lost man, aimlessly observing some birds perched on acacia branches, busy building their nests with bits of grass. Although the nests hung low, the birds made sure that the openings of each nest would never make the nestlings fall out. Young butterflies and insects were flying visibly above the twigs. A short distance away, across the field, vultures circled over the unlucky carcass of some animal. The men saw an anthill under a *marula* tree where there were many graves and Dube's mind was drawn back to all his family members who had died because of his callousness. He hated himself. He hated Sibanda whom he felt had stabbed him deep in broad daylight. He was startled by a duiker which sprang across the pathway and disappeared into the thick forest. The springing duiker made him forget his pain for a while, fascinated by the life bounding off and away into the forest just ahead of him.

They passed another field of young corn which revealed itself with liveliness. Sorghum, groundnuts, and finger millet plants were dancing in the morning sun. Reaching the field, the Dubes kept to its boundary as they marvelled at its happy crops. The year seemed promising, unlike the previous one which had seen the maize plants turning yellow before even their tassels were out. It was hard to believe that these fields had lain bare and desiccated a few weeks before. During the hot, wet season, they planted sweet potatoes and green vegetables. Their eyes rested upon the well they had dug to the east of their field on a fall. They had built an enclave around the well and covered it with wooden logs. The area surrounding the well foamed with clear spring water. It was unfortunate that they could not use the water from that perennial well for drinking. Someone had thrown a dead dog in the vast pool of water the previous year after Dube's wife had banned other village women from fetching water from the well, fouling it. The culprit had waited for it to rain and then a week or so later, thrown the unidentified decaying corpse. The matter was reported to the headman and was discussed together with other village matters, but the culprit was never found. Dlodlo had indicated that it was their own problem, for where had they ever seen someone selling or denying people free water?

* * *

At the mission school, Zanele decided to pursue the most promising opportunity in her life after the discomfort she had gone through because of her pregnancy. She went about her studies without giving much attention to anyone, not even her best friends. She was going to be that mythical bird which dies and periodically rises from the dust and ashes. Naturally, she had inward resources that made her happy even in her solitude, and she believed nobody would disturb her private dreams now. Come what may, she was going to write her examinations and ace them! Her child was to be an indelible badge of courage. With Sipho gone and her baby coming, she wanted to give herself a triumphal integrity by coming out with straight A's again and proceeding to university to study law. When Sinqobile and the other girls looked at her quizzically, she made sure her lovely face betrayed no emotion.

During the week of the examinations, she received a wishing card from Nonceba who did not know about developments after she had left. Mandla too, sent a card with beautiful words of encouragement, not that he knew anything about her situation. Her aunt sent a basket of fruits, soft drinks and biscuits for her to nibble on as she studied. Zanele kept on looking at a card Ntando had sent her. She had drawn a picture of Mpiyabo with a bag of groundnuts tied to his leg. They had been in the fields harvesting them when he refused to carry it. Zanele, Nonceba and Moya had caught him and tied it to his leg by force. That was an incident from years back when Ntando herself had not even started school. Thinking of her life with the lovely family God had given her made Zanele smile. She made sure she was never to be seen in the school yards before the examinations started as she helped her teacher with housework and set to study everyday till late at night. She did not even attend Mass with the head teacher at church.

* * *

"Hey, people, where the hell is Sipho's wife? I did not see her at church. If she has been here for a week, surely someone must have seen her!" Sinqobile asked removing her blouse.

"Do you go to church to worship God or to look for scandals about Zanele?" asked another girl, pouring water into a tumbler.

"Oh sure, ask her. Why worry about Zanele? Or maybe she now wants to take Sipho?" Tendani teased.

"I hope Zanele does not get to hear what her student is saying about her," said a voice from behind a bunk bed.

"What can Sinqobile do with Sipho? She belongs to benevolent elders who drive her to lodges."

"Ha ha ha!"

"Ha ha ha!"

"She can do well in those countries where young schoolgirls are allowed to indulge in adult activities with whoever they want!"

"Leave me alone!"

"You too, leave Zanele alone! She will never, for one day, ask for soap and food for her baby from you. You say she is Sipho's wife, were you the go-between when their families negotiated the *lobola*?" asked Hanani with annoyance.

"Yo yo yo! What have I done? It seems the whole room is now baying for my blood!" Sinqobile complained.

"You asked them, 'Where is Sipho's wife?' They are answering you. Satisfied?" Hanani unbuttoned her blouse and, as she did so, apples of virgin breasts jutted out. She removed her skirt too and hung it on a hanger and put on a tunic in a hurry. She dashed out of the dormitory.

"Girls, do not forget that Sister Feluna is waiting for all Geography and Physics students at the science laboratory," she shouted as she neared the door.

"We haven't eaten our breakfast yet!" complained some girls.

"She is waiting, and I am rushing there," Hanani said, as she ran out, accidentally brushing against Tendani's tumbler which had orange crush and spilling its contents.

"Oh, you! What have you done, Hanani? It was the last drop. You know I do not take tea," cried Tendani.

"I am sorry my dear. I can give you some raspberry syrup if you do not mind!" Hanani said, looking at her pleadingly.

"My friend does not drink any kind of syrup. They are for village girls like you, the firewood smoke girls!" Sinqobile fired back angrily.

"Thank you, Hanani." Tendani received the cupful of raspberry from Hanani. Another girl also brought a full bottle of cream soda flavoured syrup and poured half its contents into Tendani's empty bottle.

"Your statement is zero, an egg, and zero! You must be cracked!" All the girls booed Sinqobile.

Hanani winked at her, not showing any emotion.

"Stop holding yourself higher than you are. You laugh at village girls yet you run to them with all your homework. Your English is too atrocious for a town girl surrounded by libraries!" Thembeka said, laughing at her.

"Never mind her! We will meet her at Renkini terminus with a baby strapped to her back helping the touts lift an ox plough to place on top of a Marinoha village chicken bus," Tendani mocked.

"I will do nothing of the kind!"

"Talking of Marinoha, you will meet her with pushcart boys helping her with her bags of *amacimbi* from Blumberg farm near Brunapeg!"

"Ha ha ha!"

"Don't start offending me! Leave me alone!"

"Do you know where she will be going with those skimpy nightdresses she borrows from juniors on the Fridays she visits her doctor? There is no doctor. It is her sugar daddy boyfriends who organise those letters so that they can be with her for the weekends. She was sent here for rehabilitation after she was expelled from two different schools!" her foul minded friend Tendani who had suddenly fallen out with her, mocked.

"What has that got to do with anyone? It is my life!"

"Stop pouting, you started this. Zanele should be left alone with her own life too. Stay out of it," remarked Hanani, rushing out of the room. Outside, Sister Feluna was already calling and intercepting those who were trying to sneak out to the dining hall first.

* * *

The day Zanele finished writing her examinations, her aunt was waiting for her in the car park. As fate had it, she delivered a baby boy the following day at Mpilo Hospital. She was surprised that everything changed with the coming of the baby. Thoughts of Sipho caressed her. It was funny that the last time she had seen him, she had wished him dead. MaMoyo came with Dube and his uncle to see the baby who unmistakably looked like his late father. They brought a whole carcass of a big goat for their grandson as was the custom. That was the only boy to carry his father's name. Dube felt so delighted and refreshed that he wished the Hadebes would let him raise the baby. The Mahlangus appreciated the gesture with humility.

* * *

Sibanda gleefully drove his huge herd to the dip tank on a Wednesday morning. In his life, he did not want to bear the pressure of evolution which came with education and its benefits. He was a peasant through and through and for him, as for most other peasants, cattle defined wealth as they had done for their forebears. Having been raised in a family where God was never heard of but only the notorious *sangoma* Thutshubakhale, drunkenness and witchcraft were Sibanda's gods. Fights with his wife made his home a scandal, a sacrilege crying to heaven for punishment. Sibanda placed no value on education. Were it not for MaNtini, Khethiwe and Zinzile would not have gone to school. He thought that after sleeping with them to test their virginity, a custom also practised by his forebears, *nholowemizana*, he would marry them off to rich men who would give him cattle as bride price. Sikhwehle looked at him, making a glottal cawing sound from the bottom of his throat. He shrugged his shoulders which were padded with muscle and wondered if there was any man that would dare quarrel with him, Sibanda included.

"Those cursed cattle and goats from Dube will soon disappear from you before you know it," said Sikhwehle.

Sibanda looked at the tracks leading to the dip-tank. The trails were dimpled by cattle spoor. He moved slowly towards

Sikhwehle. His gaze more eloquent, he opened his thick and livid lips which were glistening as if stung by bees to reveal his tobacco-stained teeth before speaking, "I worked for them, you riff-raff. Mind your own business of driving other men's cattle to the dip-tank."

"I am far much better than you because I live with a clear conscience. You have his cattle yet his family perished as he depended on your fake medicine. Shame on you, man! Return his cattle and we shall respect you!" said Dingizulu cracking his whip.

"I want no word with both of you," Sibanda barked at them. He wiped the stubborn head which sat ridiculously on a dehydrated neck, a head obsessed with brewing more of his sex and abortion concoctions. Sibanda wore tight fitting trousers designed like those worn by polo players. Everyone thought they had been handed down by his former boss's son who was smaller than him. The trousers blatantly emphasised his bunched genitalia. His love for power was a beast inside that thing he had no control of. His appetite for women exceeded caution. He chewed medicine to get the two things he envied so much, no matter how shameful and cruel the circumstances appeared. His temper was always hot and copious like volcanic lava. Sibanda made it clear that remorse was never his emotion. With all those characteristics, nobody liked him. If you looked at him closely, he looked as if he had a deep-seated spiritual agony crying out for release. Under the medicine enamelled façade lay a miserable and empty man, unconsoled by his charms and ill-gotten wealth.

The oxen stamped their hooves on the ground to dry themselves after plunging into the dip tank waters and swung their tails to chase away the bothering flies. Siphamandla, other village men and boys were silent as they watched and listened to the battle of words between the three men. Sikhwehle brought Hadebe's cattle to the dip-tank most of the time. His herd had taken its turn and stood grazing a distance away from the dip-tank yard.

"I can see you are walking around with a bone in your mouth like a lion. You will eat your words one day. I am sure you will find yourself in hell," Sikhwehle said to Sibanda before disappearing to collect something from *umdibhisi,* the dip-tank attendant.

Sibanda made no reply to Sikhwehle but waved him away with his arm in a tired stupor.

"Hell is your home anyway, sadist," Dingizulu fired.

Sibanda looked at him with eyes like those of a wolf scenting blood, annoyed but unable to act on it.

Dingizulu moved closer to the dip-tank attendant who had beckoned them to come closer. He announced the next dipping date and also informed them that everybody should meet at Headman Nkiwane's court for a developmental meeting the following Wednesday.

* * *

On a Saturday morning, Nonceba went to the terminus to meet MaNkomo and MaNleya who were arriving from Emlanjeni. They were coming to see Zanele's baby. She found them sitting on their bags, wondering and looking lost. They had brought her presents; strips of *amarula* bark and other wild herbs for her to sit on every morning before taking a bath. Nonceba's skin glowed with health and was as unblemished and lustrous as ivory. Her gestures epitomised her generation – educated, free and mysterious in some of their ways. MaNleya admired that and wished she too could at least go back to school and start all over. MaNkomo wondered at the girls who alighted from the same bus at Matshaemhlophe and walked slowly in their heels, wearing very offending articles of clothing. One of the girls had a belly button that winked at the moon and panties that were short of flashing under the abbreviated skirt. They held a conversation as they walked while chewing lemon scented gum. As the girls moved nearer to where Nonceba and her visitors were, they did not bother to acknowledge the presence of the elders, let alone greet them.

"All men are the same," said one of the girls.

"What has he done?"

"Who?"

"The one you are about to tell me about. Since you have a herd of them, who has roused your ire?"

"The one I love, Bheki. I saw him with a girl at the movies!"

"Taste of your own medicine!"

"Look who is talking now! Some people are good at parroting holy orders they cannot follow themselves."

"Who am I to question your judgement?" The friend turned the rebuke aside with a shrug.

The pair disappeared around a bend. Nonceba blushed but concealed her embarrassment. She was suddenly thinking of Mandla who was probably high up in the sky somewhere. There was no need to worry about him cheating on her. Mandla had somehow blended with her.

Both women looked with happiness and pain at Zanele's baby who looked like his departed father, Sipho. The consolation, at least, was that Zanele had written her examinations and was feeling well after giving birth, despite all the emotional pain she had gone through. Zanele looked at all of them with mixed feelings. She thought not even the lapse of time could obliterate the scar the baby had come along with. Sipho would forever remain a memory. Zanele was happy though that Sipho's family took the trouble to know what was happening in Nkanyiso's life and Zanele's.

"So Za, how was it at the delivery bed?"

"MaNkomo! I will never go back there. I wonder how mothers with ten babies have done it."

"The problem with you mothers of these days is that you are not strong. What with this overprocessed food you indulge in! Our mothers used to work in the fields during the day and deliver babies at night. Afterwards, they rested for only a few days before they were back to the fields!" observed MaNleya while rocking baby Nkanyiso in her arms.

"Serious abuse of women!" Nonceba remarked.

"Nonceba, it was not abuse. Women were supposed to be strong!" MaNkomo said.

"They are too lazy, MaNleya, and that is why women get operated on in their first pregnancies. So, they are forced to end up with two or three children because after an operation, one is allowed only two more births or she dies," Mrs Hadebe said seriously.

"Not the Tshedu type who filled antbear and meercat holes with her many aborted foetuses," MaNleya said.

"It was a blessing in disguise that Sibanda and that roadwork man fought for her, otherwise where would we be this time with that curse of a woman?" Mrs Mahlangu spoke with a voice of deep melodious quality.

"Who is Tshedu? You always tease us, yet we do not even know her?" Zanele asked, massaging her now deflated womb.

"Sure, even Mama does the same. Who is she? I noticed that Gogo becomes uncomfortable when Sikhwehle mentions that name too. Is she related to her?"

"MaNleya, please tell them. You lived with her. During those days I never stepped my foot into that homestead!" Mrs Mahlangu said.

"She was your mother, Zanele," MaNleya said.

"My mother?"

"Yes, your father's second wife. MaNcube arranged for her to marry your father so that your mother could go back to her people."

"How did she do that? What did *malume* say? Did he accept her?"

"Have you ever heard of a man who refuses a wife?" MaNkomo asked rhetorically.

"The whole thing was silly. I wonder what Mother was thinking when she arranged something like that with Tshedu of all people. She was desperate to have your mother go back to her own people. She did not like your mother," Mrs Mahlangu explained, remembering Tshedu's flaming red wigs which seemed to communicate with her red nails and lips that were smudgy with lipstick. The thickness of the lipstick could hold a Castle lager unaided. From the way she sat with men *ekhutheni*, drinking millet or bottled beer, she seemed to have a hot blood of desire for both the men and beer."

"Yet *malume* loved and wanted her?" Nonceba asked puzzled.

"MaNcube claimed MaMoyo was lazy, a prostitute and a witch!" MaNleya said seriously.

"Ha ha ha!"

"Women like fighting each other. If it was not for my father-in-law *ubab'Hlabangana,* I would have packed my bags too and left. Remember how MaMlotshwa used to treat me. She was cautioned by the Chief's mother herself, MaNxumalo! Tshedu was from the Sithwala clan. She never had a child with your father. She never covered her hair and had those huge wigs on."

"I always remember her with her big Afro hairstyle. She carried an okapi knife in her brassiere as if she wanted to stab whoever questioned her ways." Mrs Mahlangu exclaimed.

"What a woman!" Nonceba exclaimed.

"She refused to go to the fields saying she had no kittens or puppies to feed. When she married your father, she looked like someone who was past the time for getting married. But MaNcube did not worry about that. Even when she got married, she always had boyfriends. You know men! She beat the headmaster's wife at the shops because she had asked her to stay away from her husband. She said she would date whoever she wanted because men came to her on their own and she did not invite them. After all, she said, men were not branded like cattle to show that they belonged to someone," MaNleya said.

"Wherever you found her, she was surrounded by men!"

"Ha ha ha!"

"Men!"

"Men will always be men. It is us women who have to be in control. MaNxumalo says men smell whores the way dogs smell bitches on heat. It is not always about beauty with them. An ugly and older prostitute may come here but all men will lust for her, ignoring young women like you, Nonceba!" MaNkomo said.

"Ha ha ha!"

"How true!"

"How did it end? Where is she now?" Nonceba asked, looking at Zanele who was dozing.

"She had an affair with Sibanda who used to help her with abortions. Then she fell in love with a man who was working for a company that was constructing the St Joseph's-Brunapeg road. They fought and broke her bedroom hut door and Khulu Hadebe, the late, drove her away himself. We used to hear she was at Maphisa, then Bulawayo and finally Hurungwe!"

"Ha ha ha!"

"Actually, I heard she is back but sick now. She is being looked after by her niece at Khalanyoni!"

Nonceba served them some raspberry and scones. She had baked the scones herself, much to the delight of MaNkomo. The sight of the scones, with their lush helpings of jam, made her smile.

Chapter Twenty-Five

The people gathered at the headman's court the following Wednesday. The developmental meeting took its usual course, but room was created for Simphiwe Dube to apologise to the community. He said he was sorry that things had gone the way that they had in the case between him and the Mxotshwa family. He thanked everyone for their show of support and solidarity with him and his family. There was a very loud applause from the people after Dube had spoken.

Later that afternoon, Dube left for the Chief's court with Hlabangana and the headman. They found Chief Mlotshwa discussing with some of his advisors a case in which a hostile woman had thrown an axe and broken her neighbour's ankle for "letting" the goats wander into her field of young corn. The goats had devoured her crops, nibbling at even the sprouting cow beans and groundnuts, and leaving the fields brown and bare. Her crops were her only livelihood. The man at fault did not go to the local clinic, fearing that after the nurses got to know what had happened, they would need a police report. The woman would then be arrested and charged with attempted murder. What would the man become if the woman died of starvation in jail because of his goats? Who was going to pay for her numerous travel expenses to and from the court? And how was he to compensate her for the time they spent sitting there waiting for their case to be heard? It was said that sometimes a case was adjourned four or five times. The man's wound had become septic, almost rotting. Out of guilt, the woman had come to report herself. The victim's family understood that she was a single mother of six boys who survived on the crops her field produced. Her husband was alive but had not returned from South Africa where he had gone to look for a job a decade before. Ntuli mediated between the two families without showing any favour for either of them. The woman appealed to her companions from time to time, whenever she felt cornered and when her mute appeal passed unheeded. Her face was heavy with remorse. Ntini's loquacity was fair for a spokesperson but the Chief's silence and ability to listen carried more weight. It gave the impression of one who is straightforward and resolute. It was resolved that the injured man would go to the clinic and tell them that he had fallen so that the woman would not be taken to jail, away from her three sets of twin boys. It was also resolved that the women would bring bundles of thatching grass while the men brought poles to help with the roofing of the kitchen hut that she had, in her anger and frustration, set alight. The decision was also taken that when harvest time came, the owner of the offending goats would compensate the woman, depending on how much they would harvest.

Headman Nkiwane's party lodged their appeal to the Chief. He gave Dube a pardon and ruled that he could stay. For the first time in quite a while, Dube went home feeling relieved.

Headman Nkiwane did not sleep well that night. He dreamt of Motini Nleya and Sibanda each pulling his wife who seemed not to know what to do. He could not sleep after that and Sikhwehle's words in the beer hut, which he had addressed to Motini, 'You think we do not know what you two are fighting for,' came hard and fresh in his ears. Something must have been hitting the waters, as the old saying goes. No, there is no smoke without fire. Before sunrise, Headman Nkiwane was at Old Sikhukhula's healing hut. When he got there, he found the old healer already waiting for him. He had seen him coming in a vision well before Nkiwane himself had woken up. He removed his sandals, went into the hut, placed some rands in the wooden dish and waited. The healer stuffed some snuff into his nostrils and sneezed. He waved his *itshoba* three times then put it aside. He took some bones and shook them before throwing them onto the floor. Looking thoughtful and studious, Old Sikhukhula read the message in the bones and shook his head. He took the bones a second time and once again threw them on his reed mat. He sneezed twice before burping and spoke in a woman's voice, "You have to be strong, Baba. The perpetrator is carrying dangerous poison. You must be patient because if you are not, you will die with blood on your hands. But just be patient. I see him leaving the community very soon. The boy is bad news."

"Which boy?"

"Do not worry about him. He wants to take your wife from you using bad medicine. He will not succeed. He will be gone before his plans work for him, ha ha ha!"

"*Khulumani!*"

"Go back home and shut your mouth. Pretend not to see or hear anything. Very soon people will have rest and live in peace!"

The headman walked back feeling an elation he did not understand. He found MaMpunzi looking confused. His disappearance early that morning, uncharacteristic as it was, had unsettled her. The headman pretended not to notice her worried demeanour and sombre mood. He was going to do what the old healer had instructed him to do.

Nonceba received a peculiar Christmas present from Mandla which left her dazed and uncoordinated. She had spent a month without a whiff of scent from him. She immediately withdrew to an ice-cold reserve, her expression remaining frosty, turning hostile or giving taciturn and intractable responses when questioned about her sudden mood changes. Sometimes, she felt like she was sitting or walking on something hot and seething like a thin volcanic crust. Even though she tried to conceal her misery, her unconvincing efforts betrayed her. Her anger showed behind her grin. The words on the card stuck in her memory for days. When she read them for the first time, she felt the acute pain of a stomachache that left her feeling like she had swallowed a stone. The sharp, straight words were beyond her experience or understanding. For days, she needed something to keep her wits sharp and her blood flowing. Her store of energy and enthusiasm had suddenly become all used up, yet meeting Mandla for the first time stood out as one of the most memorable days in her life.

Mandla was now exploiting his good looks with a British-South African trainee pilot as she later told Zanele in the most injured tone. Nonceba had loved Mandla without reservation. What consoled her was that she was careful with him and always preserved her virtues. As the days went by, she became more accustomed to what had happened, although it gave her a strange feeling to think that Mandla was going to be just another faceless and nameless being in her life. She looked at Zanele's little Nkanyiso and thought about how life was, its beauty, romance and cruelty.

Mnqobi, who still found Nonceba as desirable as fruit in a neighbour's garden, trapped her slowly the way a puddle of honey attracts an insect. He would not let that smile of hers go away with her. Nevertheless, Mnqobi trod very carefully, biding his time and waiting for a sign.

* * *

In Emlanjeni, time passed with peaceful regularity. One Wednesday morning, the fragrance from a profusion of wildflowers dotted around the veld was accentuated by the beautiful scent of scores of people on their way to the Hlabangana homestead. There were butterflies, as elusive as ever, everywhere, and the birds of the air too were full of the heat of life. As if becalmed by the jade green sky, *marula* trees stood lining the path in their new sparkling leaves. MaNkomo walked on, singing softly, enjoying the green veld adorned with vegetation in its fullest and richest bloom. The fresh air beat her nostrils and nourished her lungs. There was no sluggish dust raised by pattering feet because the soil was wet. It had rained the previous night. MaNkomo took a deep breath and felt her lungs emptying luxuriously as she breathed out.

The whole chiefdom appeared to have come to the Hlabangana homestead on that morning. MaNkomo, who was normally as punctual as a clock, especially for community events, had been delayed by having to take her baby to the mobile clinic for her routine weight checks. Knowing what the time was and realising that she would be uncharacteristically late unless she did something about it, MaNkomo walked as if she would overtake the wind. She had stopped singing and was listening intently to the bird songs that seemed to be directed at her to encourage her to walk on, her reed basket of finger millet carefully balanced on her head.

"Everyone was wondering what could have happened to you!"

"I was afraid that they would," she answered MaNleya, pouring the contents of her basket into the open reed basket, *isilulu.*

"I had taken my baby to the mobile clinic."

"Oh, by the way today is the babies' day?"

"I hope you put a good excuse on my behalf to Gogo MaMlotshwa."

"She was just concerned but neither condemned nor reviled you. Everyone knows just how committed you are in community matters! Today she is as happy as a cat in a dairy. This ceremony has been put off so many times before. First, it coincided with Dube's trial and, second, the headman's fence building. It was worrying her."

"I expected that."

Women continued arriving, carrying reed baskets with chaffed finger millet. Many reed baskets were closed on top by tying tablecloths or things of such kind over them to prevent the contents from being blown away by the wind. By midmorning, two large sacks were already full, although women were still bringing more baskets. MaXaba, MaNleya, MaMoyo and other village women were busy cooking mealie rice and meat in large earthen pots on open fires in the makeshift shades. Khulu Hlabangana, Headman Nkiwane, Dlodlo and Sikhukhula sat in the shade of a *mbondo* tree in the yard. MaNleya had since cooked the *isitshwala* which they ate with fried goat liver and roasted ribs in the morning. They sat chatting, Hlabangana carving a hoe handle and Dlodlo chiselling another.

After lunch, the women put away the dishes and their crafts and started the ceremony in dance. The period of darkness for the Dubes had lapsed. Some women blew whistles as they danced to the drums, creating a buoyant mood at the ceremony. The drums boomed away into the evening. Male bodies, thin from planting and weeding, jerked and pulsed in time with the drums while frail but cheerful women swayed like a field of young corn in a high wind. Volunteers went into the circle to show their prowess in traditional dance. People clapped and cheered willy-nilly, drawing the attention of those passing by. The sound of drums went cosmic and brutal, reducing the drunken and happy dancers into a rhythmical yet frenetic frenzy from which the dust rose and sweat, like raindrops, pounded the dusty ground. A female dancer wiggled her bottom furiously before jerking spasmodically like an epileptic. Women looked up, thrilled by fear and anticipation, and men imagined whatever their fancies bade them to do. They secretly hoped that the woman would not stop her erotic dance. Sure enough, she jerked again and lay down in a trance with only the whites of her eyes showing. She was a member of the Nkiwane clan. The headman was called immediately from where he was sitting with Dlodlo and Sikhukhula. Those of the woman's clan ran with millet beer and gave her some snuff. She inhaled it and sneezed and then sat up straight. A relative beckoned to Nkiwane who came and sat legs stretched in front of her. The woman said something which was obviously not clear enough for them to understand. Headman Nkiwane called his other relatives so that they could hear together what was being said.

"*Kune mashango laha, loko ungathlarihi utalova hisvona, mara hakota kusvilungisisa ekusvinga endleki.* There is a problem. If you are not careful you will die, but we can reverse this instruction," the warning was specifically directed to the headman himself.

The spirit spoke in Tshangana which MaMoyo was called in to translate. The family members pleaded with their ancestor to do something to stop the death. The woman was seized again by the spirit and sneezed until they gave her some water to drink. Her body shook and they covered her with a colourful wrapper. She groaned, yawned and stretched her arms. Before the departure of the spirit, it spoke again, promising to stop the deaths, "*Nitavona.*"

The finger-millet ceremony, known as *inshogwana,* is a marriage ceremony performed by the bride's family after the son-in-law has paid the lobola and taken his bride. It is a collective ceremony by the community where each member brings finger millet in a reed basket to celebrate the girl's marriage. She is regarded as everyone's child and is therefore worth celebrating. The marriage is a communal affair because the daughter-in-law will be joining a community where people live together, sharing and enduring all that visits them, love and tragedy alike. People are not limited to bringing finger millet only. They are free to bring presents for their daughter to start and build her family with. It could be reed mats, baskets, earthen pots, mortars and pestles or whatever else is suitable for a newly married woman. A date is then set after the ceremony and messengers are sent to the daughter's new family with all the presents, including the bags of finger millet.

While others were dancing, some people were sitting in small groups drinking opaque beer, *amahewu* or tea. Motini sat with the grey heads, avoiding his peers because his rival and friend-in-mischief was sitting in that group. As time went on, he was forced to move because he felt he had to. He joined a group composed of Sibanda, Dingizulu, and another man who had come from eGoli and who was recounting, with hefty embellishments, his escapades in eGoli to the delighted wonder of his mini audience. Motini was greeted by Sikhwehle's remark, "Polygamy is allowed in our culture. Real men do not go after other men's wives, especially your elders' wives. They go for single girls who are plentiful. I wonder how some people think!"

"What surprises me is the nerve of them going after an elder's wife. During King Lobengula's time, these are people who were given to vultures alive!"

"We did not come here for your stupid sermons, you to-die-and-be-buried-with-rats scoundrels!" Sibanda directed his insults to the pair which had never had wives, his voice as hoarse as a crow's. Custom had it that men who died without ever having had wives were buried with rats.

"Be that as it may, we never cheated with anyone. Nobody ever saw us with other men's wives behind St Joseph's rocks, Simpathe riverbanks, behind shrubs and bushes, or in the fields!"

"The devil knows where else. Maybe even in other men's bedrooms!"

"Mend your holes and straighten your crooked ways before you…"

Sikhwehle broke into a folk song about shady liaisons between loverboys and married women.

"Uzakufa kubi kubi kubi
Uzakufa kubi
Ngabafazi babantu!"

"Quiet gentlemen. Let sleeping dogs lie. This is a serious matter. I am sure whoever you are warning has heard," Sabelo warned.

Nkiwane heard those two singing and knew what was happening. He felt his blood get hotter but managed to hold himself together.

* * *

Mnqobi had not given up on Nonceba. He kept writing letters to her that did not suggest anything about what he felt for her. Nonceba wrote back and even sent him a few photographs of herself and her friends. Mnqobi had applied to the University of Cape Town and was waiting for the granting of a scholarship. Mandla had changed schools and had moved to the Miami Aviation School in the U.S. Mnqobi knew that Nonceba was his, but he still had to prove himself as a man. He did not rush at her. He was a hunter with the patience of a predator. He had already charmed his way into Nonceba's confidence by maintaining contact and providing an ear. He could not let this woman who stood like a sunbird among a flock of sparrows go. He looked at her pictures and marvelled at how the force of her character displayed itself even in the pictures.

Mnqobi had always felt that Nonceba's relationship with Mandla was more out of a symbiotic consideration than genuine love. Nonceba seemed impressed by the social status of Mandla's lineage. Mandla came from a lettered family. His father had been a professor of Applied Sciences in Europe, twenty years before. His mother was an actuarial scientist and had once lectured at the National University of Science and Technology in Bulawayo. Mandla was born in England and spent his childhood years there. That was what gave him British manners and an accent which sent many girls drooling for his attention. Mnqobi did not care about what Nonceba felt for Mandla. He told himself that he was going to make sure that he made her love him, come what may. He felt he could make her feel like the most desirable woman in the world and cause her to forget about Mandla, the 'British' boy. On occasions, Mnqobi was pained by an underflow of doubt and self-pity when, for some reason, he began to think that he could not match his dream woman's brains by any standards. Nonceba was natural and candid. At times, her modern culture fascinated and yet still intimidated him. Most people who did not know her closely would be forgiven for thinking that she was unapproachable. Mnqobi loved Nonceba with an aching that made being with or without her equally torturous. He loved Nonceba to the extent that when he spoke about her with his friends, he used a tone of controlled excitement. There was Mkandla too, who at first looked at her like a serpent mesmerising a bird, and then tried to cut Nonceba out of the herd and brand her in his own favour. But that Mkandla had become a past, making way for Mnqobi to sneak into Nonceba's good graces.

* * *

On a Saturday morning, Sibanda woke up before the third cock and arranged to visit Sikhukhula. He was in a dilemma of sorts and had no idea if Sikhukhula was going to agree to do what he was going to ask him to do. He pondered over the issue back and forth until it became clear to him that he was going to have to go to Sikhukhula anyway. Most *sangomas* wanted money and cattle. Sikhukhula could not be any different, and he, Sibanda, had plenty of both. Rats scuffled all over his bedroom hut which had acquired a putrid smell since the departure of his wife and children. He threw away his flea-infested blankets and rushed out. He made sure his pocket had enough multi-currency. Once he got there, he placed his knobkerrie and shoes outside the healer's hut and went in.

He was impressed to find Sikhukhula already dressed for the job and eagerly expecting him. That satisfied Sibanda because his thinking was that whatever the *sangoma* was going to tell him to do was worth doing. Sibanda sat on a reed mat, legs stretched out and barefoot. The *sangoma* held his *itshoba* with both of his hands and looked down pensively. On his head, he wore an *indlukula* decorated with white and black beads on a base made of the feathers of an eagle and some other huge bird. On his neck was a wide necklace adorned with the same kinds of beads as those on the *indlukula* on his head. On his arms were many types of arm bands made from the skins of various kinds of animals. The *sangoma's* back was covered in leopard skin. He wore an *ibhetshu* made from a lion's skin sewn together with that of a cheetah. Sibanda threw some South African rands, United States dollars and British pounds into the *sangoma's* wooden bowl and waited. Sikhukhula burped so deeply that even his dogs which were used to that kind of noise thought it was an intruder and barked ferociously.

"Your matter is not an easy one."

He threw his bones again and shook his head. Sibanda greeted the spirit which did not answer but uttered something in a strange language.

"*Hirikimuna, ayiye kimuna wanke shini murisa shi*. What do you want with this Nleya boy? Leave him alone. Be careful with the headman. You already know what you did!"

"What must I do?"

"*Hirikimuna hira kinimu nini, ayishe ha!*"

He threw his bones and looked at his client with blood-red eyes and a trembling torso.

"I see death on your doorstep! You have to act fast!"

"How do I act? What do I do?" Sibanda asked desperately.

"Are you brave enough? If you are, you will do what I am going to tell you to do but if you make a mistake, you will be caught. Once that happens, it means this meeting we are having never took place and I will say I never saw you. Understand?"

"Tell me what to do and I will do it now!"

"You will do this at your own risk, but not now though. It will take four days before my medicine does the works."

Sikhukhula, the medicine man, organised a mixture of herbs from different bundles and tied them together. He then dipped them in a small calabash which was greasy with grime on its woven mouth. He mixed more powders and spat into them, asking Sibanda to do the same while saying exactly what he wanted to happen. Sikhukhula took the mixture and poured it into a small gourd placed in the back of his hut. He mixed more herbs and went to talk into the mixture with Sibanda's words before pouring some on his head and feet. He poured the remaining mixture into a small container and closed it tightly. He also took the bundle he had put in a calabash and gave both to Sibanda.

"Take these. Go home and fill a bucket with water which you will put in the centre of your bedroom hut. Put this bundle in the water and from time to time, speak with it, tell it all your heart's desires. In the evenings, bath in the same water for the next three nights and make sure you do not spill a drop or the medicine will not work. On the third night before the second cock crows, walk to Headman Nkiwane's homestead, naked. Carry a sharp iron rod with you. Dig in the centre of his homestead and pour the water you have been bathing in and cover the hole. Dig another hole next to it and defecate in it facing the west. From there, do not look back. Within a day, everything you want will happen! Did you hear me well?"

"Clearly, *Babamkhulu*!"

"Remember, my medicine does not mix with any other."

"I hear you, *Babamkhulu*!" he walked away, romancing his fantasy of having Tholiwe Mpunzi as his wife.

* * *

The fields had turned a beautiful, lively and shiny green. The green made the women forget the slight back pains which proved to be imaginary as soon as one rose to do their daily chores.

One Tuesday, late in the evening, Sikhukhula sent for Nkiwane to his hut. He had dreamt of something coming to destroy his family, so he needed to warn Nkiwane.

Sibanda rose to perform his final act of the ritual on the third night. As soon as he had done everything successfully, he smiled to himself and stood to go. Alas, before he knew it, he felt and saw some movement in the dark night. The figure was like that of a tall being, taller than the trees and the huts. It was just an illusion, he told himself, but the dark silhouettes moved ever closer to him.

By sunrise, people were summoned to Headman Nkiwane's homestead to see the once defiant Sibanda naked, tied with ropes, defied by his charms and shenanigans. Out of pity, MaSibanda, his aunt, asked for permission to give Sibanda her wrapper to hide the vital organs. Sibanda did not comprehend anything but was conscious of where he was. His world had suddenly changed, filled with meaninglessness. Thoughts spun like a fly wheel in his mind, as generous tears filled his eyes for the first time since his father's death. His ash smeared face looked like it had been pickled with vinegar. Only his mother looked at him with a softened expression. Sibanda met his persecution by nocturnal misadventure. Dingizulu and Sikhwehle were amused as usual. They had warned Sibanda against witchcraft several times before. This incident was going to vanquish him horse and foot from the community. Everyone was happy that he would be gone.

* * *

At university, Zanele was keeping to herself as she was still haunted by her humiliating experience at the mission school. When boys asked her out for drinks and ice cream, she insulted them and behaved in the most confusing manner until all her suitors dismissed her as someone possessed by demons or a spiritual husband. She felt more than just a little ashamed when people mentioned that they had read about her in the papers after she had passed her 'O' level examinations. To her, that meant that they knew the aftermath as well. Meanwhile, Nonceba was communicating frequently with Mnqobi who had been accepted at the University of Cape Town. Khethiwe was going to train as a nurse at Brunapeg Mission Nursing School, just across Semukhwe River in Plumtree. She would begin her project in May.

Glossary (in order of appearance)

izishwehswe – dresses and aprons of Tswana print
ubelomkhuhlane – he or she suffered from a disease
maheu – non-alcoholic drink made from malt
umhlambikazelusile – children left to do as they please
emakhitshini – cooking and housekeeping jobs
imikhukhu – temporary zinc shelters
geli – housemaid
umwawa – a tree that produces yellow, round fruit
senyawuthi – made from finger millet powder
amasi – pasteurised milk
smomondiya – an endearment for a female lover
sizakufa silahlane ubukele – we will die together in love as you watch
malayitsha – transporters of groceries from South Africa
umsuzwane – a herb for treating fresh wounds
mbondo – a type of tree
inkente – a game played mostly by young girls
kulungile – it is well
umsehla – a type of tree
nholowemizana – an ancient practice whereby the daughter-in-law is supposed to have sex with the father-in-law first, before her husband
mzukulu – grandchild
gogo – grandmother
koBulawayo – in Bulawayo
guwe – a type of tree
malume – uncle
muphafa – a type of tree
itshowe lakho – a heap of firewood
shamwari yangu – my friend

edakeni – rain dance shrine

amayile – rain dance and song

zalabantu ziyebantwini – a phrase used by young men asking for love from a girl

ayikho eyagana inyamazana! – proverb: no woman marries an animal

umqokolo – a fruit tree

emthonjeni – at the well

enkunini – at the gathering of firewood

okuphekwa khona utshwala – at the brewing of beer

ngiyabhadala inkomo – I will pay cattle

lobola – dowry

umhiqo – a cooked mixture of fermented corn

omazwihila – children of unknown paternity

umkhaya – a type of tree

ubuntu – humanity

isitshwala – thick porridge

ubabamkhulu wakoMpofu – spirit medium of the Mpofu family

babamkhulu – grandfather

Ngitshiye abantwabami – I left my children

Ngivalele endlini! – locked in the house

Ngitshaya amayile – to sing for the rain

Yebo – Hello

Yibukhwele? – Are you jealous?

Salibonani – I see you

Yikuvuka lokhu. Ayi lapha ubaba waswela umfazi – Is this time for you to wake up? Truly, my father did not have a wife.

Mdala – old man

Nduna yami – my chief

Ezizweni – From other countries

Umkhwenyana wakoNdlovu – Ndlovu's son-in-law

Umkhwenyana – son-in-law

Ihole – a derogatory term for a non-Nguni member of the community

Amahole sehlupile – foreigners are giving us problems

Lafa ilizwe – the country has been destroyed

si si si… lafa ilizwe – our humanity is lost

makadii zvenyu Maiguru? – how are you, aunt?

ndinofara kana muchifarawo – I am well if you are

ndoshandira hurumende – I work for the government

usulijoni? – are you now a policeman?

sizayicela isivuthiwe a – proverb: we will talk about the matter when results are out

ijumo – a cultural expedition whereby men and boys clean the community

uthi baloyiwe? – do you think they were bewitched?

wena – you

Amayile – An ethnic dance

Kuzothiwani ngalengane bantu – what is to be said about this child

maye ngomfoka Mahlathini! – woe to this son of Mahlathini!

Umtaka MaMoyo ke yena bantu! – daughter of Moyo, folks!

iwosana – spirit medium

imisisi – shredded skirts

indlukula – head gear

amahlwayi – leg shackles

amatshoba – fly whisk

muwawa – a type of tree

livuka njani? – did you wake up well?

yeyi wena – hey you

velabahleke – a flower

ulude – a type of vegetable

isihaqa – a medicine made from the bark of a tree

sangomas – traditional healers

Thetha no – talk to
Ah khulul' – to release
Ekhaya – rural home
umfushwa – dried vegetables
amacimbi – edible worms
ibhobola – pumpkin leaves
awu suka – get away
kusalobuntu lapha? – is humanity still here?
emlageni – paddocks
bhuti – brother
ububende – a delicacy cooked using the offals and blood of an animal
Kiyareboha Modimo o aka – I thank you my Lord
Inzima impilo – Life is tough
Kithi bomama – for us mothers
Ngapha ngizithwele – Here I am pregnant
Ngibelethe – carry a baby on my back
Ngiyawonga – I am looking after
Abagulayo – The sick
Abakhulayo – The growing
Emkhonyeni – a place
uMlamlankunzi – a nickname for Cecil John Rhodes
Ubabhemi bantu – donkey

ACKNOWLEDGEMENTS

My profound gratitude goes to Musaemura Zimunya who emboldened me to take my writing seriously. I also thank Memory Chirere, to whom I read the first lines and the first paragraph of this book. I acknowledge the influence of all my writing and academic friends to whom I read the notes of this book: Shimmer Chinodya, the late David Mungoshi, Jerry Zondo, Sekai Nzenza, and Monica Zodwa Cheru-Mupambawashe.

Prof. Maqhawe Prudence Khumalo, thank you for reading this manuscript before I could call it a book. Thank you, Maurice Vambe, for encouraging this work. I thank you my Sekuru, dearest Lazarus and Mbuya Hungatani for giving me space in which to type and work on this book. My dearly departed Sekuru Bruno, thank you for giving me hope and encouragement in the darkest time of my life. May your soul rest in eternal peace. Thank you, Mama MaNgulube, Daddy DB, Babomncane SaS'phiwe, and NaYamu for giving me the information I needed to make this project a success. I am extremely indebted to you all.

To the writers who gave me editorial advice, Tanaka Chidora and the late David Mungoshi, you put in a great shift.

About the author

Tsitsi Nomsa Ngwenya is the author of *Izinyawo Zayizolo* (2016) and *The Fifty Rand Note* (2017), a collection of short stories that has cemented her place as an exciting voice among the current generation of Zimbabwean writers. Two of the stories from The *Fifty Rand Note* were initially published in *Imbizo*, a UNISA journal, in 2014. *Zal'Abantu Ziy'Ebantwini* (2022) is an award-winning book.

Portrait of Emlanjeni is Tsitsi's fourth book. There is no doubt that her profession as a town planner has allowed her to create stories with care, designing worlds with the ease and effortlessness of a tour guide. The result of such careful planning are stories that allow readers to not only read, but also experience the worlds she designs.

About the author

Ingram Content Group UK Ltd.
Milton Keynes UK
UKHW041235210323
418911UK00004B/142

9 781914 287343